NEXT SEMESTER

Cecil R. Cross II

NEXT SEMESTER

KIMANI
TRU™

Recycling programs
for this product may
not exist in your area.

NEXT SEMESTER

ISBN-13: 978-0-373-83145-6

© 2010 by Cecil Cross II

www.KimaniTRU.com

Printed in U.S.A.

To my grandma Mable—an angel in the physical form.
Thank you for always being there. Because of you,
I know what it means to love.

Acknowledgments

First and foremost, I've got to give thanks to God—the source of my creativity, center of my joy, and keeper of my soul. With Him, all things are possible.

To my parents, thanks for your continuous encouragement and support. Mom, when I felt like giving up, thanks for pushing me to finish. Yes, I'm paying my tithes! Dad, thanks for all your words of wisdom. To Ebony, "straight from Star Search," you inspire me—a sister, best friend, and #1 fan, all in one. My achievements are yours. To my brother, Dre, thanks for lacing me with enough game to last three lifetimes. I'm still sticking to the script. Mark, I got your back like your spinal cord, bro. As long as I've got two dollars, you got one! To my cousins, Keuna, Kahlana & Katrice—28th & Valley will never be the same. Love y'all for life! Rod-O, we're cashing that million-dollar check you wrote. Our time is now. Doc, you're more than a mentor to me. This one is in loving memory of Uncle Mike & Uncle DJ.

To my agent, Regina, thanks for always having my back, helping me stay patient, creating new opportunities, and keeping it 100% with me at all times. Tareia, thanks for being the best publicist in the world! Holiday, Colby, Slim—you already know it's Plush Blue Ent. for life! We can't be stopped! A big shout out to the "206," all my brothers of Kappa Alpha Psi Fraternity, Inc., Two-Tray J, "Catfish Are Delicious" Kev, Icky, K-Dubb, Mama Nia, Kun Luv, Aunt May, and my Images USA fam. To D-Baby & Nana—"the trip" made me who I am. Thank you. To all of my friends and family members, thanks for all your love, prayers, and support. To my niece, Sierra, nephew Darin, and Goddaughter Amaria, let this be a reminder that you can accomplish ANYTHING you put your mind to!

And last but not least, to all of the refund check splurging, spring break wildin', all-nighter pulling, step show attending, term paper writing college students, this book is especially for y'all. May your next semester be as memorable as your first.

PROLOGUE

I'd almost gotten over it all.

All of the nights I couldn't sleep. The nightmares—watching my own funeral from the front pew of a church. Not making it to Katrina's room in time to stop her from pulling the trigger, her brains splattering before my eyes. Waking up in cold sweats. Nervously gnawing my fingernails. The anxiety of awaiting my HIV test results. Tormenting myself daily about whether or not students at the University of Atlanta would ridicule me because they thought I was HIV positive. The fear of facing the rumors. Contemplating withdrawing from college altogether.

Nearly one month had passed since the day Katrina told me she was HIV positive. The day ESPN reported that her main squeeze—Downtown D, a top NFL prospect—would be ineligible for the draft because he, too, was HIV positive. The day my involvement in a love triangle led to my staring death in the face.

It took spending Christmas with family and New Year's with friends for me to gather myself, restore my swagger, and put my first semester behind me. I'd almost completely moved on.

Almost.

The name on my caller ID showed up as *unknown*. But the moment I heard the voice on the other end, I knew very well who the number belonged to.

"J.D.," the soft voice said.

For a moment, I was caught off guard. It was still early in the morning on the West Coast, and I was right in the middle of pouring a bowl of cereal. I paused and stood there tight-lipped, waiting for her to speak again.

"J.D., are you there?" she asked. "Can you hear me?"

"Kat?" I said, knowing very well it was her.

"Hey," she said, sounding unsure of herself. "Yeah, it's me—Katrina. Ummm. I know it's early in the morning out there. I wasn't expecting you to answer. I was actually going to leave you a message. But, I'm glad you answered. How are you?"

I didn't quite know how to respond to that question. The typical answer would have been, "Fine, and you?" But that would have been a lie. Truthfully, the mere sound of her voice made my stomach quiver. I felt nauseous. Thankfully, I was taking this call on an empty stomach and I had enough common sense and compassion not to blurt out how I really felt.

"I'm straight," I said, being purposely short.

"Well, I suppose that beats being lopsided," she said with a half laugh. "Anyways, it's good to hear your voice. I really don't know what to say. After everything that happened last semester…"

I abruptly cut her off.

"I don't want to talk about last semester."

"Oh...okay," she said, sounding incredibly nervous. "Well, I just finished unpacking all of my things, just kinda cleaning up in my dorm room a bit now. Have you made it back to Atlanta yet?"

"Nah."

"I figured you would have, with school starting in a few days and all," she said, continuing on as if everything was all good and we'd been talking on a regular basis. "Well, I know you probably have lots to do before you come back. You are coming back, right?"

"What difference does it make to you?" I asked as the milk I was pouring overflowed and spilled onto the counter.

I cursed under my breath as I gathered some paper towels.

"Look, J.D.," Katrina said, "I know that you are probably still upset with me about how everything unfolded. And it's not my intention to argue with you. I just wondered if you were coming back. That's all."

"Yeah, I'm coming back."

"Well, that's great!" Katrina said, sounding genuinely happy. "I remember you stressing about being on academic probation and needing to get at least a 2.5 GPA. You must've met your goal, huh?"

"Just barely," I said.

"That's what's up! How'd you do in biology?"

"I got a C."

"You passed! At the end of the day, that's all that matters. How'd you make out on the *other* test?"

"What other test?" I asked.

"*The* other test," she said. "How's your health, J.D.?"

"You just don't get it!" I shouted. "I was really feeling you last semester. At one point, there was nothing I wouldn't have done to be with you. *Nothing!* I've only felt that way about one other girl in my entire life and I was with her for *five* years! But that's neither here nor there.

All I'm saying is, I ain't heard from you the entire break and all of a sudden you wanna just up and call me on some 'how you doing'? I almost caught HIV messing with you and you want to ask me how's my health? I never would have been in danger had you been honest with me and told me you were still screwing Downtown D!"

I was heated and my heart was beating fast, but I was careful to lower my voice, remembering that my mom and sister were home and might be listening in. Still, I'd been waiting to get some things off my chest.

"Look," I said, "what you did last semester wasn't cool. Thank God I tested negative. I'm just ready to put that chapter of my life behind me and move on. Honestly, I'm still hostile about the whole situation. This conversation brought back a lot of feelings that I'd rather not deal with. So I think its best you do your own thing. And I'ma do mine. On the real, I don't feel comfortable associating myself with you on any level. You put my life in jeopardy and that ain't kosher. So when I see you, I'ma act like I don't. I think you should do the same."

The line was silent. So silent, in fact, I had to look at my phone to make sure she hadn't hung up.

"You know," she said, sniffling, "I thought about calling you plenty of times over Christmas break. I just wanted you to know how sorry I was and how much I wanted to go back in time and change things. I prayed that you wouldn't be HIV positive. I wouldn't wish this disease on my worst enemy. When I finally gathered enough nerve to call you, it was simply because I didn't want things to be weird when we saw each other. I mean, I understand if you don't want to be friends anymore, but I figured we could at least be cordial. I had no idea you would respond this way."

"Yeah, whatever!" I said.

"*Whatever?*" she asked.

My cheek inadvertently rubbed up against the touch screen on my phone and activated the speakerphone. As I frantically searched the scroll menu on my phone for the key to disable the speakerphone, Kat continued her tirade.

"Oh, that's how it is now?" she asked. "*Whatever?* How immature of you! I fully understand you being upset, but at the end of the day, *you* are not HIV positive. I am. After all of the time we spent together last semester and the good times we had, I would have expected you to be more understanding. But I guess I was wrong."

She paused for a moment before bursting into tears. I could tell because her voice was becoming increasingly shaky.

"You know, J.D., I can be many things, but I refuse to be the object of your hostility. Correct me if I'm wrong, but I don't recall ever asking you to take your condom off. That was *your* decision!"

I couldn't believe she had the audacity to call me and put the blame on my shoulders. Although she was right, at the moment it just didn't sit well with me. Enraged, I responded impulsively.

"Yeah, and so is this," I said, hanging up the phone.

As I stood over my bowl of cereal, taking my aggression out by crunching the Frosted Flakes with my spoon, I heard footsteps behind me.

"What was that all about?" my mom asked. "I could hear you fussin' all the way upstairs."

I wondered how long she'd been standing there.

"Oh, nothing," I said. "Just some crazy girl I met at school."

"I don't mean to be in your business, but did I hear her mention something about HIV?" she asked as she pulled a carton of eggs out of the fridge.

"I really don't want to talk about it," I said.

"Okay, J.D.," my mom continued as if I hadn't said a

word. "Now, I've told you to be careful down there in Atlanta. I ain't ready to be a grandmother yet and I damn sure couldn't stand to hear nothing about you coming back home with anything other than good grades. You hear me?"

"Yes, Mom," I said as I sat in one of the bar stools and starting munching on the cereal.

"I'm serious, J.D!" she said. "When I came down to Atlanta to drop you off at school and left you with that box of condoms, I didn't mean for them to be decorations for your room. If you are going to be having sex, you need to strap up. Period."

"I know, Mom," I said.

"Judging by what the girl on the other end of that phone said, apparently you don't! If you know better, you should do better!"

"Okay, Mom," I said in an aggravated tone.

"Don't 'okay, Mom' me on this, J.D.," she said. "We are talking about life and death here. You know good and darn well there ain't no cure for AIDS and you're gonna go to Atlanta and take a chance with your life? Come on, J.D., don't be stupid! Ten minutes of lust is not worth a lifetime of agony. You remember that."

My mom's impromptu AIDS awareness speech was killing my appetite. I just dropped my spoon in the bowl, propped my elbow up on the counter and rested my forehead in my hand as she continued on.

"I am not paying for you to go to school for you to be down there acting like Deuce Bigalow, Male Gigolo," she said. "I was fooling around my freshman year at FAMU and got pregnant. I am not ashamed of the decision I made, nor do I regret bringing you into this world. But that one decision changed my entire life. I couldn't finish college. But you can! Hell, nobody in our family has a college diploma, but you can be the first. And you will, as long as you make responsible decisions. Normally, I wouldn't get all in your business like this, and you know that. But I love you too much to lose you to ignorance. So Momma's gotta keep it real on this one. You feel me?"

"Yeah, Mom," I said. "I feel you."

"Fa sheezy!" my mom said, mocking my slang. "Now you know I'm gonna cook you a big breakfast since this is your last day here before you go back to school. Why you gonna ruin your appetite with that cereal?"

"I ain't ruined jack!" I said. "I'ma eat that, too. What you making?"

"Your favorite!" she said. "Some homemade waffles, cheese eggs, hash browns and bacon."

"Man, that sounds good! Do I have to go back to school?" I asked with a laugh.

ONE

HOME

Of the three holiday parties I attended while back home in Oakland for winter break, all three got shot up. A couple of my close friends had been hit, caught in the crossfire. In less than two months, I'd been to four funerals—all guys I'd grown up with. In fact, violence in The Town had gotten so bad, just going to the mall was a risky move. Growing up in Cali, I was used to being around ignorance and violence. But it seemed like it was worse now than it had ever been. It was to the point where I had to watch my back every time I stepped out of the house.

And the fact that I'd returned home from college didn't help. It only increased the size of the bull's-eye on my chest. In my hood, there is more of a celebration for a guy being released from prison than for one who'd returned home from college. As irrational as it sounds, that's just the way it is. The fact of the matter is, misery loves company. Other than my best friend, Todd, who got a full ride to Crampton on a football scholarship, none of my friends left home for college. Most of them didn't go at all.

Over winter break, I noticed a lot of the guys I hung around starting to hate on the fact that I'd left for college in an underhanded way. Snide remarks like "You think you're better than us now that you went to college?" and "This nigga been in college for one semester and swears he knows everything now" were becoming more frequent by the day. Guys who were supposed to be my friends were turning on me, all because I'd decided to do more with my life than they had. When mixed with envy, the crab-in-a-barrel mentality gave way to genocide in the hood. Home wasn't safe anymore.

That morning I was headed back to school, when I threw my last bag in the trunk of the car, I was determined to study hard and do whatever it took to get off academic probation and stay in school, so I could one day remove myself from harm's way for good. But when I saw my younger sister, Robyn, take the driver's seat, I figured my luck had finally run out. She'd just gotten her license and wanted to practice. I couldn't quite fathom why my mom decided to let her at six in the morning, while it was still dark out. But after Robyn accidentally flicked on the windshield wipers, hazard lights and the wrong blinker before we made it to the highway, I knew she needed all the practice she could get. I still couldn't understand why her in-flight training had to come while driving me to the airport. *At least let one person in this family graduate from college,* I thought, as we risked life and limb cruising down I-580 en route to the airport. I could tell my mom was a bit nervous, her head on the constant swivel, double-checking Robyn's blind spots each time before she merged lanes. But not even

Robyn's no-driving-skills-having-self could stop my mom from going through with her State of the Union address as we neared the terminal.

"Are you sure you got everything?" she asked.

"If I didn't, it's too late to turn around now," I said from the backseat, with a hint of sarcasm.

"Hey! I'm just checking to make sure you haven't left anything behind. You know the weather has changed since the last time you were down there in Atlanta. It's probably going to be chilly until March. I hope you packed warm. You know you don't have a doctor down there, and I can't afford to fly you back home if you get sick."

"I did."

"Good. Now let me see…what am I forgetting? Hmmm. Do you have your award letter? Because you left that on the coffee table last semester."

"Yeah, I got it," I said, running my hand through my pocket to double-check.

Although I had all but severed my relationship with my high school girlfriend, Keisha, leaving without hearing her say goodbye didn't sit well with me. She was my first love. She knew I was leaving and hadn't even bothered to send me a text message to bid me farewell or wish me good luck. Although I'd never admit it, my mom knew not hearing from Keisha bothered me. My mom knew me like the back of her hand.

"Look, J.D., I know you probably don't want to talk about it, but I know you have strong feelings for Keisha," she said.

"I ain't even thinking about that girl," I said, lying.

"Come on now," my mom said. "I was born at night. Not *last* night! I know that's not the truth. Y'all dated all through high school. But the fact of the matter is, both of you are grown-up now and, quite possibly, growing apart."

"Mom, I'm telling you, it's not like that with me and Keisha anymore."

"All I'm saying is—" my mom said, butting in "—and this goes for you, too, Robyn, so listen up. Don't take your eyes off the road! But listen up. Every person who was a part of your past, isn't going to be a part of your future. And that's as plain as I can put it."

At thirty-eight, my mom was good-looking, single and still young enough to understand what I was going through when it came to relationships. She never shied away from sharing her opinion, no matter whether I wanted to hear it or not.

"I hear you," I said. "That's exactly why I'm not coming back to Oakland ever again," I said.

"Not coming back?" my sister asked fearfully, turning her head to look at me in the backseat.

All the while our car drifted slowly into the next lane, causing the white guy in the minivan next to us to swerve abruptly, honk his horn and flip us the bird.

"Keep your eyes on the road!" my mom and I shouted in unison.

"Sorry," Robyn said, placing her hands back at ten and two o'clock on the steering wheel, regaining control. "What do you mean not coming back *ever?*"

"I don't know about ever," I said. "But you know how crazy it is out here. People getting shot and killed left and right. Plus, now that I'm in school, I've been noticing a lot of envy coming from the homies. Everybody's hating on me, just 'cause I'm going to college. Other than Todd, I think I'ma just cut all them niggas off for good. Every last one of 'em. Keisha included. Katrina, too! I'm cutting off everybody this semester. Starting off with a clean slate."

"Well, J.D., you know I've never told you how to pick your friends," my mom said. "And I know how jealous friends who didn't go off to college can be. Some of my girls did me the same way back in the day. All I can say is, I know for a fact that you have some good friends. At least a couple."

"*Maybe* a couple," I said.

"Everybody's not going to go off to college like you," she continued. "But that doesn't make them any less of a friend. As for Keisha and Katrina, you're on your own there. I don't know what you're looking for in a woman, but until you find it, my advice is don't settle for less. Just be careful *who* you decide to *cut off*. People are resources, and you just never know when you will need somebody to come through for you. Growing up, my grandmother used to always tell me, 'You should never burn a bridge, unless you have a boat.'"

"Well, I got me a cruise ship," I said, cockily. "So I'ma just do me."

"A cruise ship, huh?" my mom asked, giggling. "Well, unless you wanna go down like the *Titanic,* you might wanna think about being more involved in extra-curricular activities on campus this year. I think it would be good for you to get your mind off of Keisha, Katrina and your so-called friends here. Do something constructive with all of the idle time you seem to have on your hands down there. Maybe you should try running for office in student government. I think you'd be good at that."

"Yeah, right!" Robyn said, laughing. "The only reason you're telling him to do that is because you wanted to run for office in college."

"*Wanted* to?" my mom asked. "I *did* run!"

"What happened?" Robyn asked.

"I would have won, but..."

My mom is good for a barrage of run-on sentences. But stopping in midsentence was definitely not her forté.

"But what?" Robyn asked.

"Never mind that. I just think that it would be good for J.D. to take on some extra responsibility."

"I wanna know why you didn't win," Robyn said.

"Well, if you must know, when I got pregnant with J.D., it was kind of a big deal. Unlike today, it wasn't a very popular thing back then for a teenage girl to get pregnant without being married. At any rate, I was running for student body president, and the only thing standing in between me and winning was this snooty little thang named Jocelyn Paige. I'll never forget her."

"What did she do?" my sister asked.

"Well, see, your momma was fine back in the day. Fine and popular. Everybody loved me. Anyway, I had so many people on campus saying they were going to vote for me, the election was going to be a landslide. So Jocelyn did the only thing she knew to do."

"What?" Robyn asked.

"Became a player hater. That girl started spreading rumors about me being pregnant and telling everybody I didn't know who the daddy was. Which was a lie! I'd been with J.D.'s father for years. Kids can be so cruel. At any rate, the rumors got so bad and I was so embarrassed, I just quit. It's one of the few things in my life I regret. Looking back, I would have rather competed and lost than lived life not knowing if I would have won. That's why whenever you commit to doing anything, whether it's trying out for the varsity cheerleading team, or trying to make good grades in school or whatever, my only advice is that you give it your all. That way, you can be content no matter if you win or lose."

"That was my first time ever hearing that story, Mom," Robyn said. "Shoot, listening to you just now, makes me want to run for student government."

"Not me!" I said emphatically. "I couldn't ever see myself running for nobody's student body nothin'. Y'all can keep all of that campaigning, speech writing and public speaking crap. I didn't even know you were into that though, Mom. How come you never told us?"

"You never asked," she said. "The moral of the whole story is, you should never let another person or group of people dictate how far you go in life. And if you start something, never ever quit."

"Which terminal?" Robyn asked.

"I'm flying Delta," I said.

"Oh, and J.D.," my mom continued. "Just so you know. Financially, times are really tough for me right now. Until I find a full-time gig, I won't be able to help you out and send you money as often as I did last semester. I'm gonna help you when I can, but I'm just letting you know."

"I understand, Mom," I said.

"All right, well I guess that's about it then," my mom said, opening her door.

"You'd better get going. You don't have long to get to your gate."

My sister followed her lead. Both of them met me at the trunk, but neither offered a hand to lift my heavy suitcase.

"Love you, Mom," I said, giving her a big bear hug and a kiss on the cheek.

"I am so proud of you," she whispered in my ear. "Keep making your momma proud!"

I couldn't leave Robyn without reinforcing some words of wisdom I'd shared with her a couple weeks ago.

"And you… You better remember what I told you," I said.

"About what?"

"Just 'cause you got your driver's license, that don't mean you need to be out here like the rest of these hot mommas. I heard about that boy you're talking to on the basketball team. Uh-huh. Didn't think I knew about that, did you? Don't get homeboy beat up. I'd hate to have see his future go down the drain."

"Yeah, yeah," she said. "A-n-y-w-a-y-s! Don't you have a plane to catch?"

"Not before you recite the rules I gave you," I said.

"Never go over a guy's house to watch a movie."

"Exactly! That's what theaters are for. Keep going."

"Don't let a guy talk me into giving him a massage and always say no if he asks to give me one."

"Precisely! Oldest trick in the book. It always starts out with an innocent massage. Then, before you know it, your bra is unstrapped and… Anyway. You're doing good. Keep going."

"Never go over a guy's house after 11:00 p.m."

"Because…"

"'Cause ain't nothin' open that late but fast food restaurants, gas stations and legs."

"That's right," I said, nodding my head, with a slight smirk. "Keep 'em coming."

"Don't drink and drive or ride in a car with anyone who has been drinking."

"I lost one of my good friends in college just last semester behind that. Carry on."

"Uhhhm. Uhh. Dang, J.D., it's way too early in the morning for this!"

"C'mon, now! I got a plane to catch."

"Shoot," she said, snapping her fingers repeatedly, her eyes rolled up like she was in deep thought. "I don't know. Ummm. Oh, yeah. Don't drink or smoke weed. Okay, that's it. 'Bye."

"But if you do slip up and have a drink…"

"If I do, never leave my cup unsupervised."

"That's my little sister," I said, reaching out to give her a hug. "I love you."

"Love you, too," she said, hugging me tight.

With that, I waved at my mom, turned up my iPod, and walked into the airport. I was actually more excited about leaving to go back to school than I thought. I was still nervous about how people at my school would react to me and what they'd think about me after all the rumors they'd heard. I didn't quite know how the hell I'd manage to pull off a 2.5 GPA without Kat's help tutoring me. If it hadn't been for her, I'm almost certain, my grades wouldn't have been anywhere near good enough to even think about going back to the University of Atlanta. But choosing between ducking strays in Oakland or going off to college to pursue a better life for myself was a no-brainer. I had to leave. And there was no reason to look back. Too much to look forward to.

TWO

BACK ON THE YARD

I was excited when my Uncle Leroy finally showed up at the airport to pick me up. I'd been waiting outside for over twenty minutes, and it was cold as hell. The short-sleeved shirt I was wearing didn't help. As hot as it was first semester, I had no reason to believe it ever got cold in the South. My mom was right.

"What took you so long, unc?" I asked as he hit me with a bear hug—all three hundred-plus pounds of him. "You must've been taking your sweet time, like Morgan Freeman in *Driving Miss Daisy.*"

"You know these fools out here in Atlanta can't drive," he said. "Traffic was crazy! Besides, I know you ain't talking, Larenz *Fake.*"

"Everybody always got the Larenz Tate jokes," I said.

"I see you didn't take any prisoners when it came to scraping your plate this holiday season."

"Well, you know how your auntie does it. Let's just say turkey and dressing didn't miss me!"

"Apparently neither did chitterlings, collard greens, potato salad, fried chicken, candied yams…"

"All right now, youngster," he said, hoisting my overstuffed luggage into his trunk. "Don't let your mouth write a check that your ass can't cash. I don't usually box featherweights. Don't be the exception."

"You know I'm just kidding, unc," I said with a smile.

"That's what I thought," he said, chuckling. "How were your holidays?"

"Pretty straight, I guess," I said. "I didn't do much. Ate good. Hit up a few clubs for Christmas and New Year's Eve. They got shot up. You know, the regular."

"Sounds like Oakland to me," he said. "How's your girlfriend?"

"I don't have one of those."

"What? Since when? You and that girl been dating since…"

"We just kinda decided to go our separate ways," I said, interjecting.

"Oh, yeah?" he inquired. "Well, it's not like you're too old to explore your options. I don't think a young man should be locked down like that in college anyway. You've got the rest of your life for that. Shoot! All them honeys I seen last time I dropped you off on campus…there's no way I'd settle down. Not me! I'd be more single than a dollar bill!"

"I feel you on that," I said. "I mean, these girls down here are cool, but I don't know if I could take any of them seriously. Especially not after what happened to me last semester."

"Yeah, you dodged a real bullet there. You definitely gotta be safe."

To my knowledge, my Uncle Leroy had no idea about

what happened between Katrina and I last semester. I hadn't told anyone remotely affiliated with anybody in his circle, or in my family for that matter. The only person I'd told other than Todd was Robyn. And the only reason she found out was because her nosy butt picked up the other phone in the house when I was on the phone with the doctor. Even after ear-hustling, she still had to pry the entire story out of me. But I made her promise not to tell anyone.

"What do you mean, I dodged a bullet? Did you hear something?"

"Man, you know you can't hide nothing like that from family. If you get sick, who else is gonna be there to take care of your sorry behind? Of course, I heard."

"From who?"

"Well, your auntie told me. And I suppose she heard from your momma. And I don't know who she heard from."

Robyn can't hold water, I thought.

"Don't worry," he said. "I'm not gonna preach to you. All I've got to say is, never jump in the middle of an ocean without a life jacket. You catch my drift?"

"Yeah," I said, slumping down into my seat, shaking my head back and forth in disbelief. "I got you."

"You got tested and everything, right?"

"As soon as I got back to Cali," I said. "Got my results back. I'm straight. Thank God."

"Say that then, nephew," he said, having a quick look. "Well, at least you know you're straight as far as that is concerned. And hey, don't feel bad about what happened. I mean, we've all slipped up before. Hell, between me and you, that's how a couple of your cousins got here. I was satisfied with one kid. Anyway, that's a whole 'nother story. The point I'm trying to make is, when things like that happen, you just take it as a lesson learned and try not make the same mistake again."

"Believe me, that is one you don't have to worry about me repeating," I said.

"I know that's right," he said, turning up his Earth, Wind & Fire album.

I don't know if it was the song "September" blaring from the speakers, the huge So So Def billboard off the side of the highway or the fact that a guy actually raised his hand in the rearview mirror to thank my uncle for letting him over in traffic, but something about cruising up I-85 North, headed to campus, just felt right. I felt like I was at home. A second home. For the first time in a long time, I was at peace. I couldn't help but smile as we pulled off the exit and I saw the sign that read Atlanta University Center. My eyes lit up when we drove by the Elman—the all-girl college right around the corner from mine—and I saw their parking lot was jam packed with ladies being dropped off by their parents. When we pulled into the parking lot outside my dorm, there were so many cars in the small lot, we had to park illegally, beside the garbage can.

"Marshall Hall," I said aloud to myself, as I got out of the car and stretched, looking around at everybody's parents helping them take their things in their rooms.

I thought about my mom. I missed her already. Apparently, my uncle missed the college life a little more than he led on to. He was leaning up against his door, eating some funions, shaking his head side to side slowly as a girl in skin-tight jeans bent over to tie her shoe.

"Man, it feels good to be back on the yard again," I said, grinning wide.

"You ain't lying," my uncle said, devouring a handful of chips as he stared recklessly.

"You mind popping the trunk though, unc?" I asked.

"Oh, okay," he said, reaching through the window to press the button, without ever taking his eyes off of the sexy, chocolate-complexioned girl. "I wonder if she needs some help."

"Not from you, with your breath smelling like sauerkraut," I said with a chuckle.

As I struggled to loosen my suitcase from all of the junk my uncle had piled up in his trunk, I heard a very familiar voice behind me.

"Well look what the wind blew in," someone said. "This stud swear he's flickin'!"

With that all that Midwest slang, I knew who it was before I even turned around.

"My guy!" I said, giving Fresh a handshake, then a hug. "Fresh!"

"In the flesh!" he said.

"What's up with you, blood?"

"Tryna spit my game at all of the top notches on campus before you get a chance. I thought I had more time."

"Time's up, playboy," I said.

As always, Fresh was rockin' the newest J's, accompanied by the matching black-and-red Jordan jumpsuit, of course. Fresh and I were about the same height, but he had a little more weight on him than me. His complexion was one shade shy of pitch-black, but he had teeth as white as piano keys and waves for days. As important as a rifle is to a soldier, Fresh's brush was never out of arm's reach.

"I see you didn't waste any time getting fly," I said, popping his collar.

"Well you know they call me Fresh, so I try to give 'em a reason," he said, calmly removing his brush from his back pocket and gently stroking his waves.

"Where's Moms?" he asked.

"She couldn't make it out here this time."

"So who picked you up from the airport?"

"My Uncle Leroy. You met him when he dropped me off last semester, right?"

"Nah," he said.

"Yo, unc! Lemme introduce you to my boy," I said, wrapping my arm around Fresh's neck, and pulling him around the car. "This is my boy Lamont, from Chicago. We all call him Fresh."

"Well, how are ya, *Fresh?*" he asked, chuckling as he extended his hand to dap Fresh up. "I'm J.D.'s uncle, Leroy. They call me Uncle Leroy. If you don't mind me asking, how did you get a nickname like Fresh?"

"It's kind of a long story. But basically because of the way I dress. I guess I've always been fly."

"Well," my uncle said, cracking up, "I don't think there's anything wrong with that. He says he's always been fly. He's incredible! So what part of Chicago are ya from?"

"West side."

"I'm familiar with Chi-Town. I've got some family there. Whereabout on the west side?"

"K-Town."

"Oh, well that explains plenty. That neighborhood is full of pimps and hustlers. Yeah, I know that area well. It can be pretty rough."

"Certain parts," Fresh said.

"Well, you two are definitely cut from the same cloth as far as your upbringing is concerned. As I'm sure J.D. has told you, Oakland is no walk in the park. I'm glad both of you made it out and are doing something positive with your lives. I wish more of our young men would do the same."

I don't know whether or not my uncle continued to speak after that sentence. It didn't matter. Nothing could have been more important than the girl walking through the parking lot. She was pecan-complexioned, with dimples, a short, Halle Berry-like hairstyle and the body of a goddess.

Her sleek, hourglass figure seemed to glide across the asphalt in her black patent leather heels. Her ass was so big, it looked out of place on her tiny waste, leaving the belt loops on her True Religion denims bunched in the back.

"Who the hell is that?" I asked Fresh, grabbing him by the arm, my eyes fixated on her body.

"I don't know. Wish I did, though. She must go to Elman, because I damn sure ain't see her around here last semester."

"Well, if she goes to Elman, why is she going down the steps by our dorm?"

"That's a hell of a question," Fresh said. "I would chase her down but I've got my hands full already. You know I'm single now, so I got chicks lined up for days! Rashida from Detroit. Tiffany from Houston. Sandra from L.A. Man, the list goes on, fam."

"Y'all young boys are something else," my uncle said, his eyes glued to the same treasure as ours. "I need to get outta here before I get into trouble. You got all of your things from the trunk?"

"I'ma see what ol' baby is talkin' about," I said, speed-walking in her direction.

"Get her!" Fresh growled.

There were a lot of pretty girls going in and out of the dorm, but none close to as fine as the one I was chasing. The closer I got, the faster my heart pounded. Normally, I may have just waited until the next time we crossed paths to try to get at her. I've never liked the idea of chasing a girl down. Ladies generally assume those kind of guys are too thirsty. But with Uncle Leroy and Fresh watching, I had to at least give it a shot.

"Excuse me," I said, reaching out and caressing her elbow.

"You're excused," she said, pulling her arm away, and looking back with an expression of disgust, as if I was aggravating her.

"You don't have to be that way, sweetheart," I said, still trailing her. "I was just trying to find out your name."

"My name is Leslie," she said without looking back, still walking a few paces ahead of me.

"Well, my name is James," I said, careful not to drop my nickname on her right away, in case she'd heard any rumors. "What school do you go to?"

"I thought you just wanted to know my name," she said, stopping abruptly, then finally turning toward me.

Her beauty was on a whole 'nother level. Other than lip gloss, it didn't seem like she was wearing any makeup at all. And still, she looked like she could be walking the red carpet at the Grammys. My eyes scanned for imperfection and found none. That was, until she moved her head slightly to the left. That's when I noticed a fresh scar just below her bottom lip. Upon further examination, I saw that her mouth was a little puffy on that side, too. I tried not to stare.

"Actually, I just wanted you to stop so I could properly introduce myself," I said. "So, thanks. You look great from the back, but you are so much more beautiful from the front. So now that I seem to have your attention, what school do you go to?"

"What school do *you* go to?" she asked.

"University of Atlanta."

"I knew it. Gotta go," she said, turning and walking away.

"What's that about?" I asked, flat-footed.

"I'm done with U of A guys," she said. "I only date Lighthouse men now."

"Who said anything about dating?"

"Maybe I'll see you around, *James*," she said, as she turned to wave goodbye. "It was nice meeting you."

At least she remembered my name, I thought to myself, as I watched her sashay out of my life. After her little comment about exclusively dating Lighthouse men, it would be fair to assume that she definitely went to Elman. Since Lighthouse was the all-male school right across the street from Elman, and both were considered black Ivy League institutions, they tended to prefer dating each other over us. I don't think my Uncle Leroy or Fresh cared to hear that whole explanation. To them, it would sound more like a poor excuse of why I didn't get her digits. I pulled my phone out of my pocket and started fooling around with it, to make it look like I'd gotten Leslie's number and spare myself the embarrassment. As I approached the parking lot, I didn't see my uncle, but Fresh was standing there with a big grin on his face, both hands hoisted in the air like a referee signaling a made field goal. I responded with a hand gesture that signified me slitting my throat. His hands dropped immediately and confusion riddled his face.

"No?" he asked.

"Not this time," I said.

"Damn!" he said. "I just knew you pulled her when I seen you walking with your phone out. What was she on?"

"She was talking 'bout how she only dates Lighthouse dudes."

"Who said anything about dating?"

"That's what I said!"

"Damn," he said. "She was fine! You'll probably see her again."

"Yeah. That's what she said."

"Next time, tell her you transferred to Lighthouse," he said, laughing. "Or better yet, lie, and tell her you're Greek."

"*Greek?* You mean, like fraternity Greek? Why would I tell her that?"

"Trust me, she would've never shot you down if you had letters, G. Greeks never get turned down."

"How you know?" I asked. "You ain't Greek!"

"Not yet."

THREE

ROOMY

The smell hit me before the door swung open. It was a familiar stench. One of x-chromosome overload, musty armpits, feet, Raid, dirty clothes hampers and corn chips, mixed with humidity. Aaaah, Marshall Hall—the only all-male freshman dorm on campus. My home away from home. Much like an acquired taste, the foul aroma drifting through the hallways took some getting used to.

"Somebody needs to spray some Febreeze up in this piece," I said to myself, grimacing as I lugged my suitcase through the hallway behind me.

The trek from the front door to my room was also familiar. I could always tell who'd made it to their rooms and make an educated guess about where they were from by the music blasting from their stereos. And by the sounds of the reggae tunes blaring from some guy's stereo system in the middle of the hallway, I figured we had at least one new guy living on the first floor this semester. As I neared my door at the end of the hall, I expected to see my neighbor Lawry come flying out of his room asking to borrow something. But his door, which was right before mine at the end of the hall, was shut and I couldn't hear any music playing. I started to bang on his door, just to let him know I was in the building, but I decided to drop my things off in my room first. I still remember the horrific experience I had last semester when I opened my dorm room door for the first time, and an overgrown roach was waiting for me, doing the two-step in the middle of my floor. I hadn't been inside my room for a while, so as I turned the key, I braced myself for the worst. Who knew what would be waiting for me inside this time?

I wish it had been a roach.

One step inside, and I thought I had entered the wrong door. My room looked like the international Alpha Mu Alpha frat house. There was paraphernalia everywhere. Timothy's half of the room was painted gold. He had the black-and-gold Alpha Mu Alpha floor mat. The black Alpha Mu Alpha comforter, with gold sheets. He had paddles hanging on the wall. His line jacket hung neatly over his computer chair. An Alpha Mu Alpha mouse pad. An Alpha screen saver on his laptop. And a large poster of a black guy's arm reaching down to pull another black man up by his forearm, with the phrase "He's ain't heavy, He's my brother" inscribed underneath. This was a classic example of going Greek, then going overboard.

"You can't be serious," I said to myself, precariously walking into my room in awe. "Ain't this about nothing. I can't believe this fool."

Timothy wasn't there. But I could tell he'd been there. And by the looks of things, I knew this would be a long semester. After thoroughly sweeping my side of the room, hanging my clothes and arranging my shoes, I called my mom to let her know I'd made it in safe.

Just as I hung up with my mom, my roommate—Timothy McGruden III—came waltzing in. Timothy couldn't have weighed more than a buck thirty soaking wet with bricks in his pockets. But one look at him, and it was evident he wasn't the same Timothy I'd roomed with last semester. He was missing the Coke-bottle glasses. His pants weren't hiked up to his underpits like they used to be. And it was the first time I'd ever seen him wear anything other than penny loafers. Granted, the Adidas shell-tops he wore were laced extremely tight, which looked lame as hell. But he'd made a complete swag transformation. As miraculous as when Steve Urkel morphed into Stefan Urquelle on *Family Matters*. Timothy's parents hadn't changed a bit though, dressed in their Sunday's best, as usual. All of them were carrying Wal-Mart bags.

"Hello Mr. and Mrs. McGruden," I said. "Timmy."

"It's T-Mac, now," he said, placing his bags on his bed.

Now, I'm no expert on Greek fraternities or sororities, but I overheard some Kappas on campus last semester ganging up on one of their new members, talking about him for wearing a hat with their fraternity letters on it and a matching T-shirt at the same time. They called it "double-nalia." When I saw Timothy bust through the door in his Alpha Mu Alpha T-shirt, matching hat, tube socks, dog tag and key chain, I immediately wondered what the rules and regulations are for "quintuplet-nalia." Something told me Timothy had to have been breaking some of 'em. *Even though he joined a fraternity last semester, he was still as lame as he could be,* I thought.

"Hello, James," Mr. McGruden said. "Great seeing you again, buddy. How was your winter break?"

"It was just fine," I said.

"And your mother?"

"She's fine, too," I said.

"Well, that's good to hear. I plead the blood of Jesus over you and your entire family and wish you nothing but success this year. Timothy told me about your little academic probation situation last semester. How were your grades?"

I cut my eyes at Timothy.

"I got a 2.67," I said proudly. "Good enough to come back."

"Well," Ms. McGruden said, with a hint of disapproval in her tone.

"You made it, son," Mr. McGruden said. "That's all that matters. Now, it's time to take it up a notch. I'm not going to preach to you. I do enough of that on Sundays. And by the way, you're always welcome to come to service with Timothy the third, anytime you please. Just remember one thing."

"What's that?"

"It's something I tell Timothy the third all of the time," Mr. McGruden said. "Never let good enough be good enough. Or as one of my favorite college professors used to say, 'Always shoot for the moon. That way, if you fall short, you will still land on a star.'"

"I know that's right," I said.

After helping Timothy unload all of his school supplies and restock his snack drawer, his parents dipped. As they were leaving, Fresh was coming in.

"Yeah!" Fresh said, walking in. "My nigga J.D. is back in the…"

He stopped talking and walking in midsentence. His feet frozen, he just looked around the room, his eyes carefully scanning Timothy's side in disbelief. The face he made was identical to the one I made the first time I walked in—pure shock and disappointment.

"Gaaatdamn, joe!" Fresh screamed, with Timothy's parents still well within earshot.

I could hear Mrs. McGruden in the hallway.

"Lord, have mercy," she said.

"What the hell happened up in here?" Fresh continued, looking around in awe. "This looks like something straight outta *School Daze*. What is this, a mural on the wall?"

"I am actually just proud to be a member of Alpha Mu Alpha," Timothy said in a defensive tone. "Thank you."

"Well, somebody must've dropped a pair of nuts in your Christmas stocking," Fresh said.

I started cracking up.

"Ol' Timothy standing up for himself," Fresh continued with more sarcasm. "I ain't mad at you. But on some the real though, folk, you deserve some kind of Greek fraternity interior decorating award or something. This is extraordinary, fam."

Timothy rolled his eyes, sat down at his desk in front of his laptop and logged on to the Internet. Facebook, to be exact.

"Can you believe this guy?" Fresh asked me, nodding to the decorations.

I just shook my head with a slight grin.

"Hey, at least my roommate don't stink," I said. "Last time I was in your room, I damn near died trying to hold my breath."

"You got a point there," Fresh said. "He does smell like horseshit."

"You wouldn't know class if it was staring you in the face, Lamont!" Timothy yelped, without looking away from his computer screen, apparently still annoyed by Fresh's comments.

"You wouldn't know a dime if it was staring you in the

face!" Fresh retorted. "You might wanna keep cyber surfing, sending friend requests and anonymous honesty box messages and maybe…just maybe you'll get lucky this semester. Oh, and for the record, I go by Fresh. From now on, when you address me, that's what you call me, choirboy."

"Well, my name is Timothy. But everybody calls me T-Mac, now. So from now on, that's what you call me."

"Oh, it's *T-Mac* now, huh?" Fresh asked, cracking up. "Okay, J.D., I've heard enough. I'm outta here. What you on? What's demo?"

"What's *demo?*" I asked. "What the hell does that mean, blood?"

"Oh," Fresh said, laughing. "My bad. I thought I was back in the Chi for a minute. When I say, 'What's demo', I basically mean, 'What's up'? Or as you would say, 'What's crackin'?"

"Oh, okay," I said. "Well, tell me something, man. I thought we had a lot of slang in Cali. Just when I figured out that 'joe' really means 'homie,' here you come with 'what's demo'? I got it now, though."

"Good," Fresh said. "So, what's demo, G?"

"I can't even call it, blood," I said, laughing. "To tell you the truth, I'm feeling kinda jet-lagged right now. I think I'ma lay it down until our meeting with the RA's at eight."

"Damn, that's right," Fresh said, removing a brush from his back pocket, stepping in front of the mirror and touching up his waves. "I forgot all about that. Well, I'll see you there. I'm 'bout to meet up with Tiffany in the caf. I'm starvin' like Marvin, joe."

"Tiffany who?" I asked.

"Big booty Tiffany from Houston," he said. "I'm kinda feeling her right now."

"You'sa fool, blood," I said, bending over to pick up a flyer that someone had just slipped under my door. "The semester just started, and you already got too many for me to keep up with."

"Hey, I'm single," Fresh said, grinning wide and throwing his hands up. "Anyway, what's that?"

"A flyer for some back-to-school party," I said.

"Man, I had about eight of them under my door when I first got to my room," Fresh said. "I damn near slipped and busted my ass when I came through the door."

"That's a bad look," I said, checking out the flyer.

There was a superthick, caramel-colored chick on the front of it, with no shirt on, covered in soap suds, sucking a red lollipop.

"They say the foam party is gonna be going down tomorrow night," Fresh said. "That's our last night of freedom before classes start. Plus, Ludacris is performing!"

"I think..." I said, flipping the flyer over, and seeing Ludacris's album cover. "Yep, this is the flyer for that party right here. You think it's gonna be crackin'?"

"Does a bear shit in the woods and wipe his ass with a rabbit?" Fresh asked. "You already know! We there, joe."

"I don't know if I'ma be able to make it," I said. "I don't wanna be all sluggish on our first day of class. You know I gotta buckle down this semester. Plus, my money is kinda funny. So..."

"So you'll have your ass ready by ten, so we can get in for free!" Fresh said. "You got the rest of the semester to study and worry about class."

"You got a point there," I said, still weighing my options. "But you know me. I ain't really a morning person as it is, blood."

"That's why I'm glad this party is at *night!* I don't care if you miss every other party this year, you know we gotta make this one. It's the first party of the year!"

I hadn't even been on campus for a week, and already I

was going back on the promise I'd made to myself before I came back to campus—to get my priorities together, and put school first. Just when I thought I could resist the temptation, I succumbed to it.

"Well, since you put it that way, I guess I better find something to wear," I said. "But I'll tell you right now, the only way I'm going is if we catch a ride. I need to check with Lawry and see if he's driving, because catching the shuttle is what I ain't gon' do! You remember what happened last semester, when the shuttle left us and we had to walk home from the club."

"Nigga, I'll walk *to* the club I have to," Fresh said. "You see the girl on the front of the flyer?"

"She is fine," I said. "Yeah, fools are probably gonna be going dumb up in that thang! I already know there's gonna be hella breezies there. Plus, it says you get in free before eleven-thirty, with this flyer."

"There you have it," he said, dapping me up and opening the door. "Hold on to that. We need to get out there early, 'cause I damn sure ain't tryna pay, either. I'll see you at the meeting later tonight."

"Fa sho!" I said. "I'ma try to get a nap in first, though."

Timothy shook me out of my slumber.

"Hurry and get yourself together so we can get to this meeting," he said. "We've only got five minutes, and I'm not trying to be late. Especially not after the way Varnelius chewed you out for being tardy to the meeting last semester."

"I know right," I said, wiping sleep from the corner of my eye. "I had forgot all about that."

"I'm gonna check my messages on MySpace one more time, while you get ready," Timothy said.

"You sure have been online a lot today," I said. "You looking up some classes or something?"

"No. Just doing a little chatting."

"Your dad started up some kind of Internet ministry or something?" I asked, sliding on my sweatpants.

"Actually, I'm conversing with a love interest of mine."

"Whaaaat?" I asked excitedly. "A little cyber sex, huh? I guess everybody's tryna get their willy wet these days!"

"Oh, nonsense," he said. "Amy doesn't even participate in those type of activities. She's a church girl."

"Amy, huh? Got you a little jungle fever there, Timmy?"

"Jungle fever?" he asked, pressing the back of his hand up against his forehead. "I'm not running a temp."

"Oh my God!" I said. "You've never seen *Jungle Fever,* the movie?"

Timothy just sat there, his fingers hovering over the keyboard, looking puzzled.

"Aaaah, forget it! I meant to say, I didn't know you liked to ski in your spare time."

"There aren't any mountains in Atlanta," Timothy said. "Well, there's Stone Mountain, but it rarely ever gets any snow. I've never been skiing a day in my life."

"Timothy, if this roommate situation is gonna ever work out, you're gonna need to learn some damn ebonics! How 'bout this one? I didn't know you had a thing for pink toes."

"Pink toes. Pink toes. Pink toes," he mumbled to himself. "Okay, I still don't get it. Do you mind using the King's English instead of all of this street slang?"

"White girls!" I said in exasperation. "With a name like Amy, I'm assuming she's a snow bunny."

"Oh!" he said. "I had no idea you were referring to...no! Amy isn't white! She's Italian."

"Last time I checked, that was white, playa," I said. "She lives in Italy?"

"No, she lives in Tubman Hall, on the other side of campus," he said.

"Oh, I probably know her then," I said.

"I doubt it," he said. "She's a chemistry major, like me. Plus, she's into church. She isn't really on the social scene."

"Oh, okay," I said, peeking over his shoulder to take a look at her profile picture. Under one of her pictures, someone left a comment that said Italian stallion!

"Italian stallion, huh?" I asked, leaning in for a better look. He quickly closed the window.

"Do you mind?" he asked, sounding agitated.

"She's a cutie," I said.

"Yes, she is," he confirmed. "But looks are temporary, J.D. Amy is a virtuous woman. A woman I can trust to do the right thing, even when I'm not around. That's why she's my girl."

"Wow," I said, laughing. "Looks like she's got you open, too."

"I'm not even gonna try to figure out what that means," Timothy said, closing his laptop. "Come on. Let's go, before we're late."

I grabbed my room key and followed Timothy down to the living room area of our dorm, near the entrance. The hallway was packed. Everyone was heading to the meeting. When I walked into the room, I noticed that this meeting was a lot different than the one we had last semester. This was no longer a group of strangers who didn't know each other. By now, everybody had pretty much clicked up and made friends. Now, guys were sitting with their crews getting reacquainted, arguing with each other about whose team was going to win the Super Bowl. Instead of walking into a quiet room of fellas still feeling each other out, I walked into one of laughter, assuredness and guys showing off new tattoos. It still smelled like the inside of a dirty clothes hamper, though.

"All right, everybody quiet down," Varnelius said,

standing up in his gold boots, army fatigue pants and purple wife beater. He was bald-headed, dark-skinned and average in height, with a husky build, and biceps as big as my head. "I know you are just getting back into the swing of things, so I want to make this meeting short and sweet."

Varnelius was flanked by his three assistant RAs. Each of them responsible for their own floor. Of course, our floor RA, Lester, a tall, lanky, light-skinned guy with an S-curl and a plethora of female mannerisms, stood out in his florescent pink Polo button up, matching Chucks and ripped jeans. I had no idea Fresh was standing next to me, until he whispered in my ear.

"Okay, so I know the ripped jean this is making a comeback and everything," he said. "But aren't the holes supposed to be around the knee area?"

"Yeah," I said. "Why?"

"I'm just wondering why Lester's holes are so high up on his thighs. That's kinda suspect, if you ask me."

"As if his pastel color combo wasn't," I said with a laugh.

"Now that Cool Cali and Chi-Town's finest are done sharing beauty secrets, we can get started," Varnelius said, staring us down. "For those of you who don't know me, my name is Varnelius, and I am the head resident assistant here at Marshall Hall. I am *not* your babysitter! You all are grown young men, and I expect you to conduct yourself as such. By now, you all should know our dorm motto."

"I can't stand that nigga, blood," I whispered to Fresh. "He's one of them cats who just takes his job way too serious."

"As a matter of fact, since my boy D.J. from Cali is so talkative this evening, I will let him refresh your memory. D.J.," he said, looking at me.

I just sat there, looking at him with a blank stare.

"Come on D.J.," he said. "We don't have all night. We're not on West Coast time. Give us that Marshall Hall motto."

"Well, if you are talking to me, my name is J.D.," I said.

"And the motto?"

"Distinguished men of Marshall give respect to get respect," I said.

"That's right. And when it comes to respect, the rules are simple. Visitation is over at eleven o'clock p.m. Not eleven-oh-one."

"Not eleven-oh-two," everyone said in unison, sounding like a choir.

Varnelius chuckled. I think it was the first time I'd ever seen him crack a smile.

"Well, I'm glad y'all know it," he said. "Eleven o'clock sharp! No loud music after ten. It's the winter. It's cold outside. And the roaches need somewhere warm and cozy to call home. If you don't clean up after yourself, they will be roasting marshmallows right here in Marshall Hall. And I'm sure none of us want that. So do us all a favor, and keep the place clean. And for God sakes, stop pulling the daggone fire alarm! In a month or so it's gonna be too cold out to be standing outside waiting on the firemen to come for a false alarm. So this semester, easy on the practical jokes."

"This fool got more commandments than Moses," Fresh said.

Everybody within earshot busted out laughing.

"Word," someone behind me said. "Son is buggin' right now, B."

I knew that accent all too well. When I turned to see who was in agreement, I wasn't surprised. It was Dub-B, in a Mets fitted, white T-shirt and sweatpants. He stood six-four, and was the only white guy I'd ever met who rocked his hair braided in cornrolls and stayed with a fresh goatee. All things considered, he was the blackest white guy I'd ever encountered. Since Dub-B lived on the same floor as me, we grew close last semester. But since he played on the basketball team, he practiced so often I hadn't even seen him since I'd been back on the yard.

"My guy," I said, dapping him up. "What's up with you, fam?"

"Tired," he said. "This new coach got us doing two-a-days. Killing me, son!"

"And last but not least!" Varnelius said with an attitude, raising his voice to let us know he was annoyed by our side conversation. "One last warning. We all saw what happened to Downtown D last semester."

The mention of Downtown D's name sent a chill down my spine. The thought of how close I came to being a victim of his love triangle was unsettling, to say the least. I discreetly looked around to see if anyone looked in my direction to see how I'd respond, but didn't notice any unordinary attention. *Thank God*, I thought. Maybe people really have forgotten about me being in the middle of that whole saga.

"This HIV thing is real," Varnelius continued. "So if you're gonna go deep-sea diving, please, for your own safety, wear a life jacket. If you know what I mean."

"What does he mean?" Timothy whispered.

"Downtown D scored one too many times without his helmet," Fresh said with a laugh.

"What does *that* mean?" Timothy asked, sounding even more confused.

"Wear a condom," I said.

"Oh," Timothy said. "Well, what the heck does that have to do with deep-sea diving and a helmet?"

"Don't even worry about it, homie," I said, with a laugh. "I swear, you're 'bout as square as my back pocket. You crack me up sometimes."

"Unless any of you have questions, this meeting is officially adjourned," Varnelius said.

"Good," I mumbled, turning to walk away before he even got the last word of his sentence out.

"Except for those of you on academic probation," Varnelius said. "I'm not going to call out any names. You know who you are. If I am talking to you, each of you will be meeting with your individual floor RAs on your respective floors, near the washroom. If you are on the first floor, stay put. You all will meet right here. Thanks everybody for coming on time, and I look forward to a successful second semester, with no problems."

"Damn," I said, making an about-face, pouting.

"What you about to do, J?" Fresh asked.

"Man, I gotta stay for this lil' meeting," I said.

"Oh, yeah, that's right. I forgot, you are on academic probation, huh?"

"Wish I wasn't. What you finna get into?"

"I can't call it," he said. "Just hit me when you get outta there."

"Aight," I said.

Just as I was about to walk back into the room, a guy wearing a Pizza Time uniform busted through the front door, hoisting a pizza bag over his head.

"I got one last pizza going for five bucks. Any takers?"

The aroma had damn near everybody in the hallway digging in their pockets for a Lincoln. I was the first to pull one out of my pocket.

"What kind is it?" I asked.

"The five-dollar kind," somebody in the hall said. "Who cares? If you don't want it, I'll take it."

"Sausage," the guy said, handing me the medium-size pizza.

"Thanks," I said. "Man, I'm glad you came through. I probably wouldn't have had time to make it to the caf."

"I'll give you two-fifty for half of it," one guy said as he passed by.

"I'm straight," I said. "You know I'm still on Cali time, and we're three hours behind, so I get hella hungry at night."

There were about six guys sitting on the couch in the room. Lester was sitting on a stool in front of them, the holes near his thighs in his jeans at direct eye level. I decided to stand up.

"Glad you could join us," Lester said. "That pizza sure smells good. Care to share?"

"Not really," I said.

"I don't blame you. What is that, sausage?"

"Uh-huh," I said.

"Mmmm," he said, licking his lips. "I love me some sausage."

"I bet you do, girlfriend," a guy said mockingly as he walked by, snapping his fingers.

A group of guys standing in the hallway burst out in laughter. I snickered, trying to hold mine in.

"Anyway," Lester said, rolling his eyes, "now that everybody is here, let's get this meeting underway. I wanna make this as quick and painless as possible. I'm sure we've all got better things to do. In short, Varnelius has instructed us to keep you all on a short leash. The retention rate of students on academic probation at U of A is too low."

"What is a retention rate?" someone asked.

"Basically, there are too many of you all on academic probation, who for whatever reason, don't make the grade and end up dropping out of school. The university feels that your behavior in the dorm is a reflection of your obedience in the classroom. So to put it bluntly, they aren't going to put up with any shit from you all this semester in terms of taking disciplinary action if you all get out of line here in Marshall Hall. Varnelius may be a little more lenient on the other guys, but you all are starting out with a red flag. Just keep that in mind, be sure to follow all of the rules that he discussed earlier and you shouldn't catch any flak from him or anyone else. As far as your course loads go, just study hard, man. By the mere fact that you are sitting here, you obviously did well enough to make the cut last semester. And just think, if you keep your grades above a 2.5 this time around, you will have this monkey off your back for good. So handle your business."

With that, the meeting was dismissed and each of us headed to our rooms. But not before Lester made one more announcement.

"Oh," he said, "I almost forgot. This really goes without saying, but I will tell you anyway. Absolutely no fighting. Any students on academic probation who are caught fighting are expelled off top. No questions asked. So if you even see somebody fighting, just go the other way."

I thought Lester would never stop talking. By the time he concluded his speech, my stomach was doing backflips. Sausage pizza never smelled so good.

"I'll give you a dollar for a slice," Dub-B said as I walked by.

"Not this time, homie," I said. "This one is all me."

When I made it to my room, I noticed Timothy was thumbing through a biology book. I knew I wasn't going to be using Kat's tutorial services anymore, so I was going to need all the help I could get passing biology this semester.

"Say, blood," I said. "How'd you do in biology last semester?"

"I aced it!" he said. "You know that's my major. I freakin' love science!"

"Oh, yeah," I said. "That's right. I forgot all about that. Man, I might need you to look out for your boy and help me out in that class from time to time this semester."

"What happened to the tutor you had last semester?"

"Who, Katrina?"

"Yes, that's her," he said.

"Man, I ain't even messing with her like that no more," I said. "I haven't even really spoke to her since all that stuff went down last semester. To tell you the truth, I ain't even tryna be seen with her."

"I heard about the way everything unfolded," he said. "That was a very unfortunate situation. I hope you got tested for HIV."

"Oh, you know I did," I said. "Thank God, it came back negative."

"That's a blessing," Timothy said. "My father always says you can either have buns or abundance. I dunno, J.D. I mean, I'm not sexually active or anything. You know that. But it just seems like so much trouble comes with...well... you know..."

"No, I don't know," I said. "What are you talking about?"

"Buns!" he said. "You have to worry about getting a girl pregnant, contracting an STD. These days, you're practically risking your life! I think I'm sticking with focusing on abundance for now."

"I never really thought about it like that," I said.

"But more importantly, to answer your question, you know I don't have any problem lending a helping hand in biology, if you need it. I'm taking a full load this semester, so my schedule is going to be rather hectic. But as long as you're willing to study, I'm willing to help."

"I'ma need that, homie," I said. "Biology is one of my

hardest classes. And I'm on academic probation, so if I don't get at least a 2.5 GPA..."

"Say no more!" he said. "We'll meet at the library once a week to study."

FOUR

BOOKS ON A BUDGET

It wasn't even noon yet, and the strip was jumpin'. The strip was a narrow street smack-dab in the middle of the yard lined by the library, the student center, dorms and campus buildings. The strip stretched all the way from University of Atlanta's main campus, past Lighthouse, all the way to Elman's front gate. In between classes, and sometimes during them, the strip is where all the students hung out. There were so many people congregating in front of the student center, you would've thought a step show was going on. As we got closer to the crowd, I saw there *was* a step show going on. In an impromptu clash of the Greeks, each fraternity and sorority were taking turns showing off their unique partyhops, strolls and chants. I even spotted Timothy in the mix, joining his frat brothers in their call and response. I couldn't help but notice the way the sorority chicks gawked at him and his crew. It was like pledging had made Timothy a brand-new person.

I looked on with a tinge of jealousy. For some reason, sorority chicks mesmerized me. They came in all sorts of shades and sizes. Some rocked the long hairstyles, others the short dos. But no matter if the colors on their jackets were blue and white, pink and green or crimson and cream, all of them carried a certain mystique about themselves. They walk with a confident air that exudes sexiness and distinction. In my eyes, their attention to detail in their appearance made them stand out. For instance, you would never catch a chick with an APA jacket without her fingernails and toes freshly manicured with French tips. And for some reason, they always smelled fragrant. At least Kat did. And the Deltas were known for dressing sharp. Even without a line jacket on, you could tell a girl was a Delta from a mile away. It was commonplace to see them walking to class in an outfit sharp enough to wear to a *Fortune 500* job interview. And they never stepped foot on campus without heels. Not in all cases, but in most, sorority chicks were the cream of the crop. And I was standing right in the thick of it.

For a moment, I didn't care if people thought that because I'd slept with Kat, I was HIV positive. And it didn't matter that the only money I had to my name was the money I was supposed to spend on my books. I was just happy to be back on the yard. Away from the gritty streets of Oakland and back on campus. For a moment, as I stood with my Jansport strapped to my back, I felt free.

A familiar ruckus catapulted me back into reality. The sorority girls stopped doing their steps and hurriedly stepped aside as the fellas inside the circle began pushing and shoving each other. All of the onlookers began backing up to give the guys some room, in case it came to blows. I took a couple steps back, not knowing what was going on.

"What just happened, blood?" I asked.

"I don't know. But it looks like the Kappas are getting mad at the Sigmas for twirling canes," Fresh said. "As soon as they started twirling, one of them got their cane snatched."

"So you mean to tell me that these fools are beefing over who can twirl a cane?" I asked. "They're going at it like some Crips and Bloods."

"These niggaz be taking that fraternity stuff serious, joe" he said. "Plus, the Kappas were founded first, so they feel like the Sigmas are biting their style."

"*Who* cares?" I asked.

"There's a lot of history behind why they carry those canes, G," he said.

"What are you? Some kind of Kappa-ologist?" I asked. "How do you know so much about Kappas all of a sudden?"

"*Sssssshhh!*" Fresh whispered. "I don't want everybody all up in my business. But, if you must know, I've done a little research here and there."

"*Research?*" I asked. "Are you serious? You wanna be a Kappa now?"

"I'm not sure just yet. But I don't think it's a bad idea. I mean, think about it, fam. They always dress clean."

"True."

"They always get the baddest chicks on the yard."

"For the most part."

"And their parties are always off the chain!"

"You've got a point there," I said.

"Plus, from what I heard, they do a lot of community service," Fresh added.

"Man, please!" I said. "You know good and well you ain't thinking about no damn community service. You're just tryna get some."

"Who ain't?" he asked, laughing. "I bet you wouldn't have any problem pulling that lil' cutie from Elman if you were a Kappa."

"I wouldn't have no problem getting with her if I wasn't," I said confidently. "Besides, I ain't even tryna get caught up chasing breezies this semester anyway. I gotta get my grades right and stay focused. Speaking of which, let's go to the bookstore real quick."

"I hear you talkin'," Fresh said, wearing a facial expression that clearly stated he didn't believe anything that was coming out of my mouth. "C'mon."

The first thing I saw when we walked inside the student center, heading to the bookstore, was a large sign on one of the walls that read Student Government Applications Available Now! It made me think of my mom. The next thing I saw made my eyes bug out. The line from the cash register inside the bookstore stretched all the way out into the hallway in the student center. For every person who walked out, the security guard let one in.

"I ain't about to stand in this line, fam," I said. "We might have to come back."

"You ain't lying, joe," Fresh said. "This line is bogus as hell."

Just as I was about to make my exit, I felt an arm wrap around my shoulder.

"What's *crackin' blood?*" Dub-B asked, mocking my West Coast slang.

I couldn't help but laugh. Sometimes Dub-B sounded blacker than us when he spoke.

"What's *demo, joe?*" Dub-B continued, mocking Fresh's Chi-Town slang, as he nudged him. "Where y'all headed?"

"I guess back out to the strip to try to kill some time," I said. "That line in the bookstore is way too long for me."

"Not a problem," Dub-B said. "Just let me know what

books you need and I got you. You know my girlfriend works in the bookstore, so I can skip the line."

"That's what's up," I said.

"Just write down what books you need, give me the dough for 'em and I will hook it up."

"That works," Fresh said. "But since your girl can get you to the front of the line and all, you think she could hook a brotha up with a lil' discount? I'm a little short on ends right now."

"If I had the hookup on a discount, I would have hooked myself up by now, yo," Dub-B said.

I was looking through my backpack for a scrap piece of paper to write on when Fats walked up.

"Did I hear somebody say something about a hookup?" Fats asked. "How much you got to spend and what you need?"

"Not a lot," Fresh said. "And textbooks."

With Fats being from L.A., he took it upon himself to show me the ropes when I first got to U of A. He was the resident super senior on the yard. Short and stocky in stature, Fats was the man when it came to getting the hookup on anything and everything on campus.

"Well 'not a lot' doesn't sound like enough, but we may be able to work something out," Fats said, struggling to hold two extralarge plastic shopping bags full of textbooks.

"There you go," I said. "What you doing with all those books you got in those bags? I know *you* ain't taking all them classes."

"C'mon now," he said. "You know I keep more hustles than janitors keep keys. I can get you whatever books you need for twenty-five percent off. They will be photocopied. But it's still the same thing."

"Twenty-five?" I asked. "That's the best you can do?"

"Well, between me and you, since y'all my little homies, I'll look out and give y'all an additional ten percent off my usual prices, but don't tell anybody."

"Can't beat that with a baseball bat," Dub-B said. "Now, I wish I woulda holla'd at you before I bought mine."

"You really be making bread off of photocopying books and slangin' 'em for the low?" I inquired.

"*Do I?*" Fats asked, with a laugh. "I'ma make a killing, cuz. My roommate put me up on the hustle. That fool made so much cake doing this last semester, he bought some chrome rims for his ride and furnished our whole apartment. Fly shit. A living room set you would see on *MTV Cribs*. Flat screen and all, cuz."

"That's crazy," I said. "All that just off selling some books for class? Wow!"

"What classes you taking anyway?" Fats asked.

"You know I'm a business major, but I'm still taking a whole lot of my prereq classes right now," I said, looking over the sheet of paper I was about to hand Dub-B. "So I'm taking Biology, English, African-American history, Algebra II, and one more class. Either public policy or intro to technology."

"Oh, that's a no-brainer," Fats said. "You gotta go with the public policy class, without question. Dr. J teaches that Intro to Tech class. And you know him. He will actually have you up in there doing some work, so you definitely don't wanna take that. But that public policy is an easy A. I know who teaches that class. Wussername? Ummm... Uh...man, it's right on the tip of my tongue. Miss... Professor Mitchell," he said, snapping his fingers. "Yep, that's her name. Professor Tessa Mitchell. That's whose class you want to take."

"Why Miss Mitchell?" I asked.

"Because I took her class last semester, and she was

about four months pregnant then. She was always cancel-ing class because of her doctor appointments. It was beau-tiful. It's been at least a month, so that means she's gonna have even more visits to the doctor. She's never gonna be there! Think about it. More doctors visits mean less homework. And less homework equals less exams. Man, I wish she taught every class!"

"Oh, hell yeah," I said, scratching intro to technology off of my list and replacing it with public policy. "Sign me up!"

"Me, too," Fresh said. "An easy A sounds good to me."

After placing our order with Fats, Fresh and I went back outside. Things were back to normal. The Greeks were still battling. Students interested in joining their organizations standing off to the side, looking like groupies. Vendors set up along both sides of the strip peddling everything from fresh fruit and water to socks, CDs and knockoff jewelry. I was strolling by the bootleg CD stand when I felt someone tap my elbow.

"What it is, folk?" Lawry asked in his signature Southern twang.

Lawry stayed next door to me in Marshall Hall. He was one of the few people I'd met on campus who was actually born and raised in Atlanta. Clad in classic ATL dopeboy garb, it seemed like Lawry had an endless supply of white tees and Atlanta Braves fitted caps. He wasted no time flashing his gold fronts and giving me a hug shake—one of those half-handshake, half-hug displays of affection guys who are good friends can share in public without being viewed as gay—and continued: "You ain't holla'd at ya boy since you been back, shawty! What the business is?"

Some things never change. Lawry's breath was one of them. There is a difference between something stinking and something stankin'. Lawry's breath crossed the threshold. His breath stank like he had food from last month stuck in the back of his teeth. And on top of that, it always seemed hot. I could literally feel the heat from his breath around my lip and nostril area every time he opened his mouth. Last semester, it got so bad, a few times I seriously had to hold my breath every time it was his turn to speak. And Lawry, of all people, had the gall to be a notoriously close talker, which further complicated things.

"I just got here a day ago, blood," I said as I quickly reached in my pocket and pulled out a pack of gum I'd had since the plane ride. Two sticks. Just enough. I offered him the first piece. Thank God he accepted. "I'm surprised you ain't came by my room asking to borrow anything yet."

"Funny you should say that," he said. "You got a dollar you can loan ya boy? I'm trying to see what this new Lil' Wayne mix tape is talking 'bout, but I only got four bucks and penny pincher over here won't let me slide."

"Same old Lawry," I said with a smile as I whipped out my wallet. "You can have this dollar as long as you make me a copy of that CD. I heard it's tight!"

"I got a couple of blank CDs in my room. I got ya!"

"Make me one, too," Fresh said. "As many times as you came to my room last semester asking for ramen noodles, I know I'm good for one."

"I know you ain't still talking about last semester," Lawry said. "Shawty, that was soooo long ago. I got you, though."

When Lawry pronounced the *th* in his last word, I heard something flick against his teeth. Unless he'd just become the first human being I'd ever seen pop a bubble while talking, there was a foreign object in his mouth.

"Did you hear that?" I asked.

"Hear what?" Fresh asked.

"Don't tell me you're still having flashbacks from when we got jacked by them dopeboys last semester," Lawry said.

As he spoke, I paid close attention to Lawry's mouth. In the middle of his sentence, I saw something metal flicker.

"Hold up, blood," I said. "I know I didn't just see what I think I saw."

"What the hell is you talkin' 'bout, shawty?" Lawry asked.

"Damn it, man!" I said. "What made you go and do that?"

"Go and do what?" Lawry asked.

"Get a damn tongue ring!" I said, pointing at Lawry's mouth.

"No, he didn't," Fresh said.

"This little thing?" Lawry said, sticking his tongue out for all to see.

"Yes, he did!" Fresh said, covering his face with his hands. "What the hell was you on over Christmas break?"

"Man, me and my girl were wildin' out one night, drinking and stuff," Lawry explained.

"*What* girl?" I asked.

"Oh, me and my girl from high school got back together for a second over the break. And you know how that is. She got a nigga drunk. Next thing you know we talkin' about getting matching tattoos. We get all the way to the parlor and she gets scared of the damn needle. So instead of getting a tattoo, she convinced me to get a tongue ring and shit. Ya know, something I can take out when I get ready."

"Nah, I don't know about that one, joe," Fresh said. "You lost me there."

"Me, too, fam," I said, a look of perplexity on my face. "Matching tattoos…piercings… You were definitely wildin' all the way out on that one. Where they do that at?"

"It ain't even that serious, shawty," Lawry said. "I can take it out whenever. Plus, people barely ever even notice it."

"Hey, I'm 'bout to see what they talkin' 'bout over here

at this pizza table. Looks like they're giving 'em away for free," Fresh said.

"I'm with you, pimpin'," I said. "I'll holla you later, Lawry. Tongue ring or no tongue ring, I still want my copy of that Gangsta Grillz mixtape."

"'Preciate that dollar, shawty," Lawry said. "I'ma burn that for you as soon as I get back to the dorm."

We hadn't taken five steps before Fresh burst out in laughter.

"What's up with your boy?" he asked, laughing hysterically. "I think he might have a couple of screws loose."

"I can't even call it," I said, shaking my head.

"You think he might be switch-hitting?" Fresh asked.

"What you mean?"

"I mean, do you think he might have a little sugar in his tank? You know, fruity."

"Do I think he's gay?" I asked.

I paused for a moment, trying to give him the benefit of the doubt.

"Nah," I said. "Hell nah. Not Lawry. I can tell a sweet dude from a mile away. I lived next door to that guy for a whole semester. If he was gay, I think I'd know."

"Yeah, you're probably right," Fresh said. "That tongue ring is suspect as hell, though."

The smell of fresh pizza attracts college students like a moth to a flame. And everybody knows that the best way to get a college student's attention is to attach the word *free* to anything. So the crowd of students hovering around the booth with the *Free Pizza* sign didn't surprise me. When we finally made our way to the front of the booth I noticed that as with most things associated with the word *free*, there was a catch. In order to get your complimentary personal pan pizza, you had to fill out an application for a credit card. After I got accepted to college, my mom warned me about traps like these. She told me never to write my social security number or sign my name on any piece of paper without the University of Atlanta seal on it—especially credit card companies. She said that those companies targeted students and viewed them as easy prey. Her entire speech replayed itself in my head as I held the clipboard in my hand, contemplating whether or not to fill it out. Fresh had completed his and was getting ready to sign when I backed out.

"I'm leery about this one," I said, placing my blank application back on the table.

"Why you say that?" Fresh asked as he signed and dated his app.

"Yeah, it's just an application," the stubby white guy working behind the booth, wearing glasses, a hat with the credit card logo in bold letters and matching polo shirt said. "What's the worst that can happen? Even if you are accepted, you can always turn it down. Hell, if I were you, I'd go for it, buddy. Get yourself a free pizza!"

"I'm not really that hungry," I said, cutting my eyes and frowning my face up at the rep for butting in. "Besides, my mom told me about little people like him. I think she called them credit predators, or something like that."

"Man, you got me feeling real paranoid all of a sudden," Fresh said, still holding on to his clipboard, giving it some more thought. "If it was so bad, the university wouldn't let them come out here. Besides, the card is accepted everywhere, so I know they're legit. I mean, look around at all these people walking around with pizza boxes on the strip. Everybody is signing up!"

"If everybody was jumping off a bridge, would you do it?" I asked. "I'm not saying don't do it. I'm just saying, *I'm* not about to do it. Did you even read the fine print?"

"I mean… I skimmed over it," Fresh said. "I read enough to know that I can be approved for up to ten G's."

"Damn!" I screamed. "For real? Ten thousand bucks is a lot of money."

"Yep! Ten big ones!" the credit card rep said, sounding like a sneaky used-car salesman. "That card actually requires you to have a parent cosign for you. I have a cell phone if you need to make that call."

"I sure could use that right about now," I said, rubbing my hands together.

"Sure you could," the rep continued. "You should really think twice about signing up, pal. I mean, hey, what've ya got to lose?"

"Everything!" I shouted. "Man, if you ruin your credit, you're jacked up for life. Plus, my mom always said, if you can't pay for something with cash, you probably don't need to be buying it. So I'm straight."

I never heard Fresh respond. By the time I'd finished my public service announcement, my feet had already begun moving away from the booth and straight toward Leslie—the Elman girl who'd shot me down the first time I tried to holler. I had a better feeling about my chances this time. When I'd met her before, I'd just gotten off a five-hour flight from Cali, so my clothes were wrinkled, my hair was matted and my breath may not have been the freshest. But today, I knew my breath was fresh and my gear was on point. My swag was complete. The closer I got, the more beautiful she appeared. Her short hairstyle was unique and fit her well. I don't usually go after girls with short hair, but she was so fine, it didn't matter. Plus, just looking at the grade of her hair, you could tell she probably had Indian in her family. In fact, with her distinct features and petite frame, she slightly resembled the actress Nia Long. She was a natural beauty.

But as gorgeous as she was, not even Leslie's face could hold a candle to her body. She had the frame of a video vixen. Short in stature, but curvy like the letter *S*. She was rockin' a white blouse and chocolate-colored wraparound skirt, leaving just enough of her thigh exposed to pique the imagination. I could tell her thighs were firm, just looking at 'em. I figured she was a former cheerleader. Either that, or definitely a track star in high school. And the ass…short yellow bus—retarded! So fat you could see it from the front. With the naked eye, one could easily assume that she'd paid for a Brazilian Butt-lift—booty implants. But I knew everything about her had to be authentic. That's why I had to give it a second shot. As I intentionally walked directly in her path, impeding her progress, I just hoped she remembered me.

"Excuse me!" she shouted. "Do I know you?"

"As a matter of fact, you do," I said, sounding as smooth as I possibly could. "The name is J.D."

"And I know you from…?" she said slowly, wrinkles forming in her forehead insinuating she had no idea who the hell I was.

"I met you the other day in the parking lot near Marshall Hall," I said.

"Are you sure about that?" she asked. "I remember being in that area, but I don't remember meeting a J.D."

"Well, that's funny, because I distinctly remember meeting a Leslie," I said. "A fine one who goes to Elman."

She blushed, smiling from ear to ear. The cut I'd noticed on her lip the first time we met was all cleared up. But this time, there was a new blemish—a slight bruise above her left eye. One that she tried to cover up with eye shadow. It wasn't major, but it was noticeable. She didn't look like much of a boxer, but I wondered if she did some sparring in her spare time or something.

"That is my name," she said. "Maybe we did meet. I apologize for not remembering, I've just been so busy registering for my classes, dealing with the people in the financial aid office and trying to get all of my textbooks, I haven't even had time to think about much else."

"It's all good, sweetheart," I said. "As a matter of fact, now that I think about it, when we met, I told you my name was James."

"Oooooh," she said. "Now I remember! Soooooo... you're the guy all of the girls at Elman have been warned about?"

"All the girls at *Elman* have been warned about?" I asked, repeating her question with my face scrunched up, as if she'd spoken in a different language. "What do you mean by that?"

"Let's just say I heard about you," Leslie said, making a precarious facial gesture, as if she'd heard some kind of negative rumor.

My mind raced. I wondered what she'd heard, who'd told her, and if all the girls at Elman were really privy to the details of the highly publicized love triangle I was a part of last semester.

"Heard what?" I asked, sounding extremely insecure. "Good things or bad?"

"That's not all that important right now," Leslie said. "Look, I hate to be rude, but I really have to get going. It was nice to meet you, James. I mean, J.D. I mean... Heck, with all your aliases, I don't even know what to call you."

"Baby, you can call me whatever you want, whenever you want," I said. "As long as I can call you, too."

"Well, I think I will call you...a freshman!" she said, laughing. "A charming one, though. I must admit. Very charming. You are a freshman, right?"

"Second semester freshman."

"Ha! That's so funny. *Second semester* freshman. Aaaaw, that's real cute," she said.

"And what's your classification?" I asked.

"I'm a sophomore. A *second semester* sophomore, to be exact," she said, giggling.

"Real funny," I said. "I like a girl with a sense of humor. Maybe we can exchange knock-knock jokes over the phone when I call you. You got a number I can reach you on?"

"Charming and persistent," she said. "Two thumbs up! Well, I've gotta be honest. I'm kinda seeing somebody right now. And I don't usually give my number out to guys around here. Especially guys who aren't Lighthouse men."

"What is it with you and Lighthouse men?"

"No offense, but the guys over at Lighthouse just seem to have their stuff together," she said.

"Dang, that's messed up," I said. "So what you tryna say about brothas from U of A?"

"Well, I try not to stereotype people. But it just seems like guys of U of A like to play games. And that's not me. You seem pretty cool, though. Plus, you're kinda cute. Anybody ever tell you that you look like...umm..." she said, snapping her finger, deep in thought. "What's his name? He was in *Dead Presidents, Love Jones*...umm...I know you know who I'm talking about."

"Larenz Tate?" I asked, knowing good and well that's who she was referring to.

"Yeah!" she said. "That's his name! It was right on the tip of my tongue. Man, you two look just alike. I know you get that all the time."

"Every now and then," I said.

"Well, look *Larenz*," she said, laughing. "We can be friends. Just hit me up on Facebook sometime."

"That's cool," I said. "But Facebook is so impersonal. How 'bout I just call you?"

"How 'bout you hit me on Facebook first and we'll go from there," she said.

"I guess that's cool," I said, disheartened. "What's your last name?"

"Find me without it," she said, smiling.

"How am I gonna find you on Facebook, when I don't even know your last name? There's gotta be hundreds of girls named Leslie who go to Elman. It'll take me forever to find your page."

"Well, I guess we'll see how bad you really want to talk to me, now won't we?"

"And you said guys from U of A liked to play games," I said sarcastically.

Leslie hadn't even taken ten steps before some upper-classmen wearing a red and white fraternity jacket swooped her into his arms like he'd known her for years. I took note of his line name, Wallstreet, etched across the back of his jacket in huge white letters. I watched on help-lessly as the two of them walked off together in the opposite direction, seemingly enjoying each other's company. I've never wished I was anyone else in my entire life. But at that moment, on that day, I envied him. I wished I could be in his shoes. Even though Leslie had just played me to the left with the whole "look me up on Facebook" spill, I still felt like I could have her. And the fact that she was making it a challenge made her even more intriguing to me.

"Ain't that the same girl who turned you down the other day?" Fresh asked, standing next to me holding a half-eaten box of pizza in one hand and a fresh slice in the other.

"Yeah, that's her," I said.

"See, look at her, walking off all playful with the dude in the Kappa jacket," he said. "I'm tryna tell you. If you wanna pull a top-notch like her, you might wanna think about pledging Kappa."

"Why do I feel like you're tryna recruit me into a fraternity that *you're* not even in?" I asked, laughing.

"Laugh now," he said. "We'll see who's laughing when I'm on the next line coming out."

"You ain't finna be on nobody's line, blood," I said. "Everybody knows freshmen can't pledge."

"Neither can sophomores, juniors or seniors if they don't get chosen to be on the line," Fresh said. "That's why I'ma start putting my work in this semester, so when sophomore year rolls around, I'll be in the game."

"What you mean, 'putting work in'?" I asked.

"Never mind that," Fresh said, his eyes still glued to Leslie's fatty as it bounced down the strip. "Damn, she's fine!"

"Who you tellin'?"

"That was the come up of the century! You got her number, right?"

"Kind of," I said.

"What you mean, kind of? Either you got the digits or you didn't. She gave you her dorm extension or something?"

"Not exactly," I said.

"Well, what did she give you, her e-mail address?" he said sarcastically, laughing.

"She gave me her Facebook," I mumbled under my breath.

"Her *what?* Did you just say she gave you her Facebook, G? That is hilarious!"

"At least I got something," I said.

"Correction," he said. "You got nothing. Man, anybody can look her up on Facebook."

"Whatever, blood," I said. "Anyways. What kind of pizza did you get?"

"Hawaiian."

"How much did you get approved for?" I asked.

"Ten stacks!" Fresh said, proudly. "I had to gas my mom up a lil' bit, though."

"What'd you tell her?"

"I just told her that the interest on the card was a lot less than the interest on a student loan, so I would use the card to get my books and pay my tuition for next semester," he said.

"And she went for it?" I asked. "That's what's up! Ten thousand dollars is a lot of money, bro. Be careful."

FIVE

FOAM PARTY

I couldn't stop thinking about that comment Leslie made about me being the guy all of the Elman girls had been warned about. I wondered what she meant by that, and how many other students *really* thought I was HIV positive. And even if they did, how the news traveled from our campus all the way to Elman was beyond me. For the first time since I'd been in college, I felt insecure. I hadn't even attempted to look for Leslie on Facebook yet. The mere thought of doing the research just to get in contact with her made me feel like a sucka. But I'd come to the conclusion that if looking her up on the computer was the only way I could stay in contact with her, I was willing to take my chances. Besides, I figured with her going to Elman and all, it would be a while before I bumped into her around the yard again. Little did I know, I wouldn't have to wait that long.

Less than ten minutes after Fresh and I stepped foot in the foam party, there she was again. Even half-drunk, in a club full of half-dressed, gorgeous women, she stood out like a searchlight. I was low on ends, so I watched from a distance as some other guy bought her a drink. *Better him than me*, I thought. But I kept my eye on her the entire time. Just as she brushed that guy off and headed to the dance floor, I made my way through the crowd toward her. As she danced in a group with her girls, I hesitated momentarily, not wanting to embarrass myself by getting turned down for a dance in front of her friends. Then I took a deep breath, said what the hell and crept up on her from behind. At first she stopped dancing and looked back at me like I was crazy. I hit her with a big grin and kept on grooving. The moment she recognized me, her poker face gave in to a smile, and she began swaying to the beat again. As I held her from behind I was entranced by the way her black tights clung to her curves, accentuating her juicy derriere. I couldn't help being aroused just looking at the way she arched her lower back and moved her body. The way she effortlessly gyrated her hips in a circular motion as if she was hula-hooping, looking back and biting her lip ever so often to show me she was feeling me. With my hands placed firmly on her hips, I tuned everyone else out. It was as if we were the only two people on the dance floor. I leaned in, my lip gently caressing her ear as I spoke.

"You are looking so damn fine in this outfit," I whispered.

If I could've thought of a better line to use, I would have. But at the time, I was so sprung, that was the best I could do. Judging by the grin that permeated her face, she knew it was genuine.

"Thank you, sweetie," she said, as she effortlessly rolled her hips back against my pelvis to the beat.

I don't know if it was the speed at which all of the blood

in my body rushed to my genital area, the smell of her sweet perfume, or the look in her eye when she turned around to call me by a pet name for the first time, but right then and there, I knew she could be the one for me. We danced for a few more songs, then she spun around and pulled me close. I puckered up for a kiss, to no avail.

"You're a pretty good dancer for a *second semester* freshman," she said. "I had fun."

"You leaving?" I asked.

"Yeah," she said. "I got class in the morning. Can't stay out too late. You got my number, though. Give me a call."

Now, I'm not sure if it was the liquor talking or she really didn't remember blatantly telling me to contact her on Facebook, but since she was insinuating I already had the number, I rolled with it.

"Actually, for some reason, it didn't save in my phone when I tried to put it in," I said, lying my butt off. "What is it again?"

I laughed to myself as she recited her number in my ear as if she'd already given it to me. Once I had her number safely stored in my phone, Leslie flashed her pearly whites one last time, then disappeared into the crowd. She looked so good, I wanted to tag along and walk her to her dorm. When Leslie walked away from me, I felt like I was standing in the middle of a boxing ring in Caesar's Palace with my hands raised and a referee had just strapped the heavyweight champion title belt around my waist. Of all the guys in the club, the few who weren't looking at me in amazement had their eyes glued to Leslie's booty as it bounced away to its own rhythm. I took one more look for myself. If I knew how to do a backflip without landing on my neck, I would've done one right then and there in the middle of the club. After looking around to make sure nobody was checking me out, I executed a discreet, Tiger

Woods–inspired fist pump. If relationships were based on looks alone, I was convinced I could definitely settle down with Leslie. Now, I faced the daunting task of getting her to like me as much as I liked her. But until I did, I'd made up my mind I was going to have as much fun as I could. I'd chased Kat around so much last semester, I hadn't really seen what else there was out there for me. I figured the foam party was as good a place as any to start looking.

It wasn't even midnight and the club was already packed. The Greeks were doing their thing—lined up from shortest to tallest, strolling with their signature moves, calling out their unique chants and dissing rival frats and sororities. The Kappas were the cleanest, dressed in preppy gear from head to toe, the pretty boys arrogantly shimmied through the crowd while the ladies gawked. The Q's apparently missed the memo that it was freezing outside. Dressed in cut-off purple-and-gold tees, army fatigue pants and tattered Timbs, they were jumping around like madmen, stomping and clapping in unison. When I saw Timothy lined up with the Alphas mimicking gorillas as they strolled in their suits and loafers, I couldn't help but laugh. In one semester, he'd gone from Teenage Mutant Ninja Turtle pajama-wearing bookworm to an uncoordinated *Stomp the Yard* extra. The sorority chicks immediately changed my focus. The Deltas were deepest in number. They ranged from drop-dead gorgeous to "She must have a high GPA," enormous to petite, caramel-skinned to coal-complexioned. They stepped with distinction—all of them overdressed, wearing heels way too expensive and fancy for the club. The APAs weren't far behind. The storm of pink-and-green jackets came through strolling with their noses to the sky, their freshly pressed perms swinging from side to side as they pretended to adore themselves in invisible mirrors.

At first, moving out of the way so the Greeks could

make their way through the crowd was cool, but after a while, it became annoying. I felt like I was stuck on the set of *Drumline*. Dub-B, apparently clueless to the well-known fact that *nobody* is to step through a line while they are strolling, had little regard for the unwritten rule. When he nudged me and pointed out his girlfriend, Jasmine, on the other side of the club, I had no idea he was about to risk life and limb to speak to her. Without hesitation, Dub-B darted in between the line of APAs, in the middle of their coordinated routine.

Bad decision.

In a heartbeat, Dub-B was surrounded by the entire line, being pushed and shoved by an angry mob of no less than thirty sets of freshly manicured nails. In a matter of seconds, the expression on his face turned from "Oops, my bad" to sheer terror. Dub-B's lanky white frame bounced around like a bowling pin before being hurled away from them in a heap. His Yankees hat flew off his head and was trampled by the second half of the APA line, who picked up where they left off. Fresh and I were cracking up as we watched Dub-B pick up his mangled fitted cap from the floor, attempting to dust it off.

"What the hell was he thinking, joe?" Fresh asked. "Your boy was tweeking!"

"What's crackin', lil' homies?" Fats asked, dapping us up with a huge grin on his face. "Did y'all just see your boy Dub-B get manhandled by them APAs? That fool was rattled, cuz! When them girls crowded around him, he looked like he was about to shit his draws!"

"I know," I said, laughing. "That was the first time I've ever seen Dub-B actually look white. His face started turning red and all that! Man, that was hilarious!"

"Pure comedy, fam-o," Fresh added.

All jokes subsided and laughter ceased immediately

when Katrina popped up, seemingly out of nowhere, in front of me. For a few seconds, she just stood there, staring into my eyes, inaudibly asking, once more, for forgiveness. She opened her arms wide and smiled gingerly, gesturing for me to embrace her. Lord knows I wanted to. With no sign of Leslie in sight, Kat was hands-down the finest girl in the club. With her beauty, body and swag, there wasn't even a close second. Even in the club, I could smell her sweet perfume from where I stood, entrancing me like a fish to a lure. I wanted to let bygones be bygones and move on, but my pride wouldn't let me. Not in front of my boys. I had a reputation to consider. Hugging Kat in the middle of the club like that, with everybody watching, could have ignited a whole 'nother slew of rumors that I didn't want to have to deal with. So instead of stepping into her open arms or acknowledging her at all, I just tapped Fresh and nodded toward the other side of the club, signaling him to keep it moving. I left Kat standing there with her arms open.

"I can't believe you just played her like that, cuz," Fats said, shaking his head in disbelief.

"Yeah," Fresh agreed. "That was cold as hell, G. Can't say I blame you, though, but damn."

"I ain't even thinkin' 'bout that girl, blood," I said confidently. "After what she put me through, as far as I'm concerned, she doesn't exist."

After Dub-B's debacle, the encounter with Kat and a few shots of Patrón, the party really started jumping. Every ten minutes or so a huge gust of foam would squirt onto the dance floor. I don't know where it was coming from, but after a few hours, I was damn near up to my knees in suds. I had a weird urge to wash dishes. And my Jordans were all but ruined, soaked from the inside out. The good thing about it was, for some reason, the foam was driving the females wild. They frolicked in it like it was winter snow. By the time Ludacris finally the hit stage, it was nearly two in the morning.

"You tryna hit this after-party?" Fresh asked.

"*After*-party? Man, it's already damn near two in the morning. You know the first day of class is tomorrow."

"I know, but it's supposed to be live though, G," he said. "At least that's what I keep hearing. Let's just fall through for a minute. If it's bogus, we'll dip."

"That's cool," I said. "Where's it at anyway?"

"Near the campus," Fresh said. "Matter of fact, they say it's poppin' over there right now. That's where all of the upperclassmen are partying. You ready to dip?"

"Let's do it!" I said.

SIX

THE AFTERPARTY

We just left in time to catch the last shuttle heading back to campus. Thank goodness, because it was cold outside and the walk back to campus woulda been no joke. The closer we got to campus, the more I had second thoughts about going to the after-party. Partially because I was already tired and needed sleep for class in the morning. But mostly because I was sweaty, my clothes were wrinkled and my Jordans had been stepped on at least twenty times in the club, not to mention soaked by the suds. And if there were going to be upperclassmen at the party like Fresh said, I would have preferred to be looking and smelling as good as possible. The shuttles dropped us off in the Elman parking lot. From there, I followed Fresh to a house just around the corner from campus. I could hear the base pumping from the speakers a full block away from the house, and by the look of all the cars outside, I could tell the party was crackin'. But for some reason, I still didn't wanna go.

"You think there's some kinda dress code for this party?" I asked, trying to back out.

"Not that I know of," Fresh said. "We're about to find out, though."

The closer we got to the house, the more I noticed Kappa Beta Psi tags on all of the cars. There were others, too—mostly Delta Delta Theta and Alpha Pi Alpha—so I knew there were gonna be some fine girls up in there. The music was coming from a house that was painted red. In the middle of the front yard, three huge, five-foot-tall letters—KBP—painted red and white, were standing upright.

"The party is at the Kappa house?" I asked as we scaled the stairs.

I suppose the question was so stupid it didn't deserve an answer, because Fresh just kept on walking up the steps without ever turning around to acknowledge it. We didn't have to knock on the door. As soon as we reached the porch, one guy wearing a Kappa jacket stumbled out of the house with two girls escorting him down the stairs—one kissing his earlobe the other rubbing his chest. I was so busy checking out the two chicks, I didn't even get a chance to see his face, but I read the back of his jacket as clear as day. Konceited.

"Damn!" I said. "It's like that? Maybe I do need to join."

"It's funny you should say that," Fresh said, laughing as he opened the door.

I didn't know quite what he meant by that. But after being in the party for less than five minutes, I didn't care. There had to be six girls to every guy in that house. And damn near all of 'em were drunk. Plus, it was dark. The only light in the house was coming from under the microwave in the kitchen. I heard whispers of an open bar in the kitchen, but it was so packed, we couldn't even make it that far. Everywhere I turned, there was a female grabbing on me. It was as if I'd walked into heaven. I couldn't miss. Fresh wasted no time pushing a girl up against the wall and getting freaky when the DJ slowed it down and played a slow jam. By the end of the first verse he had scooped ol' baby clean off her feet and was grinding on her as he held both of her legs up and she gripped the back of his neck. I was in the middle of the living room, all up on some chick I'd never seen before, grinding like a blender. I couldn't see how cute she was, but I didn't need light to tell she was a super freak. I'd only been dancing with her for half a song when she stuck her hand down my pants. I didn't know whether to keep dancing or sneak her to the bathroom. All I knew was all of a sudden, I was harder than a football helmet. All I could do was smile and shake my head. That's when baby girl retracted her hand and leaned in to whisper in my ear.

"What's so funny?" she asked.

"You just had your hand down my pants and I don't even know your name," I said.

"They call me Peaches."

"Why do they call you Peaches, baby?"

"Because I'm thick like a peach, sweet like a peach, juicy like a peach," she said very matter-of-factly, before taking a huge sip of her drink.

"Is that right?" I asked.

"Yep," she confirmed. "And if you ever get your letters, call me. I can't wait to put it on your fine ass!"

Before I could respond, she stepped off. I wondered, damn, is it really *that* easy when you're Greek?

"C'mon, let's grab a drink," Fresh said, grabbing me by my shoulder with one hand, motioning for me to follow him to the back with the other.

I looked at my watch and saw that it was already fifteen

after three. There was really no reason to have another drink when I knew I had class in less than five hours. But peer pressure is a mutha, so I followed Fresh's lead. The closer we got to the kitchen, the stronger I could smell something burning. It was an unfamiliar scorching scent like nothing I'd ever smelled before. I was a few steps away from the kitchen when the countdown began. There was a guy, wearing a long-sleeve shirt sitting at the table with one sleeve rolled up. He was surrounded by guys who I presumed were Kappas based on how they were dressed, and the fact that they were all in on the countdown.

"Kappa!" they yelled in unison.

The guy sitting at the table lowered his head into his hand.

"Beta!" they screamed excitedly.

That's when I noticed the guy at the table's knees shaking profusely. He was a nervous wreck. Two of the larger guys in the kitchen grabbed his arm, one at the shoulder the other at the wrist, holding it steady.

"Psi!" they hollered.

That's when a guy holding what looked like a bent wire hanger rushed over from the stove with it red-hot and steaming, and mashed it into dude at the table's forearm. He held it there for about three seconds, but just watching it felt like an eternity.

"Aaaaaaargh!" the guy screamed, as his arm sizzled like bacon, the skin peeling back like a banana, revealing the white meat, blood oozing around toward his elbow and down his wrist. I turned away momentarily, becoming light-headed and weak at the knees. I couldn't believe anyone in their right mind would voluntarily allow someone to burn the shit out of them like that. I was blown away.

"For life!" everyone said together, clapping and slapping high fives.

The guy at the table stood up, grimacing in pain as he proudly showed off his badge of honor—a perfect circle with the letters *KBS* in the center.

"Want a Jell-O shot?" a girl asked, carrying a full tray of those little really small, plain paper cups you get in the hospital.

After what I just saw, I figured I needed one, just to get my mind right. My hand was hovering over the tray, when I felt someone yank my arm back with so much force it damn near popped my shoulder out of the socket.

"What the hell are you doing?" Fresh yelled in his most abrasive whisper tone. "You tryna get yourself killed up in here?"

"What's the big deal?" I asked. "You're the one who brought me over here to get the damn drink!"

"Do you want one or not?" the girl asked, still holding the tray out in front of me.

"No thank you," Fresh said. "We're good."

"You're trippin', blood," I said, rubbing my shoulder.

"*I'm* trippin'?" he asked. "I might've just saved your life, fool! Did you not see all of those Jell-O shots were *red*?"

"So they were cherry Jell-O shots," I said. "Duh. What does that have to do with anything?"

"Look, just know you don't need to touch or put your mouth on anything red up in here if you're not a Kappa," he whispered in my ear. "That was a setup. And your ass almost fell for it."

I was green to virtually all of the dos and don'ts of fraternity life, mostly because I never gave joining one much thought. Back home, the only thing niggaz from my hood ever talked about joining were gangs. And even that was rare in Oakland. Where I'm from, it was all about the neighborhood or "turf" you were from, as opposed to what gang you were in. We pretty much left the gangbanging to L.A., so I never really had to adhere to any organization's rules and regulations. Besides, I didn't even know I was coming to a frat house party in the first damn place. I was just out to have a good time.

"Having fun?" someone asked.

I figured it was probably someone I knew from Marshall Hall. But when I spun around, I was standing next to a complete stranger. He was a light-skinned, slender guy with a goatee, and stood a little taller than me. I could tell he was intoxicated because he was leaning up against the wall, cheesing so hard I could see his front tooth was chipped. I noticed he was wearing a silver Kappa dog chain around his neck, so I deferred to Fresh to respond to him.

"Hey, w'sup, Dex," Fresh said. "This party is juking, folk."

"Do I know you from somewhere?" Dex asked.

"I go to school at U of A," Fresh said. "I don't think we've ever formally met, though. My name is Lamont but everyone calls me Fresh."

"It's a pleasure meeting you, *Lamont*," Dex said. "Who invited you to the party?"

"Well, we heard about the party…"

"Who is we?" Dex asked.

"Me and my boy, J.D."

"Who?"

"James Dawson," I said, extending my hand. "This party is turned up, blood. It's crackin' in here!"

"Turned up," he repeated. "Crackin'. You must be from the West Coast. Where you from?"

"The Town," I said.

"Oh, Oakland, huh? Okay. I'm from L.A."

"That's what's up," I said.

"So who invited y'all, again?"

"Nobody really," Fresh said. "To keep it one hundred with you, Dex, we just kinda came."

"Why?" Dex asked.

"We heard a lot of good things about your organization, and we were interested in learning more," Fresh said.

"Oh, so y'all are *interested,* huh?" Dex asked obnoxiously loud so the other guys standing around could hear him. A couple of them peered over his shoulder to get a look at us. "Stick around for the after-party."

Something about the way Dex said that and walked off left me with an eerie feeling. Besides, I thought this *was* the after-party. I jabbed Fresh in his ribs with my elbow.

"How you gon' volunteer me for pledging a *fraternity?*" I asked. "That's not something you do!"

"It's not pledging," he said. "It's not like we're on line or anything. I just let Dex know that we were interested. Worst-case scenario, we might do a little prepledging, but nothing too serious."

"*Pre*pledging? Are you serious right now, blood? I'm not even sure if I wanna pledge...."

"*Sssssshhhhh!*" Fresh hissed, placing his finger over his lips. "Keep your voice down, joe."

"Oh, yeah," I said, whispering. "I'm not even sure if I want to pledge once, let alone twice!"

"It's not what you think," Fresh said, pulling me in the back hallway. "The Kappas only bring out new lines once a year, in the fall. So it's not like we're gonna have to do too much this semester."

"Look, I'm not saying I don't want to get down," I said. "But if they're not bringing out a line until the fall, what's the point of doing anything this semester?"

"It's the only way we'll even have a chance of getting on the line in the fall!" Fresh said. "Do you know how many niggaz show up to try to get in this frat? Hundreds! And they never have a line over ten. So you do the math on that. The shit is rigged, joe. Prepledging is the only way in."

My eyelids were getting heavy. I looked at my watch again. It was almost four in the morning.

"That's cool," I said. "But on some real shit, I ain't feelin' sticking around for no after-party, blood. I'm hella tired. The first day of class starts in a couple hours. I gotta go."

The second I said that, the music stopped and someone cut the lights on. The DJ thanked everyone for coming out, and people started to file out. Fresh leaned up against the wall, staring me down. He was determined to stay. I had a different agenda. I was on academic probation. I had more at stake and I didn't want to get the semester started on the wrong foot. I decided to try to mix in with the crowd and discreetly duck out. I made it all the way to the porch and thought I was scot-free when I heard someone call me.

"What's crackin', West Coast?" someone hollered out.

I kept walking as if the question wasn't directed at me, knowing good and well I was likely the only person from the West Coast leaving the party.

"Yo!" the guy yelled. "I thought you were gonna stick around for the after-party, *James.*"

I was hoping he hadn't remembered my name. I could've just kept on walking and pretended I didn't know he was talking to me. But there was no getting out of this. Now, I had to face the music. Either turn around and tell him that my sleep was more important than their after-party and ruin any chance I'd ever have of getting in, or...

"Hey," I said, spinning around wearing a fake smile. "I didn't know you were talking to me."

"C'mon, now," he said. "You know it ain't that many of us out here from the West Coast. Where you going, homie?"

"I was..." I said, struggling to find the words to complete my lie. "I was just coming out here 'cause I thought I saw this girl I knew."

"Oh, okay, because it looked to me like you were tryna bounce, dog," he said.

"Nah," I said. "I was gonna come back in."

"Oh, you don't have to," he said. "I mean, if you've got something better to do, handle you business. It's just that inside, I thought you said you were interested."

"I am," I said.

"Well, come on back inside," Dex said, throwing his arm around my neck, and half-playfully, half-forcefully, walking me back inside. By the time we made it up the stairs to the porch, surprisingly the house was dead silent. Everyone had cleared out. When Dex opened the door, he patted me on back, then kind of shoved me inside.

The front room was pitch-black and there was no one in it. I stumbled over a beer bottle and gripped the wall with both hands, attempting to get my bearings. I could vaguely hear someone talking in one of the rooms, but I had no idea where the voice was coming from. I quickly spread my legs shoulder-width and assumed a defensive stance, ready for whatever. But inside, I was terrified.

"C'mon, man," Dex said, grabbing me by my arm, leading me down a narrow hallway, then down a flight of wooden stairs that creaked with every step.

"What's down here?" I asked, nervously following him.

We were almost at the bottom step when I heard the door slam shut behind me. I had no idea anyone else was even in the house. That's when I really got scared. The basement was extremely dark, too. One small lightbulb hung in the middle of the ceiling emitting a dim light. Although it was too dark to make out any faces, I could sense there were at least fifteen Kappas standing on one side of the room. On the opposite side, there were seven guys lined up, each of them crouched with their knees bent in a squatting position and their backs against the wall. They were grimacing. Their knees were shaking. And all of them had their hands stretched out with their palms up.

"Go ahead and have a seat in the chair at the end of the wall," Dex said.

"Chair?" I asked, slowly looking around the room.

"Yes," he said, sighing deeply in exasperation. "The imaginary chair up against the wall. C'mon! Don't play stupid. I ain't got all night to be up in here with y'all!"

I took my spot on the wall right next to Fresh and assumed the position. Immediately, I knew why the other guys' knees were shaking so vigorously. While sitting in an imaginary chair with your arms straight out looked easy to the naked eye, actually holding that position was hard as hell. In less than two minutes, I was trembling, too.

"So y'all wanna be Kappas?" Dex asked, pacing to and fro in front of us, his red-and-white cane in one hand, a bottle of water in the other. "What y'all know about Kappa?"

"Not a damn thing!" one of the guys standing behind him said.

"They just wanna twirl canes on the yard," Dex said. "And look pretty like me."

"They could never do that," one said.

"Yeah, you're right," Dex said. "Maybe they wanna join Kappa Beta Psi because they heard we get all the girls on the yard. Maybe they think getting these letters will mean they'll be able to get with any girl on the yard."

Ya got me, I thought, half-smirking when he said that.

"I can," one of the guys said. "I don't know about them, though. Right now, they just look like some sorry ass GDIs to me."

"I think you're right," Dex said, laughing.

Dex stopped right in front of me, swirling his unopened bottle of water in my face. After sitting in the chair for about fifteen minutes, all of the liquor I drunk was seeping out of my pores. Not only were my legs wobbly, but I was sweating profusely from my armpits and temple.

"I bet you J.D. knows what a GDI is, don't you?"

"Nah."

"Nah?" one guy asked as if I'd disrespected him. Seconds later, some dark-skinned guy with a low haircut emerged from the shadows and ran up on me. He was at least six-five and couldn't have weighed less than 250 pounds. He was huge.

"Nah?" he repeated, banging his large hand against the wall right next to my head. Instinctively, I flinched.

"This nigga is flinching and all that," he said, laughing. "And I ain't even touched you."

He paused.

"Yet," he said, under his breath, snickering. The rest of the guys standing behind him started cracking up laughing. My stomach wrenched.

"Maybe he's just nervous," Dex said.

"From now on, any time any member of Kappa Beta Psi asks you anything, you address him as 'sir.' You understand me?"

"Yes," I said.

The huge guy slapped his hands together one inch away from my lips.

"Oh, so you're just gonna be an ole disrespectful ass nigga?" he asked. "I told myself I wasn't gonna put my hands on anybody tonight, and this fool is about to make me..."

"Fall back, Khaos," Dex said.

"I just asked him if he understood and he didn't even answer that right," he said. "Where did you find this guy?"

"Stand up and get yourself some water," he said, pulling me up by my elbow. "Here you go."

I thought he'd never ask. I unscrewed the top and guzzled half the bottle. I stopped when I heard some of the other guys grunting in agony, smacking their lips. I was so thirsty I hadn't even noticed I'd left them out to dry.

"Feel better?" Dex asked.

"Yes, sir," I said.

"How do you think watching you guzzle that water made the other guys on the wall feel?"

"I don't know, sir."

"Aaaaaah!" one of the guys said.

"That's fucked up, dog!" another shouted.

"What you mean, you don't know?" another asked.

"Do you know what a GDI is, J.D.?" Dex asked.

"No, sir," I said.

"I bet one of these guys knows," Dex said. "Y'all stand up."

"Whew!" the guys sounded off together in a sigh of relief, slowly returning to an upright position.

"I planned on sharing half of my bottle of water with y'all, but since you're thirsty friend drank your ration, this is all I have left for the five of you to share," Dex said as he poured a few drops of water into the bottle cap, and gave it to Fresh. "Take a sip and pass it down."

All of the Kappas standing behind Dex burst out in hysterical laughter. Meanwhile all of the guys I was on the wall with were looking at me like I'd snitched on them and they'd just been sentenced to life in prison.

"Now, which one of you sweaty, stinky underclassmen can tell J.D. what a GDI is?" Dex asked.

Fresh raised his hand. Dex acknowledged him.

"GDI stands for *gatdamn individual,* sir," Fresh said.

"A gatdamn individual is right," Dex said. "And would any of you GDIs be able to define the word *individual?*"

There was a brief moment of silence as each of us looked around at one another to see if anyone had an answer.

"Didn't think so," Dex said. "An *individual* is one

person existing as a distinct entity. And indivisible whole. An individual thinks about himself and himself only, with no regard to altruism. The kind of guy who can drink water in front of a group of thirsty guys without thinking to offer them a sip. A GDI is selfish. And y'all are GDIs because y'all don't know the true meaning of brotherhood. And that's what the men of Kappa Beta Psi fraternity are all about. Brotherhood."

Silence returned.

"And you say you want to be join Kappa Beta Psi," Dex continued. "Well, over the next twelve weeks, you will have an opportunity to prove to us and yourself just how bad you want it. I can tell you right now, it won't be easy. You will sacrifice your sleep, free time and freedom, for a chance to make our line next semester. The only thing I can promise you is that if you make it through this semester of prepledging, and maintain a 3.0 GPA this semester..."

"*Three* point GPA?" I accidently murmured.

"Yes, three-point-zero GPA," Dex continued. "I can guarantee that you will be on our fall line. If these requirements are more than you are capable of achieving, I implore you to gather your things and leave now."

Bolting came to mind. Coming away with a 2.67 last semester was a milestone in my academic career. And I didn't have anything to worry about except for keeping my grades up. So securing a B average while prepledging didn't sound like a lofty goal. It sounded impossible. But maybe it was just what I needed. Maybe higher expectations would force me to rise to the occasion. Maybe a new set of friends—upstanding upperclassmen with good grades and nice cars—would do me some good, like my mom said. When I thought about the upside, I decided to stay put.

"Since it seems you guys have decided to stick around, I guess I can let you go home for the night," Dex said.

Thank God, I thought, taking a deep breath of relief. It was going on six in the morning, and I figured I could still sneak a quick nap in before my nine o'clock class.

"After you guys clean up the mess upstairs," Dex said.

The eight of us let out a collective groan of disgruntlement.

"Where is Konceited?" Dex asked.

"He left with some chick," one of the guys said.

"Nah, he left with two," another corrected. "The Italian stallion left with him, too!"

"Oh, forreal?" Dex asked. "She's a fine lil' brizzle, too! Aight, well, since Konceited ain't here, y'all boys follow Khaos. He'll show you where to find the vacuum, trash bags, broom, mop bucket, Windex and toilet cleaner so you can get started."

Even though I was pissed off about having to clean up the house, I couldn't help but wonder if the girl they referred to as the Italian stallion was the same girl Timothy was dating. *Couldn't be,* I thought. It was probably just a coincidence. At least, I hoped it was.

SEVEN

CLASS

I was out on my feet by the time we left the Kappa house. The sun was up and people were walking to class. Thankfully, my first class didn't start until nine, so I had a few minutes to freshen up. I wasn't even in my room five minutes before Lawry came knocking. As usual, he wanted to borrow something. This time it was my iron, ironing board and mouthwash. I was exhausted, tired as hell and moving like a zombie. My legs were so sore from sitting in that damn imaginary chair, I could barely walk.

"You look like hell, shawty," Lawry said. "Must've had a long night."

"Basically," I said, being intentionally short.

"What is that I keep smelling in here?" Lawry asked, sniffing as he frowned up his face.

"It's probably your breath," I said.

"Smells like garlic up in here," he said, still sniffing.

"Then it's *definitely* your breath," I said, walking over to my closet to pick out something to wear.

"Why you limping around like that?" he asked. "You must've been tryna do that damn stanky leg in the club!"

"Something like that," I said.

"I see you're still wearing the same outfit you wore to the foam party," he prodded. "What time did you get back?"

I wanted to tell him I couldn't walk because I was getting hazed all night and I'd just gotten back five minutes ago, but Lawry was nosy, and I'd been sworn to secrecy.

"I got back around three," I said, lying. "I was so hammered, I wound up passing out on my bed before I could get out of my clothes."

The last thing Dex told us before we left the Kappa house was to make sure nobody found out that we were involved in any prepledging activities. He said if word got back to anybody in the frat that one of us was talking, our entire process would be over and we'd have just as much a chance to make the line as the other hundreds of guys who showed up with their applications in the fall. Fresh was right. If there's one thing I'd learned about going Greek in the last 24 hours, it was that the selection process was everything but fair. But after busting my ass cleaning the Kappa house last night, I'd taken the first step to solidifying my spot on the fall line.

"Around three, huh?" Lawry asked, still snooping. "That's funny, 'cause I was walking to the gym this morning, and I could have sworn I seen you leaving the Kappa house."

"*Ssssshhhhh!*" I hissed, placing my finger over my mouth. "Man, that wasn't me, homie."

"If it wasn't you, what you shushing me for?" he asked, smiling. "You know I was on line with the Alphas just last semester. You can't run that G on me, shawty."

"Okay, okay, all right," I said. "Look, man, I'm doing a little prepledging or whatever, but it's nothing serious. Whatever you do, don't say nothing to nobody about this."

"C'mon, now," he said. "I know what it is. You know I ain't gon' say nothin'."

"*Nobody,* Lawry!" I repeated.

"Your secret is safe with me, shawty," he said. "I ain't seen nothing."

I paid for last night on the first day of class. I could hardly keep my eyes open. Thank God, my first class was an easy find. The stroll from Marshall Hall to Washington Hall was a familiar trek for me because that's where I took Dr. Johnson's first-year seminar course last semester. I took solace in the fact that this public policy course would be an easy A, according to Fats's inside information. Let him tell it, he wouldn't be surprised to hear that the pregnant professor cancelled the first class of the semester so she could review her sonogram at the doctor's office. I hoped to see that note on the door as I turned the corner. But to my angst, it was propped wide open. There was no professor in sight. I hadn't even taken my notebook out of my book bag before the murmuring commenced.

"I think it's safe to say the professor ain't coming," one impatient girl wearing a head scarf said. "Let's get outta here before she gets here. It ain't our fault she's late."

"Don't be silly," Timothy said, checking his digital stopwatch. "It's only been six and a half minutes since class was supposed to start. I'm sure she's on her way."

"I'm with you, shorty," Dub-B said. "Somebody start up a roll so we can leave it on her desk before we dip."

"I got some paper," Fresh said, pulling his binder out of his bag. "I'll start it up."

I was sitting at my desk dozing off. Not just any dozing off, either. The embarrassing kind. The half-falling-over-out-of-my-desk, half-snoring, popping-up-like everything-is-all right kind. Similar to the way you see someone fading out in church. I awoke from my temporary state of unconsciousness to the sound of people around me laughing and snickering.

"Yo, are you all right, papi?" a Latina girl sitting beside me asked, laughing. "It looks like you might need some more sleep."

"Nah, it looks like he was going too hard at that foam party last night, yo," Dub-B said.

"He'll be aight," Fresh said, patting me on the back extra hard to wake me up.

Just as Fresh removed the cap from his pen, the last person I expected to see come through the door waltzed in. The moment she stepped in the room, I got my second wind. It was as if she'd taken center stage to perform a monologue in *The Color Purple* on Broadway. The spotlight was on Katrina and all eyes were on her. Seemingly unfazed by the attention, Katrina walked to her seat with her head high. I would be lying if I said she didn't look as attractive as she did the first time I saw her. In fact, she wasn't a penny short of a dime. Her hair was just as bouncy and full as I'd ever seen it, pressed to the *T,* as if she was going to a nightclub instead of a morning class. Much like everyone else's, my eyes scanned for imperfection, but found none. Even with no makeup on her face, Katrina looked like a doll. Her naturally long eyelashes, light brown eyes and pouty lips made it hard for me to stare at her for more than ten seconds without getting an erection. Not to mention her perky C-cups poking out from under her pink-and-green APA line jacket or her butt cheeks shaking like maracas with her every step. HIV positive or not, there was no denying Kat's beauty. It kinda made me wonder how many other cute girls parading around campus were infected.

"Yeah, that's her, girl," one girl sitting behind me whispered to another. "Mmm-hmm."

I was so focused on Kat, I didn't even notice that the guy sitting in front of me had passed back the sign-in sheet, until the girl sitting beside me tapped my shoulder.

"Are you gonna sign that or what?" she asked. "I ain't tryna be in here waiting on this professor all day."

"The campus manual of guidelines and procedures actually indicates that a professor has up to ten minutes to be late to class before we are free to go," Timothy said.

"Well, if she ain't here by the time that list makes it around to me, I'm gone," the girl said. "As high as tuition is at this school, the teachers need to show up ten minutes *early!*"

"I know that's right!" someone in the back seconded.

No sooner had I turned to pass the sign-in sheet back, Dr. Johnson came strolling through the door, his black leather Gucci briefcase in tow. He carried himself with a certain confidence that I admired, walking with his back and shoulders straight, dreds draping beyond his shoulders. Standing well over six feet and built like a professional bodybuilder, Dr. Johnson was a hulking figure who commanded respect without opening his mouth. And when he did, he spoke and conducted himself in a manner that exuded a self-assuredness that I envied. Even if you didn't like him, you had to respect him. Dr. J was a no-nonsense type of guy. He was as demanding and shrewd as he was fair. There was no way public policy class was going to be an easy A if he was teaching it. I hoped he was just subbing for the day.

"Good morning, ladies and gentlemen," he said, perching on the desk. "My name is Dr. Oliver Johnson, but you can call me Dr. J. As long as your name is on the roll sheet that I will have by next week and you are financially enrolled, I will be your professor for public policy this semester."

"Ain't this about a blip," I mumbled under my breath.

I noticed a few other students slump into their seats at the news.

"I see someone has already taken the initiative to start up a roll," he said with a chuckle. "I just know you all weren't planning on trying to pull the old 'let's sign the roll sheet before the teacher shows so we can leave early' move. So whoever's idea it was to get that started, I offer my sincerest thanks. I'd appreciate it if you all could continue to pass that sign-in sheet around for me, so I know who showed up today. I see some familiar faces and a few new ones. I'd like to take this time to welcome you all. As I'm sure you can tell by now, I am not Professor Tessa Mitchell—the instructor whose name should appear on most of your schedules. She has decided to take this semester off for maternity leave. So that, my scholars, leaves you with me. For those of you who have taken one of my courses in the past, you know my philosophy. It's plain and simple. Everybody in my class starts of with an A plus. *Everybody*. As a student, it's your job to keep that grade by coming to class on time, doing your homework, studying for exams and doing well on them. As your professor, I can promise you one thing. I won't grade you. But over the course of this semester, you will grade yourself."

As if on cue, in walked a fashion-forward, light-skinned guy wearing oversize Fendi aviator shades, matching ascot, button-up shirt, a pair of extremely snug Rockin' Republic jeans and a pair of Ferragamo loafers. He strolled in as if he hadn't a care in the world, careful to switch his hips with every step, lightly brushing the bangs he'd so neatly pressed away from his forehead, before taking his seat.

"So glad that you could join us today, *sir,*" Dr. J said. "If you didn't know, class started fifteen minutes ago."

"I'm aware of that," the student retorted.

"Well, why is it that you are so late today, if you don't mind me asking?"

"Unless you plan on picking me up from my apartment complex before class for the rest of the semester, I mind," he snapped.

"Well, also be mindful that your attendance makes up ten percent of your overall grade in this class. So due to the fact that I will absolutely not be picking you up from anywhere at any time, it's imperative that you get to this class on time if your grade is of any importance to you. In fact, it's important that you all practice being punctual. In the real world, tardiness is not acceptable and I won't make any exceptions here. My mentor always told me, half an hour too soon is better than half a minute too late."

"But Dr. J, you were late to class today yourself," one girl sitting in the front row noted.

"Valid point," he said. "Next time you have one to make in my classroom, be sure to raise your hand first so I can call on you. Point taken, though. The fact of the matter is, I didn't find out I would be filling in for Professor Mitchell until this morning. That being said, I apologize for my tardiness. Those of you who know me can attest to the fact that I won't be making a habit of it."

As Dr. J walked around the class passing the course syllabus out to each student, getting a feel for the new faces and personally greeting the familiar ones, I braced myself for what was sure to be a longer, much more arduous semester than I'd planned for. I just knew Dr. J had something up his sleeve. It was inevitable.

"Mr. Dawson," he said, hulking over my desk in a gray cardigan sweater and checkered dress shirt. "Man, it's great to see you back! How was your break?"

"It was cool," I said.

"I'm looking forward to big things from you this semester," he said, looking me in the eye as he handed me a copy of the course description. "Don't let me down."

After passing out the packets, careful to make sure everyone had a copy, Dr. J returned to the front of the class, picked up a marker and went to the board.

"Does everyone have a copy of the course syllabus?" he asked.

Everyone nodded in unison.

"Good. Have you had a chance to review it carefully?" he asked.

Confusion riddled the faces of nearly everyone in the class, each of us looking around at one another to see if anyone knew where he was coming from. I had no idea, but I sensed a curveball coming. Timothy hesitantly raised his hand.

"Yes, sir," Dr. J said.

"Well, Dr. Johnson, I was just wondering what you meant by that, seeing that we just received our course descriptions less than five minutes ago," Timothy said. "I've skimmed through the syllabus, but haven't had time to review it in its entirety."

"Yet another valid point. Thank you for raising your hand before making it. Well, as Mr.... What's your name, son?"

"McGruden. Timothy McGruden."

"As Mr. McGruden has noted, none of you have had time to review the syllabus. And none of you will need to. As a matter of fact, everybody grab the packet I distributed to you and hold it above your head."

Here it comes, I thought as I hoisted mine high.

"Now, rip it in half," he said.

The bewildered facial expressions returned. No one, including myself could fathom why Dr. J would take the time to pass out something he just wanted us to rip up.

"I'm serious!" he insisted. "Rip it up!"

"You don't have to tell me again," Fresh said, tearing his in half.

Everyone else followed suit.

"That syllabus outlined the items Professor Mitchell saw fit to focus on this semester in terms of government affairs. Her way of doing this is absolutely fine and by the book. It's just not my preference. I am interested in taking a more practical approach to ensuring you all learn the inner workings of bureaucracy—the good, the bad and the ugly."

The windup.

"How many of you all have already signed up to participate in the upcoming student body election?" he asked.

Of the thirty or so students in the class, only one hand was raised. It belonged to Howard Harrell—University of Atlanta's version of Barack Obama. Howard was a man of the people. Class president for the past three years, he was a shoe-in for student body president and everybody knew it. Revered for his near-perfect GPA, notorious for wearing a suit and tie at all times and heralded for his ability to effectively convey the thoughts and ideologies of the student body to the administration, in essence, Howard Harrell was the man. A man many suspected to be on the DL, but the man, nonetheless. In fact, in the last election, he ran unopposed. No one dared contest Howard Harrell.

"No one other than Mr. Harrell, huh?" Dr. J prodded.

Looking around the room, Howard revealed a cocky half-smile, before straightening his tie.

"Well, don't get too comfy, Mr. President," Dr. J said, looking at Howard. "That will soon change. From this point forward you can forget anything you've ever heard about public policy class. Don't worry about purchasing a textbook. You won't need it. No more study guides or scantron tests. Too easy to cheat. And here's the best part...no more homework! That's so passé."

"That's what I'm talking about, yo!" Dub-B said as others applauded in celebration.

Knowing Dr. J, all of this was too good to be true. I knew there had to be a catch. I wisely decided to hold my applause 'til the end.

"However," he said.

The delivery.

"All of you," he said, "those of you who don't chicken out and drop the class, that is, will be responsible for participating in the upcoming student government election in some way, shape or form. This class will involve interactive campaigning, speech writing and public speaking."

"Oh, hell nah," I mumbled under my breath, echoing the groans of my classmates.

This is what I get for listening to Fats, I thought. *Easy A,* my ass!

"You will be randomly selected to form groups," Dr. J continued. "Each group will have at least one representative who must run for a position in student government. The rest of the members of the group will act as campaign managers, responsible for marketing, promoting and assisting the candidates in your group running for office."

"Sounds like an easy A to me," Dub-B said confidently.

I raised a brow out of suspicion. Did he know something I didn't?

"What ever happened to Professor Mitchell?" Lawry grumbled.

"The way I see it," Dr. J said, intentionally inflecting his voice to drown out the complainers, "why read about policies and procedures in some textbook when you can participate in enacting social change right here on campus for yourselves? So without any further ado, let the selection process begin."

He grabbed his black fedora from the desk and held it

in front of himself. "This is my hat," he said. "In this hat, I have placed small pieces of paper with numbers on them. I am going to pass this hat around the class and each of you will take one piece of paper from the hat. On one side of the paper, you will find a number. That number will represent the group number you will belong to. It would behoove you to memorize that number, because the grade you receive in this class hinges entirely on the way you work alongside other students with that same number. On the flip side of that piece of paper, you will find a position on the class council. That position is what one member of your group will run for in the upcoming election. In the event someone in your group is already holding a post in student government, such as Mr. Harrell, that group member has free reign to run for reelection for that same position or any other position he or she chooses. Otherwise, one representative from the group you are a part of will be running for the position listed on the opposite side of the piece of paper that you select. The rest of you will support your candidate wholeheartedly, as if your grade in this class depended on it. Well, in all actuality…it does! The only way, and I repeat, the *only* way to get an A in this class, is for your candidate to win…and I repeat, *win* the election! *Capiche?*"

I looked around the classroom at the somber faces of my classmates, each of us nodding our heads in agony. At least, most of us were. The more Dr. J spoke, the wider Howard Harrell's grin grew. Dub-B wore a sly smile the entire time, too.

"You all will be responsible for meeting independently with your group members, on your own time," Dr. J continued. "From this point on, the time we spend in this classroom will be dedicated to you devising campaign strategy and breaking down the campaign practices of world leaders, both national and foreign, to give you an idea of what has been effective in the past and why. That being said, I will pass my hat to Mr. McGruden here in the front row and he will pass it around. And fellas, I know many of you wish you had a hat like this of your own, and you can, for the low price of $179.99, at any Gucci store. Don't try to be slick. The hat I pass around is the one I want back! Thank you."

Waiting for the hat to make it around to me was like waiting in line to get on the scariest, fastest ride at Disneyland as a kid. The closer it got, the more afraid I became. I wanted nothing to do with the upcoming student body election. I don't even remember ever voting for anyone in high school, and my best friend, Todd, was student body pesident. Other than Obama, Clinton, Bush and the guys on the dollar bills, I couldn't even name a U.S. President if I had to. Politics just wasn't my thing. By the time it came around to me, my hands were actually trembling. I reached down and pulled out a piece of paper without looking in the hat, then passed it back. I waited until Dr. J had the hat back in his hands before looking down to see what number I'd picked.

I've always hated group projects. There were always one or two people who always did all of the work and carried the whole group. I was never either one of those people. Still, I figured if I was gonna flunk out of college because of a bad grade in a class, I'd rather do it on my own merit than entrust a group of total strangers with my fate. I immediately contemplated dropping the course.

"What number did you get, joe?" Fresh asked.

"Six," I said.

"So did I!" he said. "We're gonna be running for student body president! Can you believe that? I already know what suit I'm gonna wear when I give my acceptance speech!"

Strike one. Nothing about Fresh said student body president.

"I'm in group six too, yo!" Dub-B shouted.

Strike two. With the basketball season in full swing, there was no way Dub-B would be able to contribute to a project of this magnitude. Amid the chatter, I overheard Katrina's petite, cute, sorority sister Destiny yell from across the room.

"I got number six!" she said. "What number did you get?"

With all of the commotion in the room, I couldn't hear Kat's answer. But I read her lips clear as day.

"I got six, too, girl," she said.

Strike three. If Katrina is in, I'm out!

There is no way I'm working with Kat, I thought, slumping into my seat. Just last night, I'd dissed her so cold at the club, I'm sure she wasn't too thrilled about working with me, either.

"What number did you get, kid?" Dub-B asked Timothy.

"Nine," he said.

"There are only six numbers," Dr. J interjected.

"Oh!" Timothy said. "I had mine upside down. I'm in group number six."

That's a relief, I thought, taking a deep breath. At least there was one person in the group who I was sure would really do some work. One person I wouldn't mind working alongside, that is. My moment of comfort didn't last long.

"This is gonna be a breeze," Howard said, boasting that anyone in group number two was in for an easy A.

"With your track record, it would seem that way," Dr. J said. "But well done is always better than well said."

After meeting briefly with our groups to compare class schedules and find a time and place suitable for us to meet, the class was dismissed. Katrina and I had only exchanged eye contact once the entire time. An emotionless stare-down that was over in the blink of an eye. She tried to grab me by my arm as I walked out of the room, but I jerked away, giving her a dirty look. I wasn't ready to talk to her yet. Only Atlanta's brisk winter air was colder. Surprisingly cooler than it had been when I walked to class, I bundled up as I stood outside Washington Hall, checking my schedule to see where my next class was. The fellas huddled up around me.

"So what you gonna do, shawty?" Lawry asked, slinging his arm around my shoulder. "I saw how you just chumped Kat off back there in class."

Immediately, my face frowned up. Lawry's breath smelled like he'd just gargled with spoiled milk. Talking to him in such close proximity made it virtually impossible to hold a conversation and inhale at the same time. I swiftly disengaged and took a step away from him before answering.

"What am I gonna do about what?" I asked.

"What do you think?" Lawry asked. "About being in the same group as Katrina."

"What kind of dumb-ass question is that?" Fresh asked. "He's gonna drop the class. Right, J.D.?"

"To tell you the truth, blood, I can't call it," I said. "You know I'm on academic probation, so I really can't afford to be dropping no classes. I gotta think about it. Why are you so worried about what I'ma do anyway? You need to be worried about what you're gonna do about being in the same group as Howard Harrell."

"Oh, I know exactly what I'm gonna do," Lawry said. "I'm gonna get an easy A. That's what I'ma do. Yeah, everybody knows he's about as sweet as ten packs of Skittles. But he's gonna win, hands-down and everybody knows that, too."

"Yeah, I know," I said, conceding Howard's victory. "I

kinda wish I could switch groups with you, so I could get that easy A."

"Boy you'sa fool!" Lawry said. "You need to switch groups with anybody who'll let you. Ain't no way I'd stay in a group with a girl who has HIV, when everybody knows I was dating her last semester. The way people around this campus talk...please! No way in hell, shawty! Speaking of which, is it just me, or was your girl Katrina looking a little thinner?"

"For one, that ain't my girl," I said sharply. "And for two, I wasn't even looking at her like that."

"Yeah, right!" Fresh said. "*Everybody* was checking her out. And now that you mention it, her ass ain't looking as plump as it was last semester."

"Y'all trippin'," I said. "She looked fine to me."

"I thought you wasn't looking at her like that," Lawry said.

"I wasn't, nigga!" I blurted aggressively.

I couldn't help it. We'd just started the semester, and already I'd grown sick and tired of everyone implicating me with Kat at every opportunity. Already I was tired of defending myself.

"Whoa!" Lawry said. "You getting kinda defensive, ain't ya? Don't tell me you're still hitting that."

"Hitting what?" I asked. "Man, hell nah! You got me twisted, homie!"

"Y'all tweaking," Fresh said, throwing his arm around my neck. "Why would he still be hitting that knowing she got the package? Especially not after he's been tested and he knows he ain't got it."

There was a brief moment of silence, Lawry looking at me, waiting for me to speak up in my defense.

"You did get tested for that, right?" Lawry badgered.

"You need to clean the Tootsie Rolls out of your ears, man," Fresh said. "I just told you he knows he ain't got it!"

"Of course I got tested," I said. "C'mon, now! You think I'm stupid? I am HIV negative, homie."

"They didn't give you any paperwork or test results or anything to prove it?" Lawry asked. "Not that I don't believe you. I'm just curious."

"Not that I know of," I said. "I took the blood test and they said they would call me back to let me know my results."

"You sure about that?"

"What you mean, am I sure? Of course I'm sure! What about you? While you're all up in my business, when is the last time you got tested?"

Another awkward moment of silence commenced. Lawry's silence all but assured his guilt. He just kind of stood there trying to conjure up some clever way of admitting he hadn't been tested.

"To be honest with you folk," Lawry said, "I don't be out here taking chances like that, so I haven't had to get tested."

"Well, you may not need to get tested for HIV, but I strongly suggest you consult with your local dentist about treatment for halitosis because your breath is kicking like David Beckham!"

Fresh busted out laughing so hard, he became teary-eyed. Lawry blurted a sarcastic laugh, then chunked the deuces.

"I got a class to get to," he said. "I'm outta here."

"Hey, you still got my belt I let you wear to the foam party last night?"

"Yeah, it's on my bed," Lawry said. "I meant to get that back to you this morning, shawty. My bad."

"It's cool," I said. "I need that back, though. It's the only belt I got."

"You tryna go back to the dorm and grab it now?"

"I need to, but I got a class," I said.

"Well, I'm not gonna be back in Marshall until later on tonight."

"Let me hold your key then," I said. "I'll leave it in my

room, just in case I'm not there when you get back. You know my roommate will be up in there."

"I guess that'll work," he said, removing his key from the keychain. "Just leave the key on your nightstand, shawty."

"I got you, homie," I said.

"Now, let me get outta here before I'm late for my Spanish class," Lawry said. "Hopefully there are some cute *mamacitas* up in there! I'll meet up with you in the caf around lunch."

I was walking with Timothy, headed over to Wells Hall on the opposite side of campus for biology class, when I heard someone behind me call my name.

"Yo, J.D! Slow up!" Dub-B yelled, jogging across the street toward us. "Yo, why do you be playing Katrina like that, son? I know about what happened between y'all last semester or whatever, but she's mad cool, B. I was just talking to her after class, and she really wants y'all to be cordial again. Especially since we all gotta work together on this student government project for Dr. J's class."

"Oh, yeah, you are in my group, huh?" I asked, totally ignoring his plea for peace.

"Duh," he said. "We just met for like five minutes in class. Weren't you there? I coulda sworn you were."

"He was," Timothy said.

"All I know is I'm gonna need an A in that class to make sure I keep my GPA above a 3.0, so I can get off academic probation."

"I thought you said you only needed a 2.5," Timothy said.

I damn sure told Timothy that. Now, I struggled to find an explanation for why I'd hiked the academic requirements.

"I know what J.D.'s doing," Dub-B said. "He's raising his own expectations, so even if he falls short of his own personal goal, his grades will still surpass what the university requires. Right?"

I couldn't have made up a lie any better than that sounded.

"You already know, homie," I said.

"Well, don't worry about public policy," Dub-B said. "I got that on lock. I know how we're gonna win."

"How?" Timothy asked. "You know we're up against Howard Harrell."

"That's nothing, yo," Dub-B said. "You know my dad is the mayor of our city back home. I grew up helping him with fund-raisers, listening to him practicing his speeches and watching him win elections. With my dad's help, this is gonna be a piece of cake."

At that moment, it was almost as if a halo appeared over Dub-B's head, wings sprouted from his back and I could hear a choir singing, "Hallelujah!"

"That's what's up!" I said, smiling and slapping him five. "Where you headed?"

"Biology class," he said.

"So are we!" I said, hoisting my jeans again, just before we walked into class. *I need to grab my belt from Lawry's room,* I thought.

"Good," he said. "Maybe we can study together. I know I'm gonna be struggling this semester, with basketball practice and games and all."

I strategically took my seat, one row behind and Timothy, at an angle, to give myself an optimum view of his scantron on test days. Dub-B wisely did the same. Timothy looked back and flashed a smile, letting us know it was cool. A couple minutes after I heard the professor call my name on the roll, I dozed off.

EIGHT

OFF THE RECORD

I like a little sag in my jeans, but stopping to pull them up every couple steps was getting annoying, so I decided to go to Lawry's room to get my belt. Dub-B and Timothy tagged along. While we were walking, Timothy was looking at his phone, checking out new pictures his girl had just posted on Facebook.

"Check these out," he said, showing them to us.

"You are all over it!" I said. "Couldn't even wait 'til you got to your laptop to see her new pics. That's borderline stalker status, blood."

"She is pretty, though," Dub-B said.

Dub-B had a point. In fact, Amy was so pretty I couldn't help but wonder how a guy like Timothy wound up pulling her. *God really does work in mysterious ways,* I thought. Not to be outdone, Dub-B whipped his new digital camera out of his backpack. He just had to show us the pictures he'd taken of his girlfriend Jasmine the night before.

"Shorty's body is mad crazy, right?" he asked.

"What is this, show and tell?" I asked, laughing as I looked at the pictures while fishing through my back pocket for the key to Lawry's room. "Baby is hella sexy, though."

"I'ma catch up with you guys a little later," Timothy said, walking into our room next door.

"I thought you said you had to get your belt," Dub-B said. "Why are we standing in front of Lawry's door? You know I can't stand that dude, yo."

"It's in here," I said, whipping out the key.

I probably should've knocked first. But since I still had Lawry's room key, I didn't exactly consider it barging in. Besides, it was the middle of the afternoon, so I expected Lawry to be in class. Instead, I was greeted by the unexpected. Lawry was sitting on the edge of the bed. Howard Harrell was ass out, standing directly in front of Lawry with one hand on the back of his head and his slacks bunched around his ankles.

My mouth dropped. I didn't know what to say. Apparently, neither did Howard or Lawry. The two of them looked just as dumbfounded as I did. That's when I saw the camera flash right over my shoulder. Dub-B had caught Lawry and Howard in the act on his digital camera. Lawry instantly jumped up, pushed Howard aside and rushed toward me trying to get to Dub-B's camera. But by the time he reached the door, Dub-B had already tucked his camera and hit the stairs. With Dub-B's long stride, there was no way Lawry would catch him. Everything had happened so fast, I was frozen solid. I just stood there, half in a daze, half-watching Howard Harrell scramble to pull his pants up. Howard exhaled angrily as he stuffed his dress shirt into his pants and tightened his belt. Then the door swung wide open and Lawry stormed back in, huffing and puffing, placing his hands on his knees and folding over as he wheezed for air. Howard walked right up to Lawry, leaned over as if he was going to whisper in his ear, then spoke loud enough for the guys staying two doors down to hear him clearly.

"It seems we have a problem," he said, his hand cupped over his mouth as if he was telling a secret. "Fix it!"

With that, Howard stood straight up, poked his chest out, stuck his nose in the air and waltzed out of the room without acknowledging my presence at all. Lawry immediately straightened up and began talking to me without looking me in the eye.

"Look, shawty…" he started, still out of breath, his tongue ring clanking against his gold fronts. "I know what it looks like."

I abruptly cut him off.

"Look, man," I said, grabbing my belt off of his desk, "I've seen enough. I don't think I need to hear anything from you. I'm disgusted right now, dog. I don't know what you and Howard got going on. I got my belt, I'll leave your key right here on the desk."

The expression on Lawry's face was one of sheer disgrace. I backpedaled slowly toward his door, then spun around to open it. That's when he spoke up.

"If that picture gets out, so does your little secret," Lawry said. "Just so you know."

"What secret?" I asked, playing dumb.

"You know exactly what I'm talking about," Lawry said. "I mean, I don't want to go there, but I don't think the Kappas will take too kindly to hearing about you telling people you are prepledging."

"Oh, it's like that?" I asked.

"It doesn't have to be," he said. "Just make sure you get rid of that photo and we won't have any problems."

I slammed the door behind me. Under normal circumstances, keeping Lawry's little secret would have been a lot easier. But everybody knew Dub-B couldn't stand Lawry and vice versa. Ever since they met last semester, they bumped heads, almost coming to blows on a few occasions. Knowing Dub-B, he'd probably already started uploading the photo on his Facebook page.

I definitely didn't want to replay that scene in my head any more times than I had to, but I couldn't help it. Even as I climbed the stairs headed toward Dub-B's room, the visual of Lawry's head bobbing back and forth while Howard stood in front of him haunted my thoughts. I suspected something was going on with Lawry, but I never saw this coming. He was unequivocally one of the most outspoken homophobes I'd ever met. He wore baggy jeans, walked straight up with his chest out, played Madden, had tattoos, gold teeth and a phone full of females' phone numbers. Aside from that new tongue ring he had, nothing about his persona said "gay." But Lawry's tough exterior was all a facade. All of it was a front.

By the time I made it to Dub-B's room, he'd already downloaded the photo from his camera to his computer and pulled up his Facebook home page.

"Don't do it!" I said, rushing over to his computer.

"Why not?" Dub-B asked, laughing. "Yo, that shit was hilarious, B! Disgusting, but hilarious! I gotta put your boy on blast! I just have to. You know I can't stand that punk anyway. He was tryna get at my girl all last semester. Even after he knew we were together."

"I know," I said. "I just think we should keep it on the back burner, though. Use it as a trump card, just in case the election gets dirty. Ya know?"

"Trump card, my ass!" he said, reaching for his laptop. "I'm putting that shit up right now, kid!"

"Trust me, blood," I said. "I really need to pass this public policy class. It may be the difference between me going back home for good, or being able to finish college out here in the ATL. And as long as we've got that photo, we've got leverage for the election. They'll do whatever we say."

"Who will do whatever we say?" Dub-B asked. "Everybody knows Howard is gay. What's he got to lose?"

"Well, I know Lawry doesn't want that photo to hit the streets, so we'll be able to keep him in our pocket. We can use him as our own little informant. A snitch on the inside of Howard's campaign. He'll do whatever we say as long as we keep that photo on the wraps. Trust me!"

"You sure, J?" he asked.

"C'mon, now," I said. "You know I am!"

After he shook up with me and promised not to post that photo, I got outta there. The whole Lawry debacle, coupled with my impending decision whether or not to drop public policy class and the swirling rumors about my HIV status, was about to drive me over the edge. I had a migraine headache and was on the verge of losing my cool when I decided to call home. Typically, just hearing my mom's voice made things better. She had a way of assuring me that everything would be okay. And she was doing just that until I slipped up and mentioned my assignment for public policy class. My mom was so excited about me participating in the upcoming student government election, she immediately started coming up with campaign slogans and reminiscing about her days running for office. In fact, I hadn't heard her that happy since I told her I'd been accepted to college. The more she talked, the more it seemed she wanted to live out her student government ambitions through me. Truth is, I should have never even brought it up. Now, deciding whether or not to drop my public policy class was that much harder.

My options were simple. I could either stay in the class, work closely with Kat on the election and run the risk of possibly subjecting my reputation to irreparable damage and an onslaught of rumors about us still dating. Or I could simply drop the class, which would only leave me with four classes. In order for me to make a 3.0 GPA, I'd need at least a B average. By staying in the public policy class, as long as our candidate won the election, I was guaranteed an A. And that grade would offset a poor grade in another class, if I got one. Or in my case, maybe two. With that in mind, public policy class was almost like a safety valve for me. With Timothy and Kat—two of the smartest, hardest-working students in our class—in my group, and Dub-B's pops lending his expertise, public policy was the only class I was sure I could get an A in, as long as one of 'em could pull off an unlikely victory over Howard Harrell. Dropping the class for my reputation's sake would leave me skating on very thin ice.

I had a decision to make. And less than ten hours to make it. With the deadline for dropping classes impending, I decided to stop by Dr. J's office for advice. As usual, his door was propped wide open. He was sitting down, stirring a cup of Starbucks coffee, reading a book and listening to jazz music playing softly when I knocked on his door.

"Mr. Dawson!" he said excitedly, turning down the volume on his speakers. "Come on in, sir. Have a seat."

No matter what Dr. J was doing, he never seemed too busy to talk to me. That was one of the things I loved most about attending a historically Black college. I felt like most of my professors actually knew who I was and wanted to see me succeed. I assumed forging a personal relationship with a professor would be much harder at a larger main-stream institution.

"Thanks," I said. "What you listening to?"

"Miles Davis," he said. "*Kind Of Blue*. A classic. That's before your time. You wouldn't know nothing about that."

"You're right about that!" I said. "What ya reading?"

"The autobiography of Assata Shakur," he said.

"I didn't know Tupac's mom had a book out."

Dr. J leaned back in his chair and held his stomach as he laughed loudly.

"Not quite," he said. "You're thinking about Afeni, my brotha. Assata is Tupac's godmother. Surely you've heard of her."

"Assata…Asssata…Assata," I said, snapping my fingers, trying to think of where I'd heard of her. "Name sounds familiar."

"She's a political prisoner," he said. "An integral member of the Black Panther Party convicted for *allegedly* taking out a New Jersey State Trooper back in '73. Great read, man. It's deep. You should check it out."

"I'll definitely have to do that," I said. "You think they have it in Club Woody… I mean, the library?"

"I don't see why they wouldn't," he said, taking a sip of his coffee. "So…to what do I owe the pleasure of this visit, Mr. Dawson? You don't seem like the brownnosing type."

"Nah," I said, laughing. "Not at all. I just had some things on my mind. And I just thought since…well…you know… You told me if I ever needed to talk to someone about anything, I could come to you for advice."

"And I am so glad you came, brotha," he said as he got up and closed the door. "What's on your mind?"

"Man, I've been dealing with so much lately, I don't know where to start," I said. "Before I even left home, I find out my high school sweetheart, Keisha, was seeing some other guy. Then I sign up for a class that's supposed to be an easy A and *you* show up!"

I intentionally left out the part about walking in on one of my best friends on campus giving another guy fellatio. I was still having trouble registering that in my own psyche. Dr. J chuckled, cheesing from ear to ear, shaking his head back and forth as he reclined in his chair.

"My apologies, Mr. Dawson," he said, trying to compose himself. "You are something else. Carry on."

"Well, now I've got a decision to make," I continued. "I can either stay in your class and participate in this stupid student government election or drop your class and risk not making the 2.5 GPA I need in order to get off of academic probation and come back next year. Honestly, my head is all messed up right now. To tell you the truth, Dr. J, I really don't know about this whole campaign thing. I mean, I've been a lot of things in my life, but a politician ain't never been one of 'em."

"Never mind the election, J.D.," Dr. J said in a serious tone, looking me straight in the eye. "Where do you see yourself four years from now?"

I wondered what the hell that had to do with what I just said. Nobody'd ever asked me to think that far out about my future before.

"That's a tough one," I said, taking a moment to think about it. "I don't know. I really don't."

"You want to graduate, right?"

"Yeah," I said. "Of course."

"Okay, we'll go with that," Dr. J said. "Now, answer this one for me. How do you get back to your dorm from my office?"

Yet another question I had no idea why he'd asked.

"Go upstairs, out the main doors, take a right, walk

halfway down the strip then take another right on Marshall Road. Marshall Hall is the first dorm on the right."

"You see the point I'm trying to make?" he asked.

"No."

"You see, when I asked you where you wanted to be in four years, you had no idea. But when I asked you how to get from my office to your dorm, you gave me precise directions. The point is, if you don't know where you're going, how will you ever get there?"

"Great point," I said.

"The tragedy of life doesn't lie in not reaching your goal, Mr. Dawson," he continued. "The tragedy lies in having no goal to reach."

"I feel where you're coming from," I said.

"Hey, you know me," he said. "You know I'm going to hear you out and I'm gonna keep it real with you. I sat back and listened to you talk about things that were bothering you, and granted, some of those things are important. But when it comes to you graduating from college, how many of those things are you going to let stop you?"

"None of 'em," I said.

"And that is why you mustn't let trivial matters clutter your brain or cause you to deviate from the goals you have set for your life. If Keisha is meant for you, I'm sure the two of you will reconcile some time down the line. But the fact of the matter is, at this point in your life, you have got to prioritize and really start putting things in perspective. You have got to keep your eye on the prize. And for you, that means focusing on your education. You feel me?"

"I feel you," I said. "Sometimes it's just hard, though. Ya know? Trying to stay focused with all of that going on around me. Sometimes I feel like college just ain't for me."

"Who ever said it would be easy?" Dr. J asked. "This is college, man! If it were easy, everybody would be a college graduate. The fact of the matter is, any person who has ever ended up on top in anything went through something that made them want to quit along the way. But the winners are the ones who had the audacity to keep going. People who do great things overcome great obstacles. You see, my brotha, challenge doesn't build character. It reveals it. You went through a lot last semester. So the simple fact that you made it back to U of A lets me know that you ain't the type to fold under pressure when times get hard."

The more I sat back and listened to Dr. J, the more convinced I became that he'd chosen the wrong profession. The way he was able to kick knowledge and wisdom, analyze situations and give inspiration all at once, Dr. J would have definitely been a better fit as a head coach of somebody's NFL team or NBA franchise. He challenged me to step up and become a man. Still, I didn't know if I was up to it.

"You're right," I said. "I ain't that type of dude. But—"

He cut me off right there.

"But nothing!" he said. "Don't give me that word. I hate that word! When you say *but,* that means erase everything you said before that."

"Huh?"

"Like if I was to say I met a girl today and she was fine as hell, *but* her teeth were jacked up," he said. "That means the fact that her grill was busted totally diminishes her being cute. You see what I'm saying?"

"Yeah," I said, laughing.

"So when it comes to being a stand-up guy, either you are or you ain't," he said. "No buts."

"I am," I said confidently. "To tell you the truth though, Dr. J, I wanna stay in your class and all. I'm just not really feeling the whole group thing."

"It's Katrina, isn't it?" he asked.

"That's part of it."

"That's *all* of it! Why else would you, of all people, consider dropping a class where there is no homework involved and no tests?"

As I sat there trying to wiggle my way out of his class, I couldn't help but laugh. He was right about that.

"You just don't understand," I said. "I think if you knew the circumstances..."

Again, he cut me off in midsentence.

"I probably know more than you think," he said. "I know that Katrina is HIV positive. And I know that you and Katrina were dating last semester. Kids talk."

"That's the problem right there!" I said. "People on this campus gossip too much. Yeah, Downtown D is HIV positive and so is Katrina, but I ain't! I got tested as soon as I went home. I'm straight."

"Well, first off, let me say that I am extremely proud of you for stepping up and being tested," Dr. J said. "That takes a lot of courage. However, if you got tested when you say you did, that means you were tested in December."

"Yes, sir," I said proudly. "December twelfth, to be exact. HIV free!"

"Your excitement tickles me to death," he said, chuckling heartily. "Again, I must commend you for taking the initiative to know your status. That's more than I can say for a lot of your peers around here."

"Who you tellin'?" I asked.

"On the flipside though," he continued, "while I hate to rain on your parade, I must remind you that the incubation period for HIV is six months. And if your scare occurred last semester..."

"Incubation period?" I said, interrupting him. "I don't know nothing about that. All I know is I took the test, and according to those results, I'm in the clear."

"Well, son, the Good Book says 'our people will be destroyed for a lack of knowledge.' So while I definitely don't want to jinx you by any means, I will have you know that HIV can take up to six months to show in a person's bloodstream. So while your negative test results may give you some sense of confidence in regards to your health, if you want to be sure of your status, it would behoove you to retake the test toward the end of the semester. Just to be on the safe side."

There was a long, silent pause.

"Man, I never even thought about it like that," I said. "But as of right now, the test results I have say that I'm HIV negative, so that's what I'm rolling with. And I'm just sick and tired of people speculating about what they don't know. Everybody automatically assumes I got the shit. I mean...my bad for cursing... Everybody thinks that just because I was talking to Kat last semester, I'm HIV positive, too. So this semester I just wanted to create as much distance between the two of us as possible. And I can't see that happening with both of us working on a campaign together."

"Hmmm," Dr. J said, stroking his chin, contemplating what I'd said.

"I mean, everything you said about folding under pressure and being a stand-up guy...I understand where you're coming from," I said. "But..."

Dr. J cut his eyes at me.

"Oops," I said. "It's just a difficult situation, man. You don't know how it feels to walk into a room and know that everybody is talking about you. I'm tired of going to the caf, and acting like I can't hear people whispering, spreading rumors about me that ain't even true. I'm already to the point where I wanna snap on somebody."

"So what's your solution to the problem?" Dr. J asked.

"I think you should switch me into a different group," I said.

"I can't do that," Dr. J said. "That would open up the floodgates to everybody else who wants to switch into a different group."

"Well, I guess there's only one thing for me to do."

"What's that?" he asked.

"Drop the class."

"Okay," he said. "Let's say you do. You really think that's going to stop people from talking about you?"

"I don't know," I said. "But I do know Kat and I working so closely together in the same group ain't gonna help the situation."

"Look, J.D., you're your own man," Dr. J said. "I think that you are a very bright, intelligent young man capable of making responsible decisions for yourself. Do keep in mind that you are on academic probation. And if you decide to drop my class, you'd better be sure you will be able to perform exceptionally well in your other courses. That being said, I am not telling you not drop my class. What I am telling you is that if you think dropping my class is going to solve your problem, you might wanna rethink that. If you're afraid to get an F, you can never get an A."

As I was leaving Dr. J's office, I noticed two things hanging on his wall that I had never seen before. One was a paddle. Not just any paddle. A wooden Kappa Beta Psi paddle, painted red and white.

"Dr. J," I said. "I didn't know you were Greek. I've never seen you wear any 'nalia."

"I wear 'nalia from time to time," he said. "But that's where you youngsters get it twisted. You don't always have to wear letters on you when it's in you."

"Deep," I said. "Thanks for your time, Dr. J."

"Anytime," he said.

Just before I walked out, I noticed a poster on his other wall opposite his paddle. It was simple with black-and-white lettering. On the poster was a single quote from Benjamin Banneker that read "Whatever you do in life, strive to do it better than anyone dead or alive has ever done it before."

Truthfully, the odds of my group defeating Howard Harrell's in the presidential election were about as slim as David's were against Goliath. But after talking to Dr. J and reading that quote, I knew I had a chance as long as I stayed in the class. But with the deadline for dropping classes just hours away, I didn't have a lot of time to make a decision. While I didn't want to have anything to do with Kat or the election, I didn't want to let my mom down, either.

NINE

CLUB WOODY

DECISION making was a whole lot easier in high school. Things were a lot simpler then. Mostly because I was in my comfort zone. I knew what classes I could B.S. my way through and which teachers didn't play that. I could tell you which streets were safe to walk down alone at night and which to steer clear of. I knew Oakland. But after spending a semester at the University of Atlanta, the only thing I knew for certain was that Atlanta was nothing like Oakland. Sure, there were plenty of black folks in the ATL, just like back home. But the difference was, most people from my hood in Oakland were born and raised there. Their parents, too. So when it came to doing a background check on a particular young lady, her entire resume was accessible—usually no more than two phone calls away at the most.

Back home, all I needed was a first name, last name or a nickname and, after calling up a few of my homeboys, I could find out what side of town a girl grew up on, what guy she dated in high school, whether or not she was a freak and what her parents did for a living. Gathering this type of intel was virtually impossible in Atlanta. Mostly because damn near everybody in Atlanta was from somewhere else. Especially on campus. And with everyone being from various parts of the map, from Miami to Philly, Houston and Seattle, most people chose to leave their past in their hometown. So many people came to Atlanta for a "fresh start" and a "clean slate," sometimes I wondered what they were like in high school. Atlanta afforded people the opportunity to essentially become "brand-new" and build a new reputation for themselves. Atlanta gave the guy who everyone back home knew was gay an opportunity to explore his sexuality and pretend to be straight and date women. It gave the young lady known around her hometown for sleeping with every guy who owned a letterman jacket on the first date a chance to present herself as the hottest thing since sliced bread. Pure and unadulterated. A virgin, even. Without any reliable source to verify that a person really is who they appear to be, Atlanta forced you to give a person the benefit of the doubt.

And, really, is there ever any benefit in doubting?

For this reason, it was hard for me to trust girls I met on campus. Nine times out of ten, their history was a mystery to me. And after everything that went down with Kat last semester, I felt like it was important to know as much about a person's past as possible, especially when dealing with them on an intimate level. That's why I was so impressed—and half-startled—when Leslie ran down all of my priors the first time we spoke on the phone. Our conversation was like none I'd ever had with any other girl on campus before. It was as if she'd known me for years.

"So how was it growing up on the West Coast?" she started.

"Excuse me," I said, caught off guard. "When did I tell you where I was from?"

"Oakland, right?" she asked.

"Yeah," I said. "But how did you…"

"That's not important," she said. "It's a lot different out here, huh?"

"Way different," I said. "It's hella cool, though. I love ATL, actually."

"*Hella?*" Leslie said, laughing. "You're from Cali for real! Your accent is so strong!"

"Ya think?"

"I know," she said. "And I bet you do love it out here, with all these girls on campus to choose from. What is it, like eight girls to every guy?"

"Something like that," I said.

"So out of all the girls on campus, why did you holla at Downtown D's girl? I mean, you're handsome. I'm sure you could've had just about any freshman you wanted. Why Katrina? You got a thing for older women?"

It was like Leslie's mouth was a machine gun, questions were the bullets and I was the target. She was pressing down on the trigger as hard as she could. We'd only been on the phone for a minute or so and I already felt like I was being interrogated. And these weren't assumptions or presumptions, but rather questions only someone who'd done some research and came away with cold, hard facts could ask. Initially, I was taken back by her forwardness. But Leslie had clearly done her homework, so I decided to keep it one hundred with her.

"Why I gotta have a thing for older women?" I asked.

"Maybe older women have a thing for me. And how you know about all this anyway?"

"I have my sources," she said bluntly. "Soooo... Y'all still talkin'?"

"Who?"

"You and Katrina! Who else?"

"Oh. Nah. Hell nah! No! Not at all. That's old news. What's it to you, though?"

"I mean, you asked me for my number so I'm assuming that you're interested in getting to know me. But I wouldn't feel comfortable getting to know somebody who is already involved with someone else. Especially when word on the street is..."

Leslie paused for a moment, as if to think carefully about how to choose her next words.

"Awww, nevermind," she said.

"Come on," I said. "Don't do that. I hate when people do that! What were you gonna say?"

"Everybody knows that Downtown D got HIV," she said. "And everybody knows Katrina was his girlfriend, so that means she probably got it, too. And if you were talking to Katrina..."

"Pump your brakes!" I said. "Not even. I've been tested and I'm straight. That's the first thing I did when I got back to Cali."

After Dr. J's whole spill about HIV taking up to six months to show up in a person's bloodstream, I felt a little self-conscious proclaiming my status. But I sure wasn't about to let that stop me from clearing my name.

"Well, that's good to know," she said. "But you know how the streets talk. I heard you were the reason both of 'em got HIV."

"You heard *what*?" I asked vehemently.

"Well, everybody knows that Downtown D ain't gay. That boy has been with every girl and her sister on campus."

"What does that have to do with me?"

"I probably shouldn't be saying this," she said.

"No, you should," I prompted. "I've heard a lot of false rumors going around. But I don't think I've ever heard this one. Keep going."

"All right," she said, still pondering whether or not to go on.

"Go ahead! What did you hear?" I asked.

"I heard you were gay," she said. "Well, not gay-gay. But you know…swing both ways. Bi."

Since I'd been on campus, I'd had to defuse and dismantle all sorts of rumors I'd heard about my involvement in the whole Kat-Downtown D-HIV fiasco. I'd been questioned about it by my friends and overheard people I'd never met talking about it everywhere from the caf to the stalls in the bathroom. It was sickening and becoming more annoying every day. But this was the first time I'd heard my name and the term *bi* mentioned in the same sentence. And as far as I was concerned, it would be the last.

"*Bi?*" I asked. "I ain't *bi*lingual! I don't own a *bi*cycle! I don't wear *bi*focals. And I damn sure ain't *bi*sexual! Somebody got their facts mixed up! Who told you that?"

"Honestly, I can't even remember," she said. "That's just what people were saying. They say you were on the DL with one of your homeboys in Marshall Hall. Some guy named Larry or something like that."

My heart dropped. I knew exactly who she was referring to—Lawry. But I couldn't let on that I even had an inkling of what she could have been talking about. Even though the rumor was false. I refuted her information immediately.

"For one, I ain't never been on the D nothing with

nobody!" I said angrily. "And ain't none of my homeboys I kick it with in Marshall Hall gay. Or anywhere else, for that matter. I don't even know any guy named Larry! Somebody got you all messed up, baby girl. Ain't none of that in my repertoire!"

"I'm not saying I believed any of it," Leslie said. "I mean, I know how people lie and spread rumors all the time. But it's not safe to assume anything about anybody these days. You gotta ask questions. Besides, I don't wanna be out and have one of your University of Atlanta groupies run up on me."

"You don't have to worry about that," I assured her.

"So you and Katrina are *really* done?"

"Oh, you can throw some A.1. steak sauce on that relationship, baby," I said. "It's well done! I don't even talk to that girl *at all* anymore."

It didn't surprise me that Leslie had heard about my relationship with Kat. Damn near everybody knew. What did catch me off guard though was how bold Leslie was in her inquiry.

"I hope you're not offended by my apprehension," she said in timely fashion. "But you know this is Atlanta. There's a whole lot going on down here."

"I definitely feel you...*Oprah!*"

"Hey, unless you ask, you just *n-e-e-e-v-er* know," she said, giggling. "I don't give my number out often. So when I do, I like to know who I'm dealing with."

By the mere fact that she'd done a decent amount of research before talking to me, I figured she was genuinely interested. Her excuse was that she was naturally inquisitive because she wanted to be a journalist. As for the basics, I knew our personalities would mesh when she told me she was born and raised in Las Vegas, because it was so close to the West Coast. I was glad to hear that she was majoring in English, because when it came to writing papers, I sucked. When she offered her help, I knew I had a winner. But the more she spoke about her past relationship, the less comfortable I felt moving forward. She said that she'd dated the same guy for the last two years—an older guy who she'd been with since she got to college. The situation began sounding eerily familiar. She continued, adding that her ex was very popular on the yard. She alluded to the fact that he was in a fraternity at U of A, but wouldn't specify which. But she was very adamant about the fact that he could have any girl he wanted on campus. As I sat there, stirring a bowl of beef-flavored ramen noodles I'd just prepared, I couldn't help but wonder if she was referring to one of the Kappas. And if so, which one? She said that her ex made a ton of cash during his summer internship on Wall Street and spoiled her to no end—from high-fashion Giuseppe Zanotti heels to exclusive designer Birkin bags. On spring break, they lounged in five-star resorts and ate stuffed lobster tails. Let her tell it, he was a college girl's dream come true. But the one thing she really wanted was something he couldn't give her—a monogamous relation-ship. Caught up in his own popularity, her ex-boyfriend couldn't be faithful. And on top of that, she said that he was extremely jealous and became physically "aggressive" whenever he'd get drunk. I couldn't help but wonder if that's how she'd acquired the bruises I'd seen on her face. I assumed as much. The good news, though, was that after one and a half years of "staying down" for her man, Leslie decided she'd had enough. Still, I just had to ask.

"So when you say your boyfriend was physically aggres-sive," I said, "you mean, he *hit* you? Is that where the bruises I've seen on your face are from?"

"Bruises?" she asked defensively. "What bruises?"

I didn't respond. She sounded like a battered woman suffering through an abusive relationship. Denial is always the first sign. There was a long, silent pause before she continued.

"Look, there just comes a point when you know you can do better for yourself," she said, intentionally sidestepping my deliberate question. "And I think I've reached that point. So I'm moving on. It's gonna be hard. But it's time."

I'd heard that line before. The irony of the similarities between Leslie and Kat was baffling. I could do nothing more than shake my head and take a deep breath as I pondered the repercussions of dealing with a girl who was in the process of detaching herself from a longtime ex. I knew all too well the feeling of being the "rebound" guy, and I didn't like it. After the fiasco with Kat and Downtown D last semester, I promised myself I wouldn't subject myself to chasing a girl who was still in cahoots with an ex. Why couldn't I meet a cute girl who'd been single for more than six months? I thought about what I'd done to deserve such a fate—all the girls I'd snuck around with on the side while I was with Keisha and all of the hearts I'd broken in the past by telling other girls that my relationship with Keisha was "on the rocks" when, in the back of my mind, I knew I'd never leave Keisha. I couldn't help but wonder if this was some kind of negative karma I'd brought upon myself.

"Well, they say timing is everything," I responded. "Speaking of which, it's about time for me to head to the library. I got so much work to do, it ain't even funny."

"For what class?"

"You might as well say all of 'em," I said, sighing. "Shoot, I've got some homework to finish up for my algebra class and a few chapters to read before my African-American history quiz. Plus, I have a group meeting for public policy class over there in a few, too."

"That's funny," she said. "So do I. Mine doesn't start for a couple of hours, though."

"Maybe I'll see you there," I said.

When I hung up the phone, I felt like I had accomplished something. My first conversation with Leslie was a meaningful one. I thought we covered a lot of ground. And now I had even more incentive to keep Lawry's little secret. I hoped he stayed in the closet forever. Seconds after I hung up with Leslie, my phone was chiming. I could tell by the ring tone that it was a text message. I assumed it was a message from Timothy reminding me about our biology study session that was supposed to kick off in the library in about 15 minutes.

The text wasn't from Timothy, it was from Dex. It read: *We're hungry. You've got 30 minutes to bring us 20 pieces of chicken from Popeye's, a bottle of Hennessy and a 12-pack of Corona too.*

"Damn," I murmured.

This request was going to be a problem. Mostly because I couldn't say no. I had to come through. But I had no idea how I was going to pull it off. First of all, I was definitely going to be late to my first meeting with Timothy, and he was a real stickler for punctuality. I didn't want to piss him off, because he was my secret weapon to passing biology. I knew I could come up with some kind of excuse for Timothy, though. The real problem I faced was the fact that even though there was a Popeye's within walking distance of the campus, there was no way I'd be able to get the chicken and the liquor and get back to the Kappa house in under half an hour. It was impossible. I needed a car. And even if I got a car, I'd need someone who was 21 to buy the drinks for me. And even if I had a car and someone to buy the drinks, I didn't have the money to pay for all that stuff on my own. I had to think quick. I only had three options. Fats was well over 21, but he didn't have a car— only a ten-speed beach cruiser. Dub-B had a fly ride, but he didn't have a fake ID. When it came down to it, the only person I knew who was 21 with a car who would drop everything to come help me out was Katrina. But after the way I'd dogged her out, I didn't feel right calling her in this situation. Plus, she was Greek, so she would know something was up. After texting Dex, *"Yes, sir,"* I knew I was officially on the clock. I immediately called Fresh to see if he could come up with an alternative. He came through in the clutch like a champion. In less than ten minutes, he had some upperclassman he was talking to named Tiffany outside waiting on us in her car. To my surprise, when we hopped in, I saw that she'd already copped the liquor.

"Damn!" I said, surprised. "She already went to the…"

"Yessir!" Fresh said, leaning over to kiss her on the cheek, then turning around and winking at me to let me know he had her in check. "That's why she's my baby."

"Well, if I'm your baby, why do you smell like some other girl's perfume?" she asked. "Who you been kissing on this time, Fresh?"

"Perfume?" he asked, sounding guilty as hell. "Girl, you need to quit being so damn insecure. You know I ain't out here messing around on you. Cut the crap!"

"Oh, I'm not insecure," she assured him. "I just know you're a dog! All you men are!"

The two of them kept going back and forth at each other nonstop for the next few blocks. Knowing Fresh, ol' baby probably had a legitimate excuse to be mad, but from what I could tell, she was definitely on the possessive side. I decided not to jump into the middle of their argument. I was more concerned about getting back to the Kappa house in time. When I looked at my watch, we had approximately 15 minutes to get the chicken and get back.

"You said you needed to go to Popeye's, right?" she asked between fussin'.

"Yes!" I answered for him, nervously staring at the second hand on my watch. "There's one right up the street across from the BP gas station."

"Boy, I know where Popeye's is," she said.

Well, put the pedal to the metal, I thought. When we pulled up to Popeye's with 12 minutes to spare, I figured we were in pretty good shape. However, it just so happened the day we needed chicken was the same day Popeye's was offering eight pieces of chicken for four bucks. Of course, the drive-thru line was so long it spilled all the way into the street. There had to have been at least twenty cars in line waiting for chicken. Inside was no better. From the car, I could see the line snaked all the way from the cash register to the door. I knew we'd never make it waiting for the drive-thru, and waiting inside was just as pointless. After weighing out my options, I had only one solution.

"Y'all see that Church's chicken over there?" I asked, pointing across the street.

"Yeah," Fresh said. "What about it?"

"There's no line over there," I said, opening my door and hopping out in the middle of the street. "Y'all go over there and order the chicken."

"I thought you said we needed Popeye's," he said.

"Just get the chicken, and I'll meet y'all over there in the parking lot," I said, before turning around and running toward Popeye's.

Wisely, I bypassed the line and went straight to the counter, where I was told by a lady with red extensions and gold teeth that it was against store policy to give out empty chicken buckets. You'd be surprised how fast a person making minimum wage will bend the rules for a crisp five-dollar bill. By the time Fresh and his girl made it to the pick-up window, I was opening her back door and hopping in with a plastic Popeye's bag and three empty buckets. I quickly passed them up to Fresh.

"Here," I panted, out of breath. "Put the chicken in these."

"My nigga," Fresh said. "You are a genius!"

"What the hell are y'all up to?" the girl driving asked.

"Just a little back-to-school potluck for our dorm," Fresh said.

"Mmmmm-hmmmmm," she hummed in disbelief. "Whatever! I'm a Zeta. Don't forget that. Y'all just be careful. Church's don't taste nothing like Popeye's!"

She had a point. But hopefully, after a few chugs of Hennessy, they wouldn't be able to tell the difference. She dropped us off on the main drag, near Lighthouse, one block away from the Kappa house. We jogged over from there. We reached the front door with two minutes to spare—liquor and chicken in hand. Dex took his sweet time coming to the door, intentionally I'm sure.

"It's about time," he said, grabbing the bags from us. After digging through them to make sure all of his demands were met, he slammed the door in our face. He showed absolutely no gratitude whatsoever for all of our effort and hard work. No emotion at all. I shrugged it off, assuming maybe that was a good thing. At least we'd made it on time. As for my biology study session with Timothy, well, that was another story.

Not much had changed about Club Woody since I studied for finals there last semester. The majority of students in Woodruff Library were there for all the wrong reasons, hence the befitting moniker "Club Woody." You could always tell who was really there to study and who was frontin'. The girls with their faces made up, dressed like they were going straight to the club after their study groups, and fellas doused in cologne, absent of textbooks or writing utensils, were usually on the latter end of the spectrum. Those there to socialize usually congregated in the front, while students actually attempting to study took refuge in the back, where there were quiet, cubicle-like desks. On this rare occasion, I was actually there to get some work done. And even if I'd wanted to socialize a bit, that chicken and liquor run killed any time I may have had to iron an outfit suitable for mingling in the front. As usual, there were plenty of vacant seats in the back away from the action. Miraculously, I'd managed to make it to my study session with a few minutes to spare before our public policy meeting. Timothy and Dub-B were already going over the difference between protons and neutrons when I pulled up a seat.

"Yo, son," Dub-B said. "You aight, yo? Why you walking all funny like that?"

My legs were still sore from sitting in that damn imaginary chair, but I didn't even realize my limp was still visible until Dub-B mentioned it.

"Bumped my knee on a table walking in," I said.

"Well, well, well," Timothy said, looking at his watch. "Look who finally decided to show up."

"My bad, blood," I said. "I had overslept. My alarm was trippin'."

"If you say so," Timothy said. "Just remember, I don't need this study session. I can really be using this time to study for one of my more difficult courses. But since you asked for help, I'm here. I wouldn't do this for anyone else. So please, just try to be on time from now on."

Even though I didn't appreciate Timothy talking to me like a parental figure, I could understand where he was coming from. I was in no position to issue a rebuttal. With my first biology exam swiftly approaching, Lord knows I needed help. And when it came to biology, Timothy was the man. I thought the guy loved science. But that was an understatement. He knew it like the back of his hand. But after studying with him briefly, it was clear that his relationship with his newfound love thing was more serious than I thought. They were sending each other text messages the entire time.

"You must really like that girl," I said. "If y'all gonna be texting like that, you might as well just call her."

"Yeah," he said, laughing. "She's definitely growing on me. To be honest with you, I think I may be falling in love for the first time."

"Aaaawwww!" Dub-B and I sounded off simultaneously.

"Isn't that cute?" Dub-B taunted. "Timmy's got a girlfriend!"

"Not quite," Timothy said, blushing. "I'm working on it, though. Just taking things slow."

"Speaking of taking things slow, how are things going with that Elmanite you been tryna holla at?" Dub-B asked. "Fresh told me she was tryna act Hollywood with you at first."

"I just spoke to her on the phone for the first time today," I said. "She seems hella cool," I said.

"Well, if she's as half as good to you as Amy is to me, I say make her your girlfriend," Timothy said. "U of A is big on quantity, but quality is hard to find around here. I'm glad I found my queen."

"I'm trippin' on how this girl got you so sprung," I said. "You ain't even smashing."

"*Smashing?*" Timothy asked, confused.

"Hold on," Dub-B said, slamming his biology book shut. "Wait a minute, son. Don't tell me this girl got you out here talkin' 'bout you in love and you haven't even beat yet."

"Beat what?" Timothy asked.

"Sex!" I said, louder than I'd intended to, causing a

few people studying at tables nearby to look over. I continued in a whispered tone. "You haven't even gotten any yet, have you?"

Timothy looked down, fiddling with his papers, a half grin creeping on his face. He never said yes. But surprisingly, after approximately ten seconds of silence, he never said no.

"You're still a virgin, right?" I asked.

Still no answer. Timothy's grin widened. That's when Dub-B and I erupted.

"*Aaaaaaaaahhhhhh!*" we screamed, pumping our fists. I tried to give Timothy a high five, but he refused to raise his hand. That's when Dub-B grabbed his elbow and raised it for him. Timothy tried to lower his hand before I could reach it, but I slapped him five anyway.

"No wonder he's so geeked about shorty!" Dub-B said. "She took his virginity."

"Damn, *T-Mac,*" I said, laughing. "What ever happened to abundance over buns, man?"

"Can we change the subject, guys?" Timothy pleaded. "Please."

After Timothy helped me knock out my first homework assignment, I still had time to spare before our public policy class group was scheduled to meet. Dub-B left to go meet Jasmine outside her class and escort her to the library for our group meeting. I decided to knock out my algebra homework to kill some time. The answers to all of the odd problems were in the back of the book, so naturally I started working those first. I was just about to start working the even ones when I heard two very familiar voices at the desk next to me. Wooden dividers about two feet tall, separating the desks for privacy, shielded me from their view. Based on how liberally she offered up personal information, Kat clearly assumed she was alone with Destiny. I couldn't help but listen in.

"You are so strong, girl," Destiny said. "I don't see how you do it. It seems like every time I turn around I have to check one of these little chickenheads running around here spreading rumors about you. Shoot, I almost got into a fight in the caf earlier defending you. I don't care what disease you got, ain't nobody gonna be walking around here disrespecting my girl. And that's real!"

"You are so crazy, girl," Kat said. "It's good to know *somebody* has my back. It's like you don't find out who your true friends are until something like this happens. As far as people spreading rumors and hating on me goes, that kinda comes along with the territory when you're dating someone like Downtown D. So I guess you can say I'm used to it. I can't even front, though, I don't like it. I don't like it at all. But what can I do about it now? Everybody knows I'm HIV positive, and that's how it is. When I first found out I was infected, I thought my life was over. But when I went to sleep that night and woke up the next morning, I realized it wasn't. That's when I decided that I'm going to live what life I have left to the fullest. I might as well. You only get one."

"You never fail to amaze me," Destiny said, sounding like she was close to tears. "I am so glad you are taking such a positive approach, considering everything you're going through. It's like, I've heard about AIDS, and seen the commercials with the little African kids on TV and everything, but I've never been this close to anyone who has it. And it just amazes me how you take your medicine all the time, yet still manage to get your work done in class, lead our APA chapter meetings and just go on with your life."

"Yeah, well let me be the first to tell you that taking fifteen tablets a day ain't easy," Katrina said.

"Damn!" I said, covering my mouth to muffle my voice. *That's a hell of a lot of pills,* I thought.

"*Fifteen* per *day?*" Destiny asked, echoing my sentiment.

"I know it sounds crazy," Kat said. "I used to be worried how many classes I had left to take. Now, I'm even more concerned with how many T-cells I have left."

"Doesn't taking all those pills make you sick to your stomach?" Destiny asked.

"Hell, yeah!" she said. "Girl, I cried the first time I saw how big some of the pills I had to take were. But I really don't have much of a choice, so I just learned to deal with it. Now, I'm actually starting to get used to it. I have my good days and my bad days. Days where I feel weak and some where I don't have much of an appetite at all. But I've learned to count every day that I wake up as a blessing."

"You are so positive!" Destiny said. "I swear you should be a spokesperson for BET's Rap It Up campaign or something. Just talking to you makes me appreciate life more."

"I wasn't this strong at first," Kat said. "I was crying like a little baby for the first couple weeks of Christmas break. Then I started going to church more, getting into the Word, and I found strength in the Lord. It's too bad I just started really getting into it once I found out I was HIV positive, but I guess better now than never."

"Definitely," Destiny said.

"Girl, I've just been talking your ear off," Kat said. "Thanks for listening. You know, ever since the word got out that I was HIV positive, a lot of people who claimed to be my friends have disappeared."

"That just lets you know that they were never your true friends to begin with," Destiny said.

"Exactly! And it also proved who my real friends are. Thanks for being one of them."

"You know I'm here for you if you need me," Destiny said.

"Aawww, girl, you're gonna make me cry before our little meeting," Kat said. "C'mon, let's go before we're late."

When the two of them stood, I put my head down. I didn't want them to know I'd been eavesdropping.

Just as I was gathering my things, I felt my phone going off in my pocket. I hoped it wasn't Dex calling to let me know he'd snuffed out our little slick move with the chicken swap. I took in a sigh of relief when I saw that it was my mom. We weren't allowed to talk on our cell phones in the library, but I answered anyway, speaking in a whisper.

"Hello," I said.

"So I've just finished the first draft," my mom said with excitement.

"First draft of what?" I asked.

"The speech," she said.

"What speech?"

"The one Katrina is going to have to give when she runs for student body president," she said. "You really don't know a thing about elections, do you?"

"C'mon now, Mom," I said. "You already know this ain't my thing."

"Well, it's mine!" she said. "I'm gonna go ahead and e-mail you what I've got."

"Thanks, Mom," I said, trying to ease off the phone with her.

"Tell her she can feel free to doctor it up however she wants."

"Okay, Mom," I said. "I'll do that."

"I'm gonna go ahead and include some other key points I think she may want to touch on, too," my mom said. "That way, if she—"

"Mom!" I said, cutting her off. "Okay! Thank you. I can't really talk right now because I'm in the library. I'll call you later."

"Oh, okay," she said. "I didn't know. You should've said something."

"I couldn't."

"Well, you just tell Katrina if she has any questions, give me a call," my mom said. "And I've got a few cool slogan ideas, too."

"Mom!" I said.

"Just call me later," she said, laughing.

There were six members of our group—Me, Dub-B, Destiny, Timothy, Fresh and Katrina. Our first meeting was a disaster. I couldn't believe my eyes when I looked down at my watch. We'd been in the conference room for nearly an hour and gotten absolutely nowhere. We hadn't even made it through our first group meeting, and already, I wanted out. Each time the question of who would represent our group on the ballot was raised, the same number of hands went up.

Zero.

I damn sure wasn't running for student body president. My grades were much too low to even consider adding my name to the ballot. Dub-B's priority was basketball, so he wouldn't have the time to run for office. Destiny was a pretty sorority chick, but she didn't have the charisma to take out Howard Harrell. Timothy was too timid. And even Fresh, the most overzealous and ambitious member of our group, had come to the realization that he had a better chance beating LeBron James in a game of one-on-one than defeating the almighty Howard Harrell in the upcoming student government election. Katrina was our only hope. Despite being the talk of the campus, Kat's credentials were impeccable. She was the only upperclassmen in our group and her transcript was flawless—she was on track to graduate magna cum laude, honors reserved for students in the top five percent of their class. When it came to spearheading fund-raisers and event planning, Kat had the campus on lock. Although she was thrust into the rumor mill for all the wrong reasons, Kat's leg-up on Howard Harrell was that her name was buzzing in the streets. If the saying "all publicity is good publicity" holds true and there is any truth to the theory that student government elections are just popularity contests, then Kat had a legitimate chance to win off namesake alone. Still, she was reluctant to step up to the plate and accept the challenge.

"I don't know, guys," Kat said, looking down at her notepad and nervously doodling. "Y'all sure you want *me* to run for president?"

"Yes!" Destiny said for the third time. "No offense to anyone at this table, but, girl, look around. On the real, none of us stand a chance against Howard Harrell. It just ain't happenin'."

"I think she's made a very valid point there," Timothy added.

"But *me?*" Katrina said second-guessing herself. "Student Body President? I don't know. There hasn't been a female student body president here at U of A for over twenty years!"

"A woman has never been elected President of the United States, either, but that didn't stop Hillary Clinton from adding her name to the ballot!" Fresh said.

"And a black man never won the presidential election, now look at Obama!" Dub-B added.

"That's true," Kat said. "Still, though. I just can't see it."

"Look," I said, sounding restless, "honestly, I couldn't care less who wins the damn election. I just need to pass this class. And I ain't even gonna lie. As far as our group goes, I think you're our best shot."

"Preach," Fresh said in agreement.

"So y'all really think *I* can win?" Katrina asked with a smile.

"Yes!" Fresh screamed, pounding his fist on the desk. "You can! You're cute, smart, well spoken, Greek, you know how to dress and everybody on campus knows you. Why not?"

"But what about me being…" Kat said, looking down and fidgeting with her cuticles. "Well…you know…having HIV and all."

"Just look at this as another way for you to spread awareness about safe sex," Timothy said. "Another avenue for you to share your story with those who need it most—the students. Just be honest with them. In the end, I think that will help you gain their trust."

"And most importantly, their votes," Destiny added.

"Yeah, but I don't know a thing about writing speeches or fund-raisers, or any of that stuff," Kat said.

"Well, I already told J.D. and Timothy that my pops is a very successful politician back home in New York," Dub-B said. "And I know he would be down to help us come up with some strategic ways to win the election."

"That would be awesome," Timothy said. "I was actually brainstorming a few ideas on the way over. And I was thinking, maybe we can hit up Magic and solicit some financial support for the campaign. Maybe we can do some kind of event where we give out free tickets to students who get tested for HIV."

Everyone at the table looked at Timothy like he'd lost his mind.

"Magic *who?*" Dub-B asked with a laugh. "Please don't tell me you are talking about the NBA legend."

"That's exactly who I'm talking about," Timothy said with a straight face. "As big of an HIV awareness advocate as he is, he'd probably love to help out."

"You know, I've heard some pretty crazy stuff come outta your mouth," I said, laughing. "But this takes the cake! How the hell are we supposed to reach out to a Hall of Famer?"

"And even if we did," Fresh said, "with all the businesses he owns, you know he is way too busy to be helping us with this campaign. Honestly, that's got to be about the dumbest thing I've heard all day, fam."

"Hey, it was just a suggestion," Timothy said, slightly dejected.

"How 'bout making it your last one?" Fresh suggested.

"Okay, okay, okay," Kat said, sitting up straight. "Actually, some kind of 'testing for tickets' day would be really cool. Especially if we could get some big artist to perform or something."

"Yeah right," Fresh said, sarcastically.

"Okay, so let's forget about Magic and 'testing for tickets' day," Kat said. "Hypothetically speaking, lets say I put together this awesome campaign. I write a really good speech. And I do all of the things it takes to get elected. Have y'all forgotten about Howard Harrell? That man has won every election he's run in since he's been at U of A. What about him?"

"What about him?" Timothy asked. "In Romans eight and thirty-one, the Bible says, 'If God is for you then *who* shall be against you?' I'll tell you who. Nobody! That's who. End of story."

I'd never heard Timothy sound so adamant about anything. Hell, I don't think any of us had. Timothy's encouraging words were enough to get Kat to see the big picture.

"You're right!" Kat said. "All of you are right! Thank you so much for inspiring me to do this. I'm gonna do it. I'm running for student body president!"

The round of applause started with Jasmine's two hands. Her praise had a domino effect on each of us. I was last to join in. For some reason, I still had a sour taste in my mouth about the way my relationship with Kat came to an end. Maybe it was the fact that she'd lied to me last semester about her ongoing sexual relationship with Downtown D. Or maybe the fact that my gullibility landed me on death row for a week, until my HIV test results came back. Rumors swirling about the two us still dating may have even had something to do with it. But for whatever reason, I still had a great deal of resentment in my heart toward Kat. I tried not to let it show, and avoided her at all costs. But working so closely together on this group project made that mission virtually impossible.

"Well, that works for me," Fresh said, grimacing as he looked down at his BlackBerry. It had been going off the entire meeting. He hastily snatched his notebook from the table, slid it into his backpack and headed for the door.

"Whoa!" Kat said. "Hold up, for a sec. We need to figure out a time that's convenient for all of us to meet each week outside of Dr. J's class. I'm running for student body president, but I can't do it by myself. I'm really gonna need you guys. So what's up?"

"Why don't we just meet here at the same time every Tuesday?" Timothy asked.

"I'll be on time for that," Fresh said as he opened the door and bolted out.

"That's cool with me," Dub-B said. "I should be outta practice at this time every week. I won't be able to make it on nights when we have home games, but other than that, I'll be here."

"Yeah, so that works for us," Jasmine confirmed.

Once I confirmed, everyone headed for the exit. Everyone except Kat. She just sat there, jotting down a few final notes as I tussled with the broken zipper on my backpack. By the time I got it shut and looked up, Kat and I were the only two in the room. *Uncomfortable* is the best word I could use to describe the feeling in the air—an unspoken tension presided. Not knowing what to say, I just threw my backpack over my shoulder and headed for the door without looking in Kat's direction. I damn near had one foot out the door when she stopped me.

"J.D., wait!" she said.

I had a good mind to act like I hadn't heard her and keep steppin', but my feet stopped moving the second I heard her call my name. By the time I turned around, she'd already stood up and was approaching me.

"Let's talk," she said, perching on the edge of the table.

"All right," I said, still avoiding eye contact with her. "But I don't have long. I've got some studying to do for my other classes. What's up?"

"Studying for other classes, are we?" she asked mockingly. "Well that's great news! I see somebody is starting to get the hang of things around here."

"Gotta keep my grades up," I said.

"I know that's right," she said, smiling. "Keep those priorities straight."

I looked down at my watch, as if I were really in a rush.

"Well, I'm not gonna keep you long," she said. "I just wanted to try to patch things up between us. If for no other reason than for the sake of the both of us getting a good grade in this class. I mean, we do have to work together and all, so I figure, we might as well get along. Ya know?"

"I can dig it," I said. "I can respect that."

"Good!" she said, grinning from ear to ear. "I am so happy to hear that. Especially after the last conversation we had before you came back out here."

Although I knew Katrina was HIV positive, she still had a glow about her that exuded sexy. Everything from her bubbly personality down to her picture-perfect smile, and the sweet, subtle smell of the Issey Miyake perfume she wore made her desirable. Not to mention her keen sense of fashion and flawless skin. As bad as I wanted to play the hard role, the longer I stood next to her, the more I wanted to share a moment of passion with her again. Not that I would. But she was *that* fine. Any unsuspecting brotha would jump at the chance to get Kat between the sheets. As I stood there listening to her ramble on, I reminisced about all of the nights the two of us spent together talking on the phone until one of us fell asleep. All of the nights the two of us went at it like the Energizer Bunny and neither of us got any sleep at all.

"I know you've gotta go and all, but there is something I've gotta tell you," she continued.

Oh, God! Not another one of her confessions, I thought. As I sat there, close enough to Kat's face to smell the Big Red gum she was chewing, I braced myself for her State of the Union address. That's when I saw someone eyeing me in my peripheral. I hoped it wasn't who I thought it was. Less than five seconds later, my worst fear materialized. Sure enough, it was Leslie, walking with three other girls, her eyes fixed on me. With an *"I knew it"* smirk on her face, she held eye contact with me just long enough to let me know that she'd seen me. Then she shook her head, turned up her nose, slightly rolled her eyes and went back to conversing with her friends as they walked by. While nonchalant, her lack of words said it all. I felt like someone had just sucker punched me in the gut and knocked my wind out. I wanted to run out after her and let her know that it really wasn't like that with me and Kat, but I figured I'd talk to her when she was alone…if she ever picked up the phone again.

"It's really hard for me to put this into words," Kat said, her voice cracking as she teared up.

"I don't know if I've ever told you this before…. In fact, I don't know exactly how to put it. I guess the best way to say it is just…thank you," she said, wiping tears from both of her cheeks.

"Thank me for what?" I asked, still discombobulated by Leslie's random appearance.

Of all the moments for her to pop up, I thought.

"For saving my life," Kat continued, a continuous stream of tears rolling from her eyes. "I would have been dead if it weren't for you, J.D. I would have pulled the trigger. I just thank God that he sent you through that door to talk me out of committing suicide. I felt like I had nothing to lose and you convinced me otherwise. I am so sorry for getting emotional. I told myself when I had the chance to talk to you about this, I wouldn't cry. And look at me, crying like a baby."

"It's okay," I said, placing my hand on her shoulder, trying my best to console her as she poured her heart out.

Truth be told, I felt like shedding a tear myself. I hoped I hadn't blown my chances with Leslie. But judging by her demeanor, things weren't looking too good for me.

"Anyway," Kat continued, "I just want you to know that I am eternally grateful for what you did for me. I know that things have changed and we aren't the best of friends or whatever anymore, but if you are *ever* in need of *any*thing, you can call on me, and I will be there for you. *Anything.*"

After my heart-to-heart with Kat, I decided to head back to Marshall Hall to finish up the rest of my homework. As I was walking out of the library, I saw Fresh walking toward me, smoking a Black & Mild cigar.

"What was Katrina talking about, folk?" he asked.

"A whole lot of nothin', blood," I said. "Hella apologetic and shit. Tryna get back on my good side."

"You think she's sincere?"

"Yeah, I think so," I said. "She's a good person. She just made a dumb-ass decision. She gotta pay for it her whole life, though. I overheard her telling Destiny how many pills she has to take a day. That HIV ain't no joke, blood."

"Just be thankful you didn't get that shit," Fresh said.
"*Thankful* ain't the word."

When we finally made it back to Marshall Hall, I let out a big sigh of relief. Somehow, operating only on the forty minutes of sleep I snuck in during biology, I managed to get through my first day of classes, run the errands for the Kappas, knock out my homework assignments and meet with my public policy group. I was off to a good start. Everything was going according to plan, except for the fact that I hadn't heard from Leslie since our incidental run-in inside the library. No text messages or missed calls from her at all. After kicking off my shoes, I tried to call her to smooth things over, but she didn't answer. I figured that kind of thing is always better to do in person rather than over a voice mail, so I decided not to leave a message. Instead, I shot her a simple text message that read: *Good night, gorgeous*. Meanwhile, Timothy lay curled up in his bed next to mine. I was so tired, I hadn't even noticed he wasn't in it alone. At first, when I heard what sounded like a girl giggle, I thought he was just under the covers talking to his girl on speakerphone, as he usually did for some weird reason. But the second time she did it, I heard some tussling, so I peaked my head up in curiosity. And sure enough, I saw an extra hump in his bed lying next to him. T-Mac was definitely in rare form. Not only was he in bed with a girl, but he was also in bed with a girl after visitation hours. I couldn't believe it. I felt like a Peeping Tom as I peeked over at his bed from under my covers, interested to see what would happen next. I didn't see much action, but I heard a few things.

"Not with your roommate in the room, baby," she said. "I think I'd better go back to my dorm."

A few moments later, I saw her roll out of bed and slip into her jeans.

"I love you, too, baby," Timothy said as he let her out.

He can't be serious, I thought. He'd just started dating the girl and he was already using the *L* word.

"No, I love *you* more," he said just before pecking her on the lips and leaving to walk her out.

"Oh, Lord," I mumbled. "What a sucka."

It was a few minutes past midnight when I felt myself dozing off. *Thank God my first class doesn't start until 10:00 a.m.,* I thought as I set my alarm for eight o'clock. As exhausted as I was, I figured eight hours of shut-eye was just what I needed.

Four hours later, I was awakened by the thud of thunder. It was so loud, it almost sounded like someone was knocking at my door. I rolled over and wiped my eyes. The moment I saw that it was only 4:03 a.m., my head crashed right back on my pillow. That's when the knocking sound returned, even louder than before. But this time, it was definitely somebody knocking at my door. I rolled out of bed half-asleep and stumbled over to the door. Fresh was standing on the other side, wearing a baggy sweatsuit and a panicked expression on his face.

"It's about time you opened the door," he said in a frantic whisper. "I've been knocking for the last five minutes!"

"Huh?" I asked, still trying to figure out what was going on. "I mean, why? What's up?"

"C'mon!" he said. "We gotta go! Hurry up and throw some sweats on. We gotta be at the baseball diamond in five minutes."

"Baseball diamond?" I asked. "For what?"

"What do you think? Just hurry up, joe!"

"Man, bump that," I said. "I'm going back to sleep."

"What you mean going back to sleep?" Fresh said, stepping inside the room, lowering his tone once he saw

Timothy was sleeping. "If you quit now, all that stuff we did the other night would be for nothing. You can't quit, fam. Just throw on a sweatsuit—one with a hood on it."

"A hood?" I asked. "For what?"

"I don't know, man!" Fresh said. "I'm just going by what Dex told me. Just hurry up!"

Aggravated and still half-asleep, I scrambled to find some sweats. Meanwhile, it was still raining cats and dogs outside. I wondered why the hell anyone would want to meet outside in that. When I left, Timmy was still snoring like a bear.

"Let's go!" Fresh said, jogging down the hallway.

The baseball diamond was located next to the football field, clear on the other side of campus. I could do nothing more than shake my head and sour my facial expression as I darted out into the rain. Before I got one block away from Marshall Hall, I was soaked. By the time Fresh and I reached the baseball diamond, we were drenched and out of breath. It was raining so hard, there were puddles inside my socks. I could feel the water in between my toes with every step. This time, there were only four Kappas—Dex and three others. And from our original group of eight, we were now down to four. Standing on a muddy baseball field in the pouring rain at four-something in the morning, I couldn't say I blamed the quitters.

"All of y'all line up against the damn fence!" Dex shouted.

By the tone of his voice, I could tell he was upset. Once again, I was last in line, right behind Fresh.

"I don't feel like being out here in the rain no more than any of y'all do," Dex said. "But you little GDIs are already out of line! And tonight, I'ma teach y'all a lesson about disrespecting the brothas of K-B-Psi! Earlier, I sent one of y'all a message and told you to bring me some chicken. *Popeye's* chicken."

My stomach began doing backflips and I became woozy. I knew where he was going with this.

"Shit," Fresh mumbled.

"But somebody thought it would be a good idea to go somewhere else to get the chicken for cheaper instead," Dex continued, walking straight toward Fresh and holding a receipt in his hand. "Now, I'm a business finance major with a 3.8 GPA. But it damn sure doesn't take a rocket scientist to tell the difference between Popeye's and *Church's!* Especially when you leave the receipt in the bag! Who would do some dumb shit like that?"

Dex walked up and down the line, holding the receipt in front of each of our faces. I thought Fresh would've at least had enough common sense to take the receipt out of the damn bag. Guess not.

"It was probably the same fool who likes to send sweet little text messages and all that," one of the Kappas said.

"I don't think he's here this morning," Dex said. "I think he quit."

"If he knows what's good for him, he should have," one of the other Kappas said, laughing.

"Is J.D. here?" Dex asked.

I had a good mind to just act like I didn't hear him. For a moment, I just stood there with my hands at my sides looking straight forward, pretending as if he hadn't said a thing at all.

"I knew that dude was a punk," one of the Kappas said.

"I told you he didn't come back," Dex said.

"I'm right here, *sir,*" I said, reluctantly raising my hand.

"Aaa-haaaa!" Dex said, walking up in my face and standing toe-to-toe with me. "So you did come back? From what I hear, you like to send little late-night text messages to other people's girls."

The only girl I'd sent anything to was Leslie. I had no idea how the hell Dex found out about it, of all people.

"Don't get too close to him," one of the Kappas said. "I heard he got the package."

"AIDS?" Dex asked.

"That's what I heard," the Kappa said. "You know he was messing around with Katrina last semester."

"Downtown D's Katrina?" Dex asked. "The APA?"

"Yep," the Kappa said. "I heard he's the reason both of 'em got it."

"No, I'm not!" I said. "People need to quit spreading lies about me. I've been tested and I ain't got no damn HIV!"

"Ain't nobody asked you what you had, ya little GDI!" Dex said. "I know you were responsible for messing up the chicken order. And I know if you speak out of line one more time or ever use profanity directed at any of the bruhs, you're finished. Now, you done made me so mad, all of y'all are gonna pay for it. Line up at home plate!"

As I was standing there, last in line, my mind raced as I dreaded what they were going to do to us. What ensued was one of the most embarrassing, heinous things I've ever had to do. In the pouring rain, on the muddy field, we had to run full-speed around the bases and slide face-first into each one. Each time I slid, mud would spout up into my face, eyes and mouth. After the first five times around the bases, diving in the dirt felt like diving onto concrete. Every slide felt like a belly flop off of a high-dive in a swimming pool. I could feel the skin tearing around my elbows, forearms and stomach. A few times, it knocked the wind out of me. We had to complete 30 laps. That's 120 total face-first slides into the bases. I don't know how we got through it, but we did. It must've taken us an hour to complete. Afterward, I was so exhausted, I could barely stand on my own two feet. I was dizzy, panting and dying of thirst. That's when another Kappa came jogging up from across the field. It was Konceited. He was carrying a Gatorade bottle.

"Damn, where you been at, bruh?" Dex asked him. "We were sitting around the frat house, waiting for you."

"My bad," Konceited said. "I got caught up with that damn Italian stallion!"

"Again?" one of the Kappas asked.

"I can't stay away, bruh," Konceited said. "She's a beast!"

"You talking about the one who's dating that lame-ass Alpha nigga T-Mac, right?" Dex asked.

"Yeah, that's her," Konceited confirmed.

"Hope you're strapping up," one of the other Kappas said. "I know a couple of the bruhs over at G-State and Tech who hit that. She's a Greek groupie."

"C'mon now, bruh," Konceited said. "You know I stay strapped like car seats. It's not like I'm tryna wife her up."

Damn, I thought, shaking my head slightly. I knew it. Timothy was getting played by a freak. I knew I had to tell him. I'd have to figure out how later.

"Later for all that," Dex said, taking the Gatorade bottle from Konceited. "Everybody line up again. Take your hoods off, cock your heads back, and open your mouths. After all of that running, I know y'all gotta be thirsty."

Thank God, I thought, still breathing heavily, gasping for air. Lord knows, I needed a sip. Dex started at the front of the line and worked his way back, filling each of our mouths to the brim. By the time I swallowed it was too late. What I thought was Gatorade turned out to be one hundred percent prune juice.

"How did that taste, fellas?" Dex asked, laughing.

The older Kappas were cracking up as I gagged.

"Got plenty more here, if you need another sip," Dex continued. "I'm sure you guys have worked up quite an appetite, with all that running and all. So I'm gonna give you this piece of caramel to share. I want you to take the biggest bite you can, and pass it back. If you take a small bite, you will eat all of it. If you spit out any of it, you are done. Don't ever think about coming back."

With that, Dex proceeded to hand what looked like an extremely small candy apple to the first guy in line. By the time it made it back to me, I could tell it was anything but that. When Fresh turned around to hand it to me, even though it was raining and his mouth was shut, I could smell a strong aroma on his breath that damn sure wasn't culti-vated by Granny Smith. I was, however, face-to-face with a half-eaten piece of garlic that had been dipped in caramel. Dex took one step closer to me and yelled at the top of his lungs.

"Eat!" he screamed.

I held it in front of my face, my hand shaking and lip quivering. Just the smell of the fresh garlic made my stomach quiver. As bad as I wanted to force it in my mouth, like the rest of the guys had, I couldn't bring my hand to do it.

"Okay, I see we still have an individual on our hands," Dex said. "He's better than the rest of y'all. He doesn't wanna eat with y'all. Don't worry about it, homie. Don't eat it. You're different. You're special, so you should be in the front of the line. C'mon."

Dex grabbed me by my elbow and led me to the front of the line.

"Since you don't wanna take one little bite out of the apple, you can stand here and watch your buddies eat the entire thing."

As I watched the guys vigorously shaking their heads back and forth, letting me know they couldn't stomach another bite, I decided I couldn't leave them hanging like that. I had to take one for the team.

"I'll take a bite, man," I said.

"*Man?*" Dex asked. "Who the hell do you think you're talking to? You can't seem to stop messing up."

"I'm sorry, sir," I said. "I meant to say, I'll take a bite, sir."

"You are sorry," Dex agreed, snatching the apple out of my hands. "If you think your little freshman ass can take a girl from a man of Kappa Beta Psi, you got another thing coming. Get your sorry ass down and give me one hundred push-ups while your friends finish off the apple."

The way he kept bringing up that text message situation outta nowhere, I was starting to think maybe Dex was Leslie's ex. It seemed like he had a personal vendetta out against me. I was struggling with push-up number 68 when Dex pulled me up to my feet by the back of my collar and shoved me in the front of the line. I felt bad for letting the fellas down. They looked at me like they wanted to jump me. Each of them looked nauseous. That prune juice alone had my stomach boiling. We stood in a single file line and I was in the very front.

"Now, for some jumping jacks," Dex said. "If you feel the urge to throw up, which you probably will, you make sure to throw up in the guy's hood in front of you. If I see one drop spill on the ground, you're finished. You will never be a man of Kappa Beta Psi. Ready, go!"

With the rain still pouring down on us, less than three minutes into the jumping jacks, I felt the guy behind me tap me on my shoulder. I thought he'd tapped me by accident or something, so I kept right on going and didn't think anything of it. A few seconds later, I felt a strong tug on my hood, and my neck snapped back, arms flailing. That's when I heard it. The first sound was reminiscent of a burp. One of those disgustingly huge, post-Thanksgiving dinner, dessert and a six-pack burps. The next sound was eerily similar to the sound of a faucet shooting out water on full blast. The fact that the guy behind me had just earled in my hood was bad enough. But the worst part was that not all of it landed in my hood. It smelled worse than spoiled milk and felt like warm oatmeal dripping down the side of my neck. I was frozen solid. I didn't even want to move.

"Who told you to stop?" Dex asked, as he stood right in front of me. "Keep going!"

When I resumed, it got worse. I could actually feel the vomit dripping down my shoulder, sliding down my back and slithering down my ass crack. It was without question the single most disgusting thing I'd ever felt in my entire life. At least I thought it was. A few minutes later, right around the time the vomit had mixed in with my sweat and made it way down my thigh all the way to my ankle, someone creeped up from behind me and flipped the hood on my head. That's when I stopped. The collection of rain and vomit settled into my scalp and oozed down my face from all angles. Before I could guard my face with my hands, it seeped into my ears and the corner of my eyes. Luckily I closed my mouth just in time, but the vomit still made its way to the crease between my lips. All I could do was wipe my mouth with my muddy sweatshirt and bow my head in disgrace.

"I think I'm done with y'all for now," Dex said. "Try to get some sleep before class. Oh, and you might wanna think about taking a shower, too!"

The sun was just starting to come up as the four of us headed back to main campus wounded and limping, smelling like last month's trash. The other two guys lived in the upperclassmen dorms near the library. Just before we split up, one of them asked, "So why didn't you guys go to Popeye's like he asked?"

"Long story," I said. "He would've never known if Fresh hadn't left the receipt in the bag."

"Way to go, Fresh," one of the guys said.

"My bad, y'all," Fresh said, rubbing his shoulder. "I was trippin'."

"And you were the only one who *didn't* get thrown up on," I said. "I shoulda took a bite out of that damn thing and stayed in the back."

TEN

The funny thing about prepledging is, there comes a point when you've gone through too much to turn back. That's the first phase. Then it segues into a mode where you feel there's nothing worse the guys in the frat can think of to do to you. A unique dichotomy exists here—at the point when you feel weakest, you're actually at your strongest. Then you come to the realization that the more the guys in the frat disrespect you, the more they actually gain respect for you for sticking it out. Your true intentions are tested on a daily basis, and the imposters in it for superficial reasons are weeded out. When the process started, I was one of the imposters. I was interested in Kappa Beta Psi only because I thought that Leslie would be more attracted to me if I became a member. But over the course of time, I learned that joining the frat was about so much more than that. I had no idea the Kappas went out to low-income areas twice a month to help build houses for Habitat for Humanity. Since I'd been prepledging, they'd organized a canned food drive, mentored middle school kids through their Kappa League program and delivered sack lunches to the homeless. When I first got involved with prepledging, I wasn't sure I was doing the right thing. Halfway through the semester, I was positive. I'd learned the entire Greek alphabet and a lot of basic history about the Greeks, with special attention to Kappa Beta Psi, of course. They didn't share anything deep with us because we weren't officially online as of yet. Most of the things we learned, I could've easily looked up on the Internet. But the fact that I was learning the info from them instead of looking it up made it all the more special. The only drawback was the time I was putting into it. My social life was virtually nonexistent. When I wasn't in class, working on Kat's campaign or studying, I was putting in work for Kappa Beta Psi. I'd grown accustomed to functioning while suffering from sleep deprivation. I was lucky to get a nap in here and there. Most of the time, "here and there" really meant "this class and that class." At the beginning of the semester, Fresh and I made a pact to look out for one another in the classes we shared. Both of us intentionally sat in the back. I would sleep for the first half of the class, while he took notes. Then, he would wake me up, and I would take notes for the second half of class, while he got his nap on. Our system actually worked really well, for the most part. But on some days, things just didn't go as planned.

One day in particular, just before spring break, I'd dozed off in Dr. J's public policy class. I typically made it a point not to, but the night before I'd stayed up all night working on my ten-page paper for English class. I was passed out before Dr. J even called role. I was in the midst of catching some good z's when I heard something loud sound off on my desk. I popped up straight, trying to act as if I'd been awake the entire time, but it was no use. Dr. J was standing over me with a plastic ruler in his hand.

"Look, J.D., you know I don't tolerate anybody falling asleep in my class," he said. "Why do you and you friend Lamont want to test me today?"

"We don't want to test you, Dr. J," I said. "I apologize. We just had a long night, staying up working on our campaign and all."

It's always good to make professors feel like you make their class a priority. I thought I'd be able to slide on sympathy, but Dr. J wasn't going for it.

"I find that hard to believe," Dr. J said. "This isn't the first time I've noticed the two of you catching z's in my class. This is just the first time I've addressed it."

"It won't happen again, Dr. J," Fresh said. "I promise."

"Not if you want an A in my class, it won't," he said. "I'ma give the two of you a second chance. But falling asleep in my class is an instant letter grade drop. Y'all know that."

Dr. J walked back toward the front of the class, shaking his head in disappointment.

"I wouldn't think I'd have to do this at this juncture in the semester, but let me take a moment to remind everyone in here that you do *not* have to be here. This is college, not high school. No professor at the University of Atlanta is going to call home and report that you were not in attendance. We are not babysitters. You are not children. If at any point, you feel you are too tired to stay awake in my class, by all means, leave and go get yourself some sleep. But dozing off during class time is disrespectful to me and a distraction to your classmates."

The second Dr. J turned his back to the class, I jabbed Fresh in the shoulder.

"It was your turn to stay awake," I whispered.

"I tried," he said, shaking his head, wiping his eyes. "I'm tired as hell, fam."

I couldn't even be mad at Fresh. I was in the same boat. Miraculously, I was able to make it through the rest of the class without dozing off again. Slowly but surely, the most important relationships I had were going down the tubes. Dr. J was the only professor who I knew had my back for sure. I couldn't afford to get on his bad side. And I was snoozing my way right toward it. As for my personal life, things couldn't be worse. I hadn't gotten any booty all semester. I hadn't even gotten close. Not even a kiss. Nothing. And the one girl I was really feeling had been giving me the silent treatment for almost a week. Ever since I got wind that Dex was Leslie's ex-boyfriend, and he obviously had access to her text messages, I stopped sending her texts. But I still called. Of course, I was careful to press *67 before I dialed her number, so my number would show up as blocked on her screen. I was glad when she Leslie finally answered my phone call and agreed to meet me in the library to talk. My intentions were two-fold. On one hand, I really wanted to see and talk to her in person. On the other hand, I needed her help on an important paper I had to write for my English class. I figured I could knock out two birds with one stone. Leslie sent me a text message and said she'd be running a little late, so I decided to hop on Facebook to kill some time. To my surprise, the first thing I saw when I logged on was an advertisement: Howard Harrell for University of Atlanta Student Body President. Who knew people spent money on Facebook to advertise for student government elections? It was quite clear Howard was going all in. We had a lot of catching up to do. The second thing I noticed was a status update from Timothy. According to his most recent post, he was now officially "in a relationship with Amy Druzolowski." I slammed my fist down on the table.

"This is some bullshit," I murmured to myself.

Timothy and I weren't the best of friends. But he was my roommate, and as bad as I hated to see him getting played, I couldn't take the sight of him playing himself. And now, to make matters worse, he was doing it on Facebook, for all to see. He had to be stopped. As much as I knew it would hurt him, I had to break the news. At the same time, I had my own laundry list of relationship problems. Even though Leslie said her relationship with Dex was over, I assumed they were still involved to some degree. And I was sure they still shared feelings for each other. But the fact remained, they weren't together anymore. So I figured, as long as Dex didn't find out about it, I still had a chance. I knew I was playing with fire. Dating Leslie while prepledging Kappa Beta Psi was like walking a 70-story-high tightrope in the Windy City with no net. I was asking for problems. But when Leslie walked up to the desk where I was sitting, looking like a million bucks, I knew it was worth the risk. Every time I saw her, it was like the very first time. I became short on breath.

"Oh, hell no," she said, looking over my shoulder as we hugged. "I know that's not your English composition book. J.D., did you really ask me to come here so I could help you write a paper?"

"Nah," I said, trying to play it off. "Of course not. Honestly, I just wanted to see you, sit down and talk for a minute."

"Awww!" she said. "That's sweet. Well, I can't stay for long. What's been up?"

Of course, our conversation led into how badly I needed help writing my paper. She took the bait, just like I thought she would. We ended up working on the paper together for hours. I didn't know it at that moment, but that one study session was really what brought us closer together. I'm not quite sure if it was my poor use of grammar or horrible sentence structure that turned her on, but by the end of the study session, it seemed Leslie was on me. Whatever time I had in-between classes and prepledging, I spent with her. We hit the mall together, went to the movies and sent text messages to each other all day, every day. She'd sneak into my room after hours and I'd sneak into hers between classes. I had no earthly idea why she felt I was worthy of her time. She was without question one of the baddest chicks on campus. By my estimation, I was everything she wasn't looking for. I was a freshman with no car. I didn't go to Lighthouse. I wasn't Greek. And the only real popularity I had on campus was the fact that everybody assumed I had HIV. Whatever the case, Leslie was feelin' me, despite my shortcomings. She had me wide open. It must have been written all over my face, because all of my homies could seem to tell she had my head gone.

"Can you please tell me why you're always locking yourself down with one girl?" Fresh asked as I sat around the lunch table with the fellas. "I thought you would have learned your lesson about that last semester. You know these girls ain't about nothin'! And you know damn well, we ain't about nothin'! So why get involved in a serious relationship with any one chick on campus when the ratio of females to guys is like eight to one?"

"He's got a good point there," Fats said.

"Yeah, but have you seen J.D.'s girl, yo?" Dub-B asked. "She's the truth!"

"Yeah, yeah," Fresh said. "She's straight and all that, but damn, fam-o. You're on love lockdown like Kanye West! Last semester it was Kat. This semester it's Leslie. On some the real, I think you need to expand your horizons, pimpin'. Be more like Fresh!"

"More like Fresh, huh?" I asked. "You're speaking in third person now?"

"Yes, more like Fresh!" he said. "I got Rashida from Detroit on my team."

"You talking 'bout light-skinned Rashida with the freckles and the big booty?" Dub-B asked.

"Yep," Fresh said.

"She's from Dallas, yo," Dub-B said.

"Oh," Fresh said. "Well, anyway, I got her. I got Tiffany from Houston…Sandra from L.A."

"Actually, Tiffany is from L.A. and Sandra is from Houston," Dub-B corrected.

"Damn," Fresh said. "You got a good point there. You're right. But the point I'm trying to make is, I got all of 'em wrapped around my pinky finger, dog. Ready to do my homework, write my papers and wash my dirty draws if I ask them to."

"You don't even know where the girls you talk to are from," I said.

"Who cares where they're from?" Fresh asked. "I can tell you where they're going."

"And where's that?" Dub-B prodded.

"To *Pluto* if I tell 'em to!" Fresh said. "I'm having things my way like Burger King, pimp. That's how I'm living!"

"You're a funny guy, cuz," Fats said. "Swearin' you be pimpin'. You better watch your back, though. One of these days, dealing with all of those females is gonna catch up to you."

"That's what I've been trying to tell this fool," I said. "It wouldn't be so bad if all of them didn't think they were dating him."

"Hey! I can't help what they *think*," Fresh said.

"We'll see how long that excuse lasts," Fats said. "Hold my spot down. I'm going back for seconds. Nice T-shirts, by the way."

Fats was referring to the black tees Dub-B's pops had made for us that read: Vote Kat on the front, Student Body President on the back.

"I can't believe Fats is carrying a notebook this semester," I said. "He must be really trying to graduate."

Out of curiosity, I decided to peak inside Fats's notebook to see what he'd written.

"What class is that for anyway?" Fresh asked as I flipped through the pages.

"I don't know," I said.

"Why not?"

"There is *nothing* in it!" I said. "It's blank!"

"Are you serious?" Fresh asked, snatching the notebook from me. "Hell nah, joe. How the hell Fats gon' be carrying around a notebook that has nothing in it? That's why he's been here for seven years!"

"Who you talkin' 'bout, cuz?" Fats asked, returning with a plate of soul food.

"You, fool!" Fresh said. "All the time you spent on this campus, you could be *Dr.* Fats by now. And you're still walking around campus with a empty-ass notebook. You are hilarious."

I liked Fresh because he never held any punches. He was the kind of friend who would tell you if you had a booger in your nose. You had to keep those kinds of friends around.

"Well, I'm graduating in a couple months," Fats said, dousing his chicken with hot sauce. "You, my friend, will be lucky to graduate in four years. The way you chasing girls around campus, you might end up being here longer than me."

"Yeah, right," Fresh said.

All of us laughed.

"Laugh now," Fats said. "We'll see who's laughing when election time comes around. I heard y'all fools are running against Howard Harrell."

"Yeah," Dub-B said. "And?"

"And it's gonna take a whole lot more than those little T-shirts y'all got on to beat him!" Fats said. "Trust me. I've been on the yard for going on seven years now. I know. Howard is a beast when it comes to student government elections! Think about it, cuz. You don't just win student body president three times in a row for nothing! He's got it down to a science. Fund-raisers, posters, flyers, all that stuff! Y'all better be ready, 'cause I promise you, he's gonna come with it."

"Oh, we're gonna be ready, yo," Dub-B said confidently.

"I hear you talking, cuz," Fats said. "How are y'all getting graded for that public policy class anyway?"

"The only way to get an A is to win the election," I said.

I needed Kat to win the election more than anybody. Now that I needed a 3.0 to make the Kappa line, I knew I was going to need at least a few A's to balance out some of the lesser grades I was sure to get. And that was becoming a distinct possibility now that Timothy had gone AWOL on me and missed our last few biology study sessions because he was hanging with his girl.

"Aaawww!" Fats sounded off. "Man, that's ugly, cuz. I hope none of y'all are depending on getting an A up in there."

ELEVEN

NO SHOW

EVery Tuesday at six o'clock for two months straight, our group met in the conference room in Club Woody to work on Kat's campaign. Timothy had uncharacteristically missed the last couple meetings because he was "sick." I knew "lovesick" was more like it. Kat, on the other hand, really was sick most of the times we met—coughing, sneezing, nose running, nauseated. I assumed it was probably just her body reacting to all of the drugs she was taking. Even still, Kat was always the first one at the meeting. Dub-B and I were usually always the last to show. With basketball practice and games, he always had a legitimate excuse. Since nobody was supposed to know I was prepledging, I never had a valid excuse. Every time I'd come in ten or fifteen minutes late, Kat would bark out the same complaint.

"To be early is to be on time," she'd recite. "To be on time is to be late. And to be late is unacceptable!"

This time, it was almost half past the hour when I rolled up in the meeting, late as usual. I figured I would have to hear Kat's mouth and deal with the others murmuring about me being the slacker of the group. Mentally, I was prepared for it. I was not, however, prepared for Kat and Fresh to be missing in action. Neither of them were in attendance. Immediately, I noticed a worried expression on the faces of my other group members.

"Have you seen Katrina or Fresh around?" Dub-B asked.

"Nah," I said.

"Timothy?"

"Not since class earlier," I said. "Why?"

"None of them are here," Destiny said in a panicked tone.

The fact that Fresh and Timothy were MIA didn't bother me nearly as much as Kat's disappearing act. Fresh was expendable. Timothy was becoming progressively unreliable the more he fell for his girlfriend. But we needed Kat. She was the one running for office. We couldn't do anything without her. *Kat sure picked a hell of a day to go missing,* I thought, as I called her cell for a third time.

In less than thirty minutes, each candidate for student body president was to give their speech for the primary election. As a group, last week we'd agreed to meet at our usual time and location to listen to Kat deliver her speech and give her a few last-second pointers before she hit the stage. Apparently, Kat had other plans that none of us knew about.

"What happened?" Destiny asked, a look of concern on her face.

"Straight to voice mail," I said, frustrated. "Again."

"Do you think we should head down to the student center?" Dub-B asked. "Maybe she forgot about the meeting and she's already there."

"Maybe he's right, y'all," I said.

"Are you freakin' kidding me?" Destiny asked. "Kat would never forget about a meeting this important. That girl is the most organized person I've ever met. Her not answering is starting to scare me. Dub, you try calling her from your phone."

After yet another failed attempt to connect with Kat, we decided to take matters into our own hands. Quickly, we drafted a speech detailing all of Kat's accomplishments and where she stood on the issues. Just as we were putting the finishing touches on the conclusion, Destiny's phone rang. It was Katrina.

"Put her on speakerphone," Destiny said. "Hey, girl. Where in the world are you?"

"You don't wanna know," Kat said in a muffled voice. "I came to the mall to pick up the big poster we had designed at the art supply store."

"And?" Dub-B asked.

"And when I came outside, all of my tires were flat," she said. "*All* of 'em!"

"Who are you with?" I asked.

"Well, Fresh rode with me out here," she said.

"Hell nah!" I said. "That explains things. I think I know exactly what happened."

I wasn't certain, but something told me Tiffany had something to do with Kat's flat tires. Then again, any one of Fresh's women could've been to blame.

"Well, are you going to be able to make it back before the speeches start?" Destiny asked, nervously pacing back and forth. "I'm on scholarship. I can't afford a bad grade in this class."

"*You?*" I asked under my breath.

"And you can't afford to miss this speech, ma!" Dub-B continued.

"I know," Kat said, sniffling as if she was crying. "I don't know why this had to happen right now!"

"I can come pick you guys up," Dub-B said. "You're at Lenox?"

"I already called one of my line sisters to come pick us up about twenty minutes ago," Kat said, pouting. "She said she's stuck in traffic, and it's deadlocked. I don't think I'm gonna be able to make it, y'all."

"Damn!" I said, my heart beating faster. "What are we gonna do?"

"If I don't make it, I want J.D. to deliver the speech," Kat said.

"*J.D.?*" I asked. "Why me?"

"What do you mean, why you?" Kat asked. "Your mom basically wrote the doggone thing for me! You know it better than anyone else in the group. Plus, I know that you need to pass the class, so I'm sure you'll give it your all."

Judging by the looks on the faces of Destiny and Dub-B, neither of them thought Kat's idea was a very bright one. But this was Kat's campaign, and although they may have disagreed, none of them spoke up in opposition. There wasn't a bone in my body that wanted to deliver the speech in Kat's place. But she had a valid point. I needed to pass the class. About as unsure of myself as everyone standing around me was, I hesitantly agreed.

"I got you," I said without a lick of confidence.

"Girl, please try to make it back," Destiny pleaded. "Please! If not, we'll figure it out."

Ten minutes before the speeches were to commence, I'd come to the conclusion that Kat wasn't going to be in attendance and I would have to put the fate of our group on my shoulders. Of the five candidates running for student body president, only two would be voted onto the final ballot. As an incumbent, and three-time president, Howard

Harrell was a shoe-in for one of the spots based on his experience alone. The other spot was up for grabs. The way my grades were shaping up in my other classes, I figured I need at least an A in Dr. J's class in order to ensure a 3.0 GPA. The only way I'd even had a shot was if Kat's name appeared on that final ballot alongside Howard's. And now, by an ironic twist of fate, whether it did or didn't was solely my responsibility.

As we walked down the strip heading toward the Student Center, the closer we got, the more nervous I became. The speeches were open to the entire student body. And judging by the crowd filing up the steps toward the auditorium, you would've thought Barack Obama himself was giving a speech. Just before I was ushered backstage by an administrator, I took a peek at the crowd. There wasn't an empty seat in the house.

"Ain't this about nothing," I whispered to myself as I took my seat backstage in the room of presidential hopefuls.

I was the fourth candidate slated to take the stage. Just as the third—Tangy Fuller, an airhead junior who thought she'd win on her good looks alone but really didn't stand a chance—was wrapping up her speech, Howard rose from his seat on the couch and approached me. At the time, I was nibbling on my thumbnail, half-mouthing my speech to myself one last time.

"So your girl Katrina is a no-show, huh?" Howard asked before taking a sip of water.

I'd never said two words to Howard in my life—and would have been content going to my grave without doing so. But I knew he was just trying to psyche me out. Before I had a chance to answer, Howard answered for me.

"Figures," he continued. "After I take the stage it'll be like she never showed up anyway."

If his intention was to rattle me, it worked. I was already

nervous as hell. Howard's comment damn near put me over the edge. When I heard the crowd applauding for Tangy, I knew I was up next. My heart was racing like I was being chased by a stray red-nose pit bull. Like a shark smelling fresh blood, Howard could sense my anxiety.

"At this time, I would like to introduce the fourth candidate for student body president," the host said. "A junior criminal justice major from Athens, Georgia— Katrina Turner!"

Katrina Turner? I specifically told the host that I was speaking on behalf of Katrina, I thought, as my hands trembled so vigorously the speech fell to the floor.

"Katrina," one of the backstage helpers yelped, "you're on!"

"I'm *J.D.*," I said, bending over to scoop the speech up.

"Oh, yeah," the girl said. "Sorry about that. Well, you're on, J.B. Hurry up!"

"Good luck, *Katrina,*" Howard said, bursting out in laughter.

As I strutted out to the podium, trying my best not to look into the crowd, I could hear the whispers in the crowd.

"That ain't no damn Katrina," someone said.

"Who the hell is he?" one guy in the back yelled.

"Where's Kat?" one of her sorority sisters in the front row asked another.

My knees wobbled uncontrollably as I stood behind the podium. I tried to gain my composure by grabbing a hold of it, but my unsteady hands only caused the wooden structure to shudder, making my inexperience more obvious. As hard as I tried not to stare into the audience, it was impossible. I couldn't help noticing Dex and a few of the other Kappas standing near the front, off to the side, watching intently. I saw Dr. J, too. He was standing closer to the front of the stage, his bow tie protruding from his V-necked sweater. Somehow, my group members managed to get a seat front and center in the second row, sandwiched between the Alphas and APAs.

"As you can probably tell by now, *I* am not Katrina Turner," I said, inciting a few laughs from the stone-faced crowd. "But I am James Dawson, a member of her campaign team. And I am here to speak on her behalf, because I believe in her motto—*the status quo has to go!*"

The APAs and Alphas erupted in a standing ovation. To my surprise, more than half the crowd followed suit. That was my shining moment. Ten seconds of applause. I relished every last one of them. Somewhere between the first hand clap and the last, I completely blanked out. Even with my speech written out in front of me, I was overwhelmed by the pressure. I'd never spoken in front of that many people before. And all eyes were on me. All of a sudden, I couldn't read my own handwriting. I stumbled over my words and stuttered indiscriminately. By the time I made it through my intro, the heat from the spotlight was cooking me like a rotisserie chicken. I thought wiping the small stream of sweat from my temple would help me get back on track, but when my hand slipped awkwardly from my head and crashed down onto my neatly arranged sheets of paper, causing them to flutter to the stage, I completely lost it.

"Excuse me," I said, before bending over to scrape up my papers scattered across the stage.

At this point, my ineptitude was on full display. By the time I collected my speech and put it back in the correct order, the guy in the back of the room was flashing his red beam in my face, signaling me to wrap it up.

"I apologize for this," I said. "As you can probably tell, I wasn't prepared to deliver a speech today. In closing, I just ask that you look at all of the qualities Katrina brings to the table. She is more than qualified to be student body president."

"Well, where the hell is she?" a heckler in the back of the room yelled.

A few people laughed. Then, before I could muster up an answer, it started. What began as a soft chant near the back of the auditorium snaked its way to the front like the wave at a baseball game, growing louder as it approached.

"Howard! Howard! Howard!" the crowd chanted.

I tried talking over them, but it was useless. Over half the crowd was chanting Howard's name at the top of their lungs. I saw a few people waving me off stage like I was stinking it up at the Apollo. A few others held their keychains up and rattled their keys, signaling me to hit the road. To add fuel to the fire, the DJ started scratching and spinning a song before I could say "Vote for Katrina" one last time. Even as the music played, the chant continued and fists pumped. I couldn't have done a worse job representing Katrina and her campaign. I'd been given a chance to salvage my own GPA and help Katrina win the election and I blew it. Oddly enough it wasn't the hecklers rattling their keys or the DJ cueing me off the stage that hurt the most. Not even the thought of how mad Kat would be when everybody told her how bad I'd bombed. It was the sight of Dr. J dipping his head into his hands in shame and the dejected look on the faces of my group members that made me feel like the scum of the earth. I'd all but single-handedly ruined any chance of Kat being elected student body president. I hoped her support from the Greeks on campus and friends she'd made over the last three years would be enough to at least get her on the final ballot. By the look on their faces, I was certain my speech didn't win over any of the Kappas. As I walked off stage, my head slightly drooped and tears formed in my eyes. I felt hopeless.

"And now for the man who has served three consecutive terms as president," the host said as I made my way toward the backstage exit, "it is my pleasure to introduce Howard Harrell!"

The crowd went wild. I went back to Marshall Hall. I didn't care to stick around for his speech. Instead, I snuck out the back door, careful to avoid all of my group members. I'd bombed so horribly, I didn't even want to see them. Just when I'd made it to the stoop outside Marshall Hall and thought I was home free, I was spotted.

"You didn't do that bad, cuz," Fats said, catching up with me as I walked down the stairs.

"I needed that to go a lot better than it did," I said, my head sunken. "Everybody was depending on me and I blew it!"

"Pick your head up, cuz!" Fats said, patting me on the shoulder. "It was just a speech."

"It was more than just a speech," I said. "I really shot myself in the foot on my midterms, so I'm probably gonna need an A in public policy class to make the cut."

"Hey, everybody flunks a midterm exam every now and then," he said.

"Try two out of three," I said.

"Damn! That's a bad look, cuz. Well, maybe you can make up for it on your finals."

"Nah, man," I said. "I messed up real bad this time, blood. The only way I'ma be back at U of A next year is if Katrina wins this damn election. And the way I just fumbled that speech, it's a long shot."

"Ain't she running against Howard Harrell?"

"Yeah," I said.

"Ha!" He chuckled. "It was a long shot before you took the stage, homie. Good luck with that! You know that fool ain't lost an election since he's been here."

"Thanks, Fats," I said sarcastically. "I feel a lot better about it now."

"Well, hey, look at the bright side," he said.

"What bright side?"

"At least you'll be able to kick it on the beach in Miami in a few days before you have to go back to Oakland," he said. "You still going down there for spring break, right?"

"Yeah," I said. "But damn. Why you gotta kill my dreams like that, though?"

"I didn't mean to," he said. "I just gotta call a spade a spade. I mean, I'ma get as many people to vote for Kat as I can, but I ain't even gonna lie, when it comes to student government elections, Howard has the campus on lock, cuz."

"Whatever, man," I said, taking a deep breath. "Anyway, I'm 'bout to hook up with Fresh in a minute and give him my money, so he can book our room with his credit card."

"I need to do the same thing," he said. "Who's all staying with you down there?"

"Right now, it's just me, Fresh, Dub-B and my roommate, Timothy."

"Four freshmen in Miami," Fats said. "Y'all are definitely gonna need an OG like me to show you the ropes. Plus, you're gonna need me to get the drinks. You got a spot in the car for ya boy? I'll put in on it."

"As high as gas is, you know we ain't driving," I said. "If you're coming, you better hurry up and get a plane ticket."

TWELVE

SPRING BREAK

Our plane landed at Miami International Airport forty-five minutes ago, and still, there was no sign of our bags. With all of the spring breakers flying in from all over the country, I suppose the baggage claim folks were backed up. But I didn't mind the wait. The terminal was jam-packed and swarming with dime pieces—most of whom looked like they'd come from exotic parts of the world I'd only seen on the Discovery Channel. I was so sidetracked by staring at all of the females, it was quite possible my luggage had been circling for the last half an hour and I'd just missed it. We hadn't even made it to the beach yet, and already, it felt good to be away from the campus for a while. After being accused of being HIV-positive for the greater part of the semester, taking orders from the Kappas and doing all kinds of ridiculous things as part of their "prepledge" process, the whole election speech meltdown and blowing my midterms, I just needed some time to chill and clear my head. While waiting, the five of us talked about everything. Our conversations helped keep our minds off of our missing luggage and made time fly by. We started on Fresh and his credit card spending habits.

"Take it from an OG," Fats said. "Spending all your bread on those females you're trying to get with is gonna catch up to you, cuz. I heard about what happened to Kat's car the other day at the mall."

"That was an isolated incident," Fresh said.

"Yeah, right," I said. "I'm surprised it didn't happen earlier. I don't know how you were keeping up with all of those girls anyway. A Tiffany necklace for this one, a bottle of perfume for that one."

"*Tiffany?*" Fats asked in amazement. "*Tiffany,* my nig? Damn, I didn't know you were trickin' off like that!"

"Hey, Lil' Wayne said it best," Fresh said calmly. "It ain't trickin' if you got it!"

"Yeah, but when *Lil' Wayne* said that, he had like five *million* bucks in his bank account," Dub-B said. "*You* have *one* credit card, yo."

"You guys are real funny," Fresh said, laughing half-heartedly. "I mean, I know I'm smashing some of the baddest chicks on campus. I know this. But you don't have to hate."

"Is that all you guys ever think about is sex?" Timothy asked. "Who is *smashing* this girl and who is *cutting* that chick?"

I thought getting some would have made Timothy a bit cooler, but clearly he was still as square as a box of Apple Jacks. The rest of us simultaneously gave Timothy a menacing look, before sounding off at the top of our lungs, "Yes!"

"Anyways," Fresh continued, clearing his throat. "Like

I was saying before I was rudely interrupted by the twenty-year-old virgin."

"Hey, I'm only nineteen," Timothy squealed. "And for the record, I'm no longer a virgin. Thank you!"

"Wooo-hoooo!" Fresh said. "Break out the champagne glasses! Bible boy *finally* got some booty! It's too bad damn near everybody on campus already hit that. But that's a whole 'nother story. What I'm trying to express to y'all is you don't have to be mad 'cause you can't be me. None of you can do that. But that doesn't mean you have to be a hater your whole life!"

"Wait a minute, Fresh," Timothy said. "When you said, 'Every n-word on campus already hit that…' What do you mean, man?"

"Nevermind that," Fats said. "Ain't nobody hating on you, cuz. All we're saying is, if you have to buy things for your breezies just to get 'em between the sheets, it don't really count."

"Yeah," I agreed. "You're basically just paying for it."

"Trickin' in other words," Fats said.

"C'mon, now," Fresh retorted. "Every guy has come out his pocket to get some at one time or another."

"J.D.," Timothy said in a frustrated tone, nudging me with his elbow. "What the heck did Fresh mean by that comment he made about Amy?"

For a second, I contemplated telling him right then and there. Lord knows I wanted to. But I didn't want to spoil his entire trip to Miami. Plus, I didn't want to embarrass him in front of the fellas. So I decided to wait. I just continued right on talking as if he hadn't said a thing.

"Not me!" I said boldly. "I've never had to come out of my pocket to get the drawls. Never!"

"Oh, so you've never taken a girl to the movies and paid?" Fresh asked. "Never taken a girl out to eat? Never bought a new outfit or got a fresh haircut just to impress a chick?"

"Of course I have," I said. "But…"

"But nothing!" Fresh said. "It may have been indirect. But you definitely paid for it. Besides, with all this bread I got left on my credit card, I can afford to spend a little here and there. Like I said before, it ain't trickin' if you got it!"

The longer we waited for our luggage, the deeper our conversations got. Somehow, Fats's theory about college degrees came into question. Of course, Fats thought he was always schooling us about everything because he was the oldest.

"All I'm saying is, you don't necessarily *need* a diploma to be successful," Fats said. "I mean, look at Russell Simmons and Diddy. Neither of them finished college."

"You can't really compare yourself with them, though," I said.

"Yeah," Fresh said. "They're in the entertainment industry. That's different."

"Okay. Well, what about Bill Gates?" Fats asked. "He never graduated from college, either."

"He didn't?" I asked.

"Nope," Timothy chimed in.

"It's not about that college degree, cuz," Fats said. "That's why there are so many college graduates out here right now working bullshit retail jobs and gigs at restaurants! They think it's about that piece of paper, but it's not. It's all about connections. It's not what you know, but who you know. Or better yet, who knows you! It's all about networking, homie."

I knew that the pendulum would swing in my direction. But I had no idea what the topic of conversation would be when it did. By the time we corralled our luggage and hopped in a taxi, I thought I was home free. But that's when the verbal abuse commenced.

"What the hell were you thinking about when you were up there on stage giving that damn speech?" Fats asked.

"Here you go," I said.

Fresh covered his mouth with his hand and put his head down, trying to conceal his laugh. Neither Fats nor Timothy could hold in their laughter, both of them cracking up like a couple of hyenas.

"Seriously, cuz," Fats continued. "I mean, you started off so confident, like 'Hello, my name is James Dawson.' Then right after that, you just lost it."

"I think it was stage fright," Fresh said.

"Was I really *that* bad?" I asked.

"You were worse," Dub-B said with a straight face. "I don't know who was counting the votes. But I don't see how the hell Katrina made it on the final ballot after that speech you gave. I mean, we cool and all, but honestly, I thought you'd ruined us."

"Me, too," Timothy added.

I could do nothing more than roll with the punches on this particular roast. I knew I'd dropped the ball on the speech. How Kat managed to eke by the prelims onto the final ballot was anybody's guess. When I logged on to the school Web site to check the election results and saw her name listed as one of the finalists for student body president, I was convinced once and for all, that prayer really works. I felt the same way when we hit Ocean Drive for the first time. I saw the woman of my dreams on at least six different occasions before we even pulled into our hotel parking lot. When we hopped out and all of the fellas started slapping high fives, all of my previous concerns went out the window.

Miami was like nothing I'd ever seen before. I'd been to Venice Beach in L.A. a few times, but the moment I stepped out of the taxi, I could tell Miami was on a whole 'nother level. Don't get me wrong. I'd seen some of the most beautiful women in my life on the beach in Cali, but for the most part, it seemed there were more families vacationing together on the beaches out West. Whereas Miami was nothing but college students getting drunk and wildin' out. And per capita, there were way more fine females on South Beach, rocking the skimpiest bikinis one could imagine. In fact, there were so many bad breezies, I didn't even know where to start.

"This is ridiculous," Fresh said with a huge smile on his face as he adjusted his sunglasses. "I ain't gonna lie, I haven't ever even seen a real palm tree before."

"Me, neither," Timothy echoed. "This weather feels so tropical. It has to be at least eighty degrees out here!"

"Damn the weather and the palm trees," Fats said. "You see all the bad brizzies out here, cuz? Let's hurry up and take these bags in the room so we can get back out here and holla at some of 'em!"

There were five of us and only two beds in the room. But we were determined to make do. There was a couch in the corner and we ordered a cot, so everyone had somewhere to sleep. We played rock-paper-scissors to see who had first dibs on the bed. We didn't waste much time in the room. We dumped our bags, hit the showers, then headed to the beach. Fresh grabbed a Coke from the vending machine near the elevator.

"Got my chaser," Fresh said after taking a swig on the way down to the lobby. "Now, all I need to do is hit the liquor store for some Hen, so we can get right."

When the elevator doors opened in the lobby, Leslie was standing there with a few of her girls waiting to get on. Leslie was wearing a light purple, two-piece bathing suit so skimpy it looked like she borrowed it from Lil' Kim. Suntan oil glistened on her skin. My mouth watered. There were thousands of good-looking, horny girls I'd never met just steps away, strolling the beach and looking for trouble. But still, there was something about that damn Leslie that I just couldn't get enough of.

"Who you looking all sexy for?" I asked, pulling her close.

She smelled of coconut suntan oil. It immediately turned me on.

"Who else?" she asked, pecking me on the lips three times with her arms wrapped around my neck.

Just as I was going in for a little tongue action, I felt the elevator door slam into my shoulder.

"Get a room," one of Leslie's girls said, jokingly.

"C'mon, joe," Fresh said. "You two lovebirds can be all lovey-dovey on your own time."

Boy, did we ever take him up on that offer. The next three days I spent on South Beach turned out to be 72 of the best hours of my entire life. At the end of each night, I knew I was hooking up with one of the sexiest girls on the beach. But by day, we partied like rock stars. Thanks to our refund checks coming in just in time, each of us had a little dough to play with, so all of us were balling out. Every day before we left the room, all of us competed in a push-up contest. Toning up the pecs before hitting the beach was mandatory. Even though Timothy always lost, he always joined in to add a little definition to his scrawny bird chest. When we hit the sand, it was on and poppin'. There were groups of girls as far as they eye could see laid out on beach towels tanning, their bodies glistening in the sun. There were people vacationing from all over the United States. In my first few minutes on the beach on our first day out, I met chicks from Dallas, Maryland and South Dakota—three places I'd never been. A day later, while recruiting on the beach, I happened to spot Howard Harrell suntanning on a towel next to none other than Lawry, who was wearing nothing but some goggles on his head and a pair of neon green Speedos on his ass. It was by far the gayest ensemble I'd ever seen him wear. The only reason I knew it was him is because I recognized his tattoos when he stood up to shake out his towel.

"Damn," I said, taking off my sunglasses in disbelief, pointing. "Ain't that…"

"Yep!" Dub-B said. "That's your boy, Lawry! That boy done came all the way out the closet, fam."

"Hell nah, G!" Fresh said, covering his mouth with his hand. "Lawry is tweeking!"

"Tweeking ain't the word, cuz," Fats said.

"I'm pissed!" Dub-B said, bashing his fist into his open palm.

"Why?" I asked.

"Now that he's out the closet, we ain't gonna be able to post that picture on the Internet!" he said. "It'll be pointless. Everybody already knows Howard is gay."

"What picture?" Fresh asked.

"Yeah, *what* picture, Dub?" I asked, giving him a look that said "drop it."

Apparently Dub-B got the hint.

"Aw, nothing," he said nonchalantly.

"Aw, nothing, my ass," Fresh said. "What ya got?"

"Just this little picture of Lawry giving Howard some head," Dub-B said.

"Dub!" I screamed. "You wasn't s'posed to tell nobody about that. You're killing me, blood."

"Hold up, cuz," Fats said. "You got a picture of *what?*"

I was mad Dub-B leaked the fact that we had the picture to the homies. Actually, I was pissed. Even though Lawry seemed to be out of the closet, the last thing I needed him to do was tell Dex or one of the Kappas that he knew I was prepledging. I'd be finished.

* * *

South Beach was so poppin', it was hard to hold a grudge against anybody. The sun was beaming down, everybody was drunk, having a good time and people were wildin' out.

After Timothy dipped out to go visit his girl, Fats convinced the rest of us to follow him to the scooter rental stand. At fifty dollars per day, the scooters were kinda pricey, but they turned heads, so they were worth every penny. Mine was candy-apple red and it seemed everywhere I went, there was a fine chick who wanted to ride on the back. But when it came to hanging out, Wet Willie's was the place to be. We stopped by that bar at least twice a day to order drinks, courtesy of Fats's ID. The best part about it was I rarely paid for one. Most of the time, Fresh would whip out his credit card and buy rounds for all of us just to impress girls standing nearby.

"It's on me, fellas!" he'd scream.

Out of all the spots we hit, Club Mansion was the most memorable. We went there on our last night—the only night Timothy came out with us. Dub-B's girl, Jasmine, tagged along, too. I have no earthly idea why he decided to bring sand to the beach that night. But after taking a few steps inside the club, I couldn't care less. Club Mansion was packed wall-to-wall with beautiful girls. I could tell by the expression on Dub-B's face the moment we walked in he wished he'd come alone. As monstrous as two football stadiums stacked on top of one another, Mansion was by far the largest club I'd ever partied at in my life. It didn't take long for Fresh to flex his pocket muscle.

"We're going to the VIP tonight, fellas!" he said.

At the bottom of the staircase leading to the VIP area, we were met by a tall white man who looked like he'd just won the Mr. Universe competition. He towered over us, his muscles bulging through his black suit. There was no sneaking around him.

"Can I help you gentlemen?" he asked.

"We're tryna get up in VIP, cuz," Fats said.

"Okay," he said. "How many gentlemen are there in your party?"

"Five," Fresh said.

"All right," the security guard said. "That'll be twenty-five."

"Is that all?" I asked, digging in my pocket, whipping out a crisp twenty-dollar bill and a five. "Shoot, if I woulda known it was only twenty-five bucks to get up in VIP, we woulda been up in there a long time ago."

"Yeah," Timothy added. "That's not bad at all."

"I'm afraid there's been some kind of misunderstanding," the security guard said with a slight grin. "When I said twenty-five, I meant twenty-five hundred. Five-hundred dollars per person."

"Five *hundred?*" Fats asked.

"Per person?" I asked for clarification.

By this time, there was a lengthy line of beautiful ladies standing behind us, trying to get into VIP. While it would have been embarrassing to turn around and walk away, I was prepared to do just that. I figured the security guard was inflating the price to keep a little something for himself anyway. Just when I was about to tell him what to do, Fresh spoke up.

"What all comes with that?" Fresh asked.

"Who cares?" I asked. "I'm not about to let you spend all of that money on nobody's…"

The security guard started talking over me.

"Three bottles of premium liquor, a bottle of champagne, and your own private section overlooking the club," he said. "You will get a total of eight VIP bands, so you can bring a few ladies up with you if you want."

"Just twenty-five hundred?" Fresh asked, obnoxiously loud, so all the ladies behind us could hear. "Is that all?"

"Count me out," Dub-B said. "That's way too much for me, Fresh. I'ma just chill on the dance floor down here, yo."

"This one is on me, fellas!" Fresh said even louder. "We're all going!"

"You sure about that, cuz?" Fats asked.

"You're trippin', blood," I said. "Twenty-five *hundred* dollars? It's not that serious to get up in VIP. Really, it's not."

"Y'all take Visa, right?" Fresh asked.

"Sure do," the security guard said.

"I'm sure then," Fresh said, whipping the plastic out of his wallet. "Let's do it!"

Even though I knew Fresh was making a big mistake paying so much money to party in the VIP section, I felt like a real boss as I scaled the spiral staircase to the lavish VIP area. As promised, a cute waitress led us to a lavish booth, where our bottles were already waiting on ice. The group of chicks who were standing behind us in line at the bottom of the staircase had made their way into our vicinity. Of course, Fresh invited them to sit down and drink with us. As good as they were lookin', I damn sure wasn't about to object to that. Especially not after we started popping bottles. After the first bottle of Grey Goose, I was nice. After three glasses of Moët, I was tipsy. And after four shots of Patrón, I was officially hammered. My eyes were low, my speech was slurred and I had to hold on to the rail just to stand up straight. After a few shaky attempts of standing on my own two, I decided it would probably be safer for me to just sit down. But the moment my butt touched the couch, the room started to spinning. And the longer I sat, the faster it spun. Nauseated, I placed my elbows on my knees, rested my forehead on my palms, and stared at the floor, trying to regain my composure. But it was no use. I'd reached the point of no return.

"Hey," Jasmine asked Fresh, nodding toward me. "Is J.D. gonna be okay?"

"Yeah, he'll be straight," Fresh said as he patted me on the back.

"I'm cool," I said, standing to my feet, grabbing the railing to keep my balance. "I'm not as think as you drunk I am."

"Oh, cuz is hammered!" Fats said. "Keep an eye on him."

"Yeah," Jasmine said. "Somebody keep an eye on him. I'm going to the bathroom. Anybody know where it's at?"

"I got him," Dub-B said, wrapping his arm around my shoulder. "I think the bathroom is over there in the corner, on the other side of the bar."

Just then, Timothy walked over toward me and showed me his phone. There was a text message from Amy on his screen. It read: *I love you, baby. Good night :)*

"My girl is so good to me, J.D.," Timothy said. "I swear, man. There is nothing I wouldn't do for this girl. It's like God himself sent her to me."

"Is that right?"

"Yeah, man," he said, brimming with delight. "It feels good, too. Just to know that somebody is feeling you just as much as you're feeling them. I'm telling you. If my baby wasn't feeling sick, she'd be right here with me right now."

"What's wrong with her?" I asked.

"She said she thinks she ate some bad oysters," he said. "She just decided to stay in the room tonight. And I would have been right there with her if you guys wouldn't have dragged me out tonight. Man, I love that girl."

It was at that moment, as I stood there listening to Timothy profess his love for a girl who I knew for a fact was playing him like a fool, that I came to the conclusion that I had to tell him right then and there. Something about excessive alcohol consumption tends to make people brutally honest. I'd kept the truth from him for long enough. I couldn't take it anymore.

"Timothy," I said in a drunken slur. "We've been friends and roommates since we got to U of A, right?"

"Duh," Timothy said.

"Well, I've got something to tell you that you may not want to hear."

"What's up, J.D? You know you can tell me anything."

"Look, man," I said, trying to find the right way to tell him his girlfriend was a ho.

Before I could finish the sentence, I noticed a very familiar profile standing across the room. I'll be damned if it wasn't Amy across the room grinding all up against some guy.

"Spit it out!" Timothy urged.

Turns out, all I had to do was repeat myself.

"Look, man!" I said, pointing across the room.

"I'm looking and I don't see anything, J.D.," he said. "I think you're just drunk, buddy."

"And I think you need to look a little harder, *buddy,*" I said. "Doesn't that girl over there in that purple dress look familiar?"

"That dress isn't purple, J.D.," he said. "It's blue. But now that mention it, that girl grinding her booty all over that guy sure does resemble Amy."

He squinted. Wiped his eyes. Then they bugged out.

"Hey!" Timothy screamed, pointing. "Wait a minute… that *is* Amy!"

I didn't even have time to set my drink down on the table before Timothy barged over toward her. I followed Timothy over and Fresh, sensing something was up, filed in right behind me without asking questions. Amy was bent over with her palms on the floor popping her butt like she was in a strip club. Her dress was hiked up and her thong was in full view. Timothy kneeled down and whispered something in her ear. I'm not sure what he said, but when Amy looked up, the expression on her face was as if she'd seen a ghost. Swiftly, Timothy grabbed her by both wrists and pulled her to an upright position.

"What the heck are you doing here?" he asked. "I thought you said you weren't feeling good."

"I'm just having a time good," she said in a drunken slur. "I mean, having a good time."

"Have you been drinking?" Timothy asked. "I thought you said you didn't drink."

"Who the hell are you and why are you interrogating her?" the guy she was grinding on asked.

"What do you mean, who am *I?*" Timothy asked. "I'm Amy's boyfriend! Who the heck are *you?*"

I was so drunk, I hadn't even paid any attention to the guy Amy was dancing with until he spoke up. When I finally took a look at his face, I couldn't believe my eyes. Of all the people in the world Amy could have been dancing with, it just so happened to be Konceited. I hoped he didn't recognize me.

"J.D.," he said. "You better get your choirboy roommate outta here before he gets tossed up, man."

"See, this is exactly why I never come to the club," Timothy said, grabbing Amy by the hand and attempting to walk away. "C'mon. Lets go talk."

"Amy's not going anywhere," Konceited said, grabbing her other hand.

"Amy!" Timothy said, looking back at her in frustration, wanting so badly for her to pull away and follow him.

"Timothy," she said, letting go of his hand, "I think it'd be best if you just walk away. I'll catch up with you a little later, okay? Sorry."

That comment damn near knocked the wind out of me. The damage it had to have done to his pride and self-esteem was immeasurable. His own girlfriend had just chose another man over him right in his face. That was the epitome of public humiliation. She might as well have spit in his face while she was at it. At that point, Timothy should have just walked away.

"What is this all about?" he asked. "I don't understand. How long have you been seeing this guy? Where is all this coming from?"

"Oh, me and Amy been going strong for a while now, patna!" he said, smacking her on the ass.

"Craig!" she shouted. "Not in front of Timothy."

"I'm surprised your roomy, J.D., didn't tell you," he said, laughing.

"Oh, so you knew about this?" Timothy asked me.

For a moment, I was at a loss for words. I didn't want to lie to him. I felt like the poor guy had already been lied to enough. Really, what could I say?

"I'm sorry, man," I said. "I wanted to tell you before but..."

"And this whole time, I thought we were friends," Timothy said.

"He really did want to tell you, fam," Fresh said.

"Oh, so you were in on this, too?" Timothy asked. "I guess I'm the butt of the jokes, huh? I can't believe you guys. You know what? From here on out, just act like we never met!"

"Timothy," I said, grabbing his forearm, "calm down, man."

"Don't touch me!" he said, pulling away angrily. "You're gonna get what's coming to you. Just watch and see."

Seeing Timothy storm out of the club made me feel like a piece of shit. I wasn't even the culprit, yet I still felt guilty. I should have told him about my suspicions the first time it was brought to my attention, so I could've had a clear conscience about it. Even still, why did Konceited feel the need to throw me under the bus? He could've just as easily left my name out of it altogether. Not only did it cost me my friendship with Timothy, but it also could have cost me a passing grade in biology. Without Timothy's help with my homework and studying for my final exam, I didn't stand a chance.

"Hey, he had to find out sooner or later, fam," Fresh said, tossing his arm around my shoulder as we walked back toward our section. "She had T-Mac out here looking like T-Wack!"

Apparently, Timothy wasn't the only one having girl problems. When we made it back to our table, it looked like Dub-B and Jasmine were in the midst of a heated argument. Jasmine was shaking and crying and Dub-B's face was beet-red. I stood close to get my ear hustle on. It turned out I didn't have to eavesdrop at all.

"J.D., your boy is trippin'," Dub-B said. "I am really gonna have to whoop his ass, yo."

"Who?"

"Lawry!" Jasmine shrieked.

"That's *not* my boy, for one," I said. "But what did he do?"

"He grabbed my girl's ass when she went to the bathroom," Dub-B said. "I'm telling you, J.D. When I see him, I'm putting hands on him, fam. That's all there is to it. I'ma embarrass him, B."

"That's crazy!" I said. "Are you sure it was him? I thought he liked guys now."

"Yeah, I'm sure," Jasmine said. "I know that stanky-breathed bastard anywhere. He was trying to holla at me and when I walked off, he smacked me on my ass hard as hell."

"Where's he at?" I asked.

"Jasmine said he went downstairs after he did it,"

Dub-B said. "I've been trying to spot him, but there's like a million people down there. Finding him in here would be like finding a needle in a haystack. I'ma see him soon, though. Mark my words."

To ease the tension, Fresh poured up one more shot of Patrón for each of us. Getting more drunk only made matters worse. I was still sucking on a lime slice trying to deaden the tequila taste when Fresh nudged me with his elbow.

"I know I'm drunk and shit, so I might be tweakin'," he said. "Don't look now, but I think your girl Leslie is on her way over here."

"On her way over where?" I asked, instinctively turning to look over my shoulder as I'd just been asked not to.

Sure enough, when I turned around, Leslie was right in my face. Now, Leslie had no idea about me prepledging Kappa. That's just the way I wanted to keep it for now, at least. Although I didn't see any of the other Kappas near Konceited, I knew he wasn't alone. Plus, I figured he was still keeping an eye on me. So when Leslie leaned in to give me a kiss, I purposely avoided her lips and gave her a hug instead. I hoped she didn't notice.

"Hey, what was that all about?" she asked. "These lips aren't sweet enough for you to kiss in public all of a sudden?"

"Nah, it's not like that, boo," I said.

"Please don't tell me you're acting shady because of these corny little boppers you got over here in your section," she said. "I was just coming over to say hey. I'm not hating, am I?"

"Of course not," I said.

"Whatever!" she said. "I'll let you have your little fun. Just call me when you leave."

Just watching Leslie walk away in her skintight yellow dress turned me on. By the time she reached her girlfriends over by the bar, I was rock hard. One of the girls in our section who was sitting at zipper level noticed my arousal. I felt her tap me on my thigh.

"Excited?" she asked, laughing as she nodded at the bulge in my pants and showed her girlfriends.

"How'd you know?" I asked, smiling.

"Yo, son," Dub-B said. "Who is that dude all in your girl's face over there?"

When I spun around I saw some guy crowding Leslie's personal space, pointing his finger all in her face. By her body language, I could tell he was making her uncomfortable. I was so drunk, I could barely stand on my own two feet without wobbling. But I had to do something. Instinctively, I started walking over briskly. Dub-B, Fresh and Fats filed in right behind me without asking questions. Leslie was standing with her back pressed up against the bar and the guy she was having trouble with had his back to me. I was halfway to them when all of a sudden, the guy grabbed her by her neck with two hands and started choking her. His grip was so firm around her neck, she dropped her champagne glass and both of her feet were off the ground.

Leslie's girls began swinging their purses at him wildly, trying to get him to release his grip, but their pitty-pat hits seemed to do little more than infuriate him. I balled my fist, cocked it back and hit the guy with everything I had, right in the temple. He never saw it coming, but he damn sure felt it. He instantly released Leslie from his clutches and toppled over sideways. He tried to use his hand to catch himself, but it was no use. His elbow folded and he came crashing down on his face. I stood there, hoping I'd knocked him out with a one-hitter-quitter. But when I saw him squirm to get up, I knew I had to finish him. I heard Leslie gasp for air, and then an all-out brawl ensued. As I was in the midst of being overpowered, wrestling with the guy on the floor, Fats, Fresh and Dub-B had locked up with members of his crew, exchanging blows. The guy I was tussling with was so strong, I knew I wouldn't be able to maintain control much longer. Thankfully, security came and broke things up before it got too ugly. Boy, was I happy to see them. Of course, when they pulled me off of him, I acted like I wasn't.

"Yeah, boy!" I taunted. "You better be glad these security guards are pulling me off you!"

The entire fight, I hadn't even got a good look at the guy's face. But when the security guards pulled him to his feet, I couldn't believe my eyes. The guy I'd pummeled and damn near knocked out was Dex. He had a puffy eye and was bleeding from the nose. I had no idea.

"You're finished, nigga!" he said, blood spouting from his bottom lip. "Wait 'til we get back to school! You should've never got in the middle of this."

As the security guards were pulling us through the club by our shirt collars, making a point to embarrass us by parading us through the middle of the main dance floor, I tried to lower my head so nobody would recognize me. I was tossed from the club like Uncle Phil used to kick Jazz out of the house on *Fresh Prince of Bel Air*—both feet off of the ground, arms flailing. Fresh was right behind me. Dub-B and Fats were next.

As for the single most embarrassing moment of my life, getting physically thrown out of a club ranked right up there with my campaign speech debacle. But as I stood there with my shirt tattered, a hole near the knee in my shorts, looking around at my friends, all of us breathing heavily, I realized one thing. They were really my friends. In a time of conflict, none of them ran. We all stood our ground, together. Fresh had a small knot on his forehead and a long scratch on the side of his neck. A sliver of glass from broken glass had cut me on my forearm, and Dub-B's bottom lip was cut. Before long, the feeling of embarrassment turned into one of pride—each of us showing off our war wounds like badges of courage. Even with a swollen forehead, Fats was still smiling, talking trash.

"Them fools didn't wanna see us from the shoulders, cuz!" he said. "They better be glad security came when they did. I think a couple of them were Kappas from U of A."

"I *know* they were," Fresh said, shaking his head, shooting me a look that said "Why the hell would you go and do something like that?"

As we headed back toward our hotel, Fats and Dub-B were exaggerating about what they did in the fight, while Fresh and I contemplated our fate with the whole prepledging process internally. Next to stealing one of the Kappas' girlfriends, beating one of them up was right up there on the "How *Not* to Become Kappa" list. It was clear Fresh had more on his mind than Kappa Beta Psi and uppercuts.

"I hope they didn't really charge my credit card twenty-five hundred bucks," he said as we stumbled down the hallway toward our room. "We didn't even get to pop all the bottles."

While waiting to board my flight back to Atlanta, Leslie called to apologize. She felt bad for involving me in her domestic dispute. She said that Dex confronted her about coming over to our section and she told him that they weren't together anymore and she could say hello to whomever she wanted. That's when Dex snapped and got physical. Leslie concluded by thanking me for my bravery and assuring me that her relationship with Dex was officially over.

"That's what they all say," Fresh said. "She ain't going

nowhere, though. Don't believe the hype, joe. I don't care what she says!"

"How long were they together?" Fats asked.

"Not that long," I said. "Like a year and a half, I think."

"Fresh may be right, yo. That's a mad long time to be committed to someone, J.D.," Dub-B said.

"I'ma put it to you like this," Fats said, removing his iPod headphones. "I don't care how much this girl tells you she's feeling you or whatever, just know that if they've been talking for that long, chances are he's still hittin' those, cuz. Plain and simple. They may not be a couple anymore, but think about it. Of all the breezies you dated on a serious level, how many of 'em can you still get it crackin' with if you wanted to?"

"Shoot…" I said, thinking as my eyes rolled to the back of my head. "All of 'em!"

"Exactly," Fats said. "So you know ain't nobody quitting a long-term relationship cold turkey like that. Don't get me wrong. Ol' baby is bad as hell. But when you're dealing with her, just be sure to keep everything in perspective."

The good thing about having close friends is they always have an opinion on what they think is best for you. Most of the time, their advice is unwarranted and unadulterated. But some of the time, it's sound. In this instance, it was probably a little bit of both. But I listened anyway. As Fresh, Fats and Dub-B continued to chime in with their opinions, I noticed that Timothy hadn't said a word. In fact, he was sitting across from us wearing his earphones, working on his laptop. It was as if he was there alone.

"Yo!" Dub-B screamed, pointing to the TV displaying CNN overhead. "Ain't that Downtown D?"

"Sure is," Fats said, as the words *Breaking News* flashed across the screen.

"This just in," the anchor said. "University of Atlanta's star quarterback Deiondre Harris, also known as Downtown D, has been arrested in Louisiana for drug trafficking. Officials say he had over two pounds of ecstacy pills and two semiautomatic weapons in his trunk when he was pulled over this afternoon. All this after Downtown D shocked us all a few months ago with his announcement that he was withdrawing his name from the NFL draft because he was HIV positive."

None of us said a word. We couldn't. So much promise and hope down the drain. Finally, Fats broke the silence.

"Can you believe that fool, Downtown D?" he asked as we stood in line to board. "They better put homie on suicide watch. I can't imagine how it feels to be that high up and fall off like that. I mean, to go from a Heisman candidate and guaranteed top NFL draft pick to being HIV positive and on his way to prison. Whew!"

"I still can't believe it," I said. "Why would he be trying to sell some x pills anyway?"

"Probably trying to keep up that image," Fats said. "It's bad enough he caught the package. But to risk your freedom just to make it appear as if you ain't fell off, when everybody already knows you have...man, that was just retarded, cuz. It wasn't even worth it."

"Hey, look at the bright side," Fresh said. "At least he don't have to worry about nobody trying to get with him in the shower!"

Me, Fresh and Fats chuckled halfheartedly. Dub-B remained stone-faced.

"That's not even funny, B," Timothy said. "That dude needs prayer, yo. Put yourself in his shoes for a minute."

"I'm straight," Fresh said. "As a matter of fact, every time I put a condom on, it's so I *don't* end up in his shoes. But since I'm the only one in our crew who got some new-new in Miami, y'all probably wouldn't know nothin' about that."

"Hey, *I* got some," I said.

"I said *new-new,* fool," he said. "Leslie don't count. You'd already hit that before you got to Miami."

"Come on now, cuz," Fats said. "The only reason you got some ass is because you were using your little credit card to buy the breezies drinks and food and whatever else they wanted."

"And your point is?" Fresh asked.

"My point is that you're spending money like you got it to burn," Fats said. "You have *one* credit card. One!"

"Yeah, but my credit card has a ten thousand dollar limit, folk," Fresh argued. "Ten *thousand!* This little bit of money I'm spending on chicks is nothing. I ain't losing no sleep behind it. Why are you so worried about what I'm doing with my money anyway? I damn sure didn't hear none of y'all complaining when we were poppin' bottles in the club last night."

He had a point there. No complaints from me.

THIRTEEN

BALLOT BOXING

The campus wasn't the same after spring break. For one, there was a group of about eight gay guys walking around campus in pink-and-green T-shirts with line numbers and weird line names like Pig in a Blanket on the back. Apparently, it was some "sorority" the gay guys had started, mimicking Alpha Pi Alpha. They wore pearl earrings, necklaces and all. From what I heard, the APAs were pretty upset about it.

When it came to things being weird around the yard, that was only the beginning. Timothy was moping around heartbroken. He refused to talk to me, and spent most of his time in the room studying and reading his Bible. On top of that, there was a nasty rumor spreading around campus that the real reason Kat didn't show up to give her speech in the prelims was because she was hospitalized for HIV treatment. I didn't have to guess who'd drummed up that lie. I knew it had to have come from Howard's camp. Somehow word got back to campus about my scuffle in the club. Thankfully, no particulars, though. Since Leslie went to Elman, nobody really knew all of the details. Everybody just knew that the Kappas had been involved in some kind of altercation. For me, that was a good thing. I hadn't heard a peep from them since I'd been back on the yard and neither had Fresh. The other two guys we were pre-pledging with hadn't heard from them, either, so as far as I was concerned no news was good news.

As for the election, the momentum had definitely swung in favor of Howard Harrell. Walking around the yard, you would've thought he'd founded the University of Atlanta. His picture was everywhere. There were billboard-sized posters hanging from lampposts on the strip, posters on the walls in the caf and a new, full-color, high-gloss flyer with his greasy face on it under my door every time I walked in my dorm room. There was no escaping it. Howard Harrell was bigger than life. He even had his campaign slogan posted in huge letters above the urinal in the men's bathroom. It read Don't Be A Coward, Vote For Howard. Sure, we'd spent the last few weeks putting up posters here and there around the yard promoting Kat's campaign, reaching out to her supporters and Facebook friends as frequently as we could, and trying to drum up as much of a grassroots following as possible to support all of the votes she'd get from the Greeks and Greek wanna-bes. But even with all of them on board, things still looked shaky for Kat. With less than one week until the big election, word around campus was that Kat was in for a good old-fashioned ass whoopin' at the polls. And I couldn't allow that to happen. If Kat lost the election, the best I could hope for is a B in Dr. J's class. And a B in Public

Policy would significantly reduce the chance of me making the 3.0 GPA I needed to be able to pledge Kappa next semester, and could lower my GPA to the point where I couldn't even make the 2.5 GPA that I needed in order return to college for my sophomore year. Truth be told, the grades I expected in other classes were fair at best. The only way to sure things up was for Kat to guarantee me an A in Dr. J's class by winning the election. She had to win.

"Sorry I'm late, but I've got good news," Kat said, smiling from ear to ear, as she entered our conference room in Club Woody, five minutes late for the meeting. "Make that great news!"

Before she could explain, I felt my cell phone vibrate. I checked it. It was a text message from some number I didn't recognize that read, *"If it ain't broke, don't fix it. Howard Harrell for President!"*

"Well I sure hope it's good, because Howard is killing us right now," I said. "This fool is sending out mass text messages and everything."

"You got that, too?" Destiny asked, holding up her BlackBerry. "I ain't even gon' front. That's smart. We should do that, too."

"I got something even better," Kat said, still cheesing.

"What?" Dub-B asked in exasperation.

"Well, I didn't tell you guys," Kat said, "but, as soon as I found out I'd be running for president, Timothy and I got together, wrote up a letter and sent it to the Magic Cure Foundation, letting them know my situation. Just to see if they could help me out in any way."

"And?" Fresh asked.

"I'm about to tell you, if you'll let me," Kat said. "Dang! Anyway, about a week ago, I got a call from them and they said that they may be interested in sponsoring a concert on campus, free for all students who get tested for HIV. You won't believe who he got to come perform."

"Who?" I asked.

"Kanye."

"You are lying, girl!" Destiny said, her face lighting up.

"That's bogus as hell, G," Fresh said. "There is no way Kanye East is performing here on Friday. You've got to be kidding. Other than Lil' Weezy, Kanye is the biggest hip-hop artist in the game. Do you have any idea how much something like that would cost? You need to quit playing."

"Do I look like I am playing?" Kat asked, still grinning wide. "I am dead serious."

"Oh my God!" Fresh said. "We're bringin' him to the yard? That's gonna be off the chain!"

"Oh, now *we're* bringing him, huh?" Kat said, giggling. "Fresh, you are hilarious. But, yeah, we got a star coming."

"For the freeski?" I asked.

"Absolutely free," Kat said. "When they heard about my 'Testing for Tickets Day' idea, they said the foundation would cover all of the expenses. I checked with the student activities coordinator on the way over here and he said that it was short notice, but he agreed to it anyway. He got on the phone and called over to the health center to see if they were down and they were. So everything is a go!"

"Oh my goodness, girl!" Destiny yelped. "Do you know what this is going to do for our campaign?"

"It's a wrap!" I said. "Howard Harrell might as well kill himself."

"We'll see what happens," Kat said modestly. "I just hope a lot of students get tested."

"Shiiiiiit!" Fresh howled. "For free tickets to see Kanye? I'll be the first one in line! You already know everybody on campus is gonna sign up."

I figured if the whole performance actually came

through, Kat's chances of stealing the presidency would increase tremendously. As much as I'd like to think that the student government election is all about the issues, Fats told me that in the end, it would basically come down to being one big popularity contest. And what better way to put your name on the map than have the hottest artist out cosign for you?

Three days later, Kat's campaign took a drastic turn for the best. As Fresh had so prophetically claimed, the line for tickets was around the block. As a group, we'd sent out event invitations to all of our friends on MySpace and Facebook, sent text messages and called everyone in our phones. And that got people talking. But when the radio station got wind of it and a couple of the DJs mentioned it on their shows, everybody in the city was talking about it.

The concert tickets were being distributed on a first-come first-served basis, and only students who wore a red ribbon with "Vote for Katrina" on it, which they received after being tested for HIV, could get one. Even though the testing didn't start until nine in the morning, I heard that students started lining up around four in the morning. When I got out there around eight, the line snaked nearly a half mile from the testing station in the front of the student center all the way down the strip. *Professors might as well cancel class,* I thought. Damn near every student on campus was standing in line for tickets to the concert. And more importantly, to be tested.

Testing for Tickets Day worked like a charm. Careful not to let the hoopla of the event overwhelm our subliminal motive, we made sure everyone standing in line received a pamphlet highlighting Katrina's accomplishments and where she stood on the issues. Kat's sorority sisters and the Alphas put on an impromptu step show for the students waiting in line, some of whom had been standing in line for over three hours. Not to be outdone, other Greeks soon flocked, showcasing their party strolls and chants in a friendly battle. Even the campus hustle man made a killing. Once he caught wind of the event, he set up shop right on the strip, selling his fruit cups and ice water. By afternoon, a few party promoters had taken it upon themselves to capitalize on the event, passing out flyers to the "official" after-party.

Then for the grand finale, as promised, Kayne hit the stage, performing in front of a standing-room-only crowd in our packed gym later that night.

I was standing in line outside the caf when I saw the first one. It was posted at eye level on the Plexiglas window everyone had to pass while waiting in line to enter the lunchroom. It was huge—about the size of one of those Coming Soon movie posters you'd see at the theater. In fact, it looked just like one of them, with the same fonts and everything. And it had to be expensive—printed full color on a high-gloss paperstock. Right there, for all to see, was a poster with a headshot of Katrina in the center. The top read: Coming Soon to a Ballot Near You… There was a triangle drawn around Kat's photo, with arrows pointing to smaller photos surrounding hers. I couldn't believe my eyes when I zeroed in on them. On top of the triangle was a photo of Kat hugged up with Downtown D in his football uniform. Underneath, in bold letters read The Jock. There was an arrow pointing from that picture to one of me and Kat smiling, hugging each other in front of Marshall Hall. Underneath, the title read The Freshman. Then there was an arrow pointing from that photo to one of me with my arm wrapped around a sweaty, shirtless Lawry. Now, the picture was actually taken inside the club at a party we'd gone to last semester. And there were originally five guys in it. But someone had cropped everyone else out and zoomed in on Lawry and I. Underneath the picture, the caption read The DL? An arrow pointed from that photo back to the one of Kat and Downtown D. On the bottom of the sign, in large lettering was a fake movie title that read The Irresponsible Candidate. If that wasn't enough, there was a red, HIV awareness ribbon tacked next to a quote that read "Katrina Taylor turns in one of the best performances we've seen in years."

It was as disgraceful and embarrassing as it was offensive and slanderous. There was no name attached to the attack. But I knew its origin. Fresh must have sensed the fire boiling up inside of me, because he spoke before I could even open my mouth.

"Whatever you're thinking, don't do it," he said, placing a consoling hand on my shoulder. "The election is around the corner and school will be out in two weeks."

"I wouldn't give a damn if it was out in two hours," I said. "Somebody is gonna have to pay for this! On my momma, blood."

"Don't do nothing stupid, fam," Fresh said. "It ain't even worth it. Kat will get kicked out of the election and you will get kicked out of school."

"Fresh is right, J.D.," Dub-B added. "Besides, we don't even know who did this."

"Oh, I think I could take a very good guess," I said. "You know damn well who was behind this! Lawry is the only person who had that photo of us. He's gonna have to see me from the shoulders. Period."

"You got a good point," Fresh said. "And I wouldn't even be mad at you for dropping that punk. But right now, we gotta be diplomatic about the shit. We came too far with this campaign to throw it away now."

I hadn't taken ten steps inside the caf before the whispering and finger pointing began. I tried to act like I didn't hear them, but I did.

"There he is, girl," one whispered.

"Mmm-hmm, the one on the poster," another said.

"He's the one who gave Kat HIV?" someone asked.

"That's what I heard," another said.

I sat a few tables away from the hecklers, but I heard every word. Fats, Dub-B and Fresh were all at my table. The guys tried to talk loud and drown out all of the instigators spreading rumors, but it was no use. Everybody in the caf was talking about it.

"I can't believe them fools did that, blood," I said. "All this just because I stopped talking to Lawry. That's a real hater move. Now I gotta whoop his ass."

"You think they put those posters up because you haven't been talking to Lawry?" Fats asked. "Nigga, please! Obviously, you haven't been on Facebook lately."

"I haven't," I said. "Timothy won't let me use his laptop anymore. Why? What's on Facebook?"

"Somebody posted a picture of Howard giving Lawry some head in one of the rooms in Marshall Hall," Fats said. "It was the gayest thing I've ever seen, cuz!"

"Huh?" I said, scrunching up my face. "Are you serious?"

I looked across the table at Dub-B. He smiled. Before I could say anything, Fresh chimed in.

"So hold on, fam-o," Fresh said. "You telling me you haven't seen that joint? Everybody in my last class was talking about it. The girl sitting next to me pulled it up on her Blackberry and was showing everybody. Nigga, that photo is hilarious. I thought you posted it on purpose, to ruin Howard's chances of winning the election."

I looked over at Dub-B. He was grinning wide.

"You know I can't stand Lawry," he said. "And after that little stunt he pulled at the club in Miami, he had it coming."

I can't say I was mad at Dub-B for posting the picture. I would've probably done the same thing if he'd grabbed Leslie's butt—after I beat him up. But I was pissed that Lawry implicated me in his homosexual exploits. He'd gone too far. Not to mention, now I had to worry about whether or not he was going to tell the Kappas that he knew I was prepledging. Lawry had me by the balls.

"That's bullshit, blood," I said. "You told me you wasn't gonna post that picture, man."

"Why are you so mad about that picture getting out, cuz?" Fats asked. "What's it to you?"

"I was just thinking that," Fresh said. "Why are *you* so protective of that picture getting out, folk?"

I just shook my head, took a deep breath and got up from the table, without answering. All of them were oblivious to the deal I'd cut with Lawry. They had no idea how much trouble I could get in with the Kappas behind that picture getting out. At that moment, I wished I'd never told Lawry that I was doing any prepledging at all. I should have just denied it until he changed the subject, like I started to. But hindsight is 20/20. And now, I was in for it. Before I talked my way into more trouble trying to explain myself, I figured it was best for me just to evacuate the scene. On my way out, I snatched down that demeaning poster from the wall. I ripped it in half and threw it in the Dumpster just outside the caf. On my way back to Marshall Hall, I saw at least three more, all of which I tore down, too. I went straight to my dorm room without saying a word to anyone. I'd come to the conclusion that when it came down to whether or not I'd make it back to U of A next semester, it was me against the world. Nobody could study for me or take my exams. I was on my own. And I wasn't about to let any of this stop me from graduating from college. I had finals to study for. I kicked off my shoes and cracked open my biology book, determined to get some much-needed studying done before the finals. I was approximately seven minutes in, when I got a text message from Dex. It was a rather odd request, but coming from the Kappas, you never really ever knew what to expect. The message read: *Bring three pair of panties and $100 to the frat house. And be here in an hour!*

I didn't have too many options. With $38.75 in my account, I knew I'd need to borrow some dough, quick. And something told me coming up with three pair of panties wouldn't be easy—especially now that the word was out that I was on the DL.

"Damn!" I screamed in frustration, slamming my book cover shut.

After venting alone for about two minutes, then feeling sorry for myself for another three, I snapped into it. First, I called Leslie. I figured she probably hadn't seen the posters since she went to Elman and I knew she'd let me borrow the money if she had it. Thankfully, she picked up.

"Hey, baby," I said. "What you up to?"

"Baby?" she asked. "Don't *baby* me right now, J.D."

"Huh?" I asked, confused. "What you talking 'bout? What's wrong?"

"You've got some explaining to do," she said. "What's all this talk I'm hearing *again* about you being gay, man?"

"Here you go with that shit," I said. "You of all people should know better than that by now, Leslie."

"You would think, right?" she said. "I don't know though, J.D. I mean, I'm walking down campus minding my own business, and I see one of Howard Harrell's posters with you hugged up this dude with no shirt. And to make matters worse, I get to my computer, and I see the damn thing posted all over Facebook! Not to mention the guy who you're hugged up with in the picture—Larry or

Lawry or whatever his name is—just happens to be the same guy I heard about you being on the DL with when I met you. And you denied knowing even him. And on top of all that, I heard there are pictures floating around on the net of that same guy giving head to Howard Harrell. And you're all hugged up with this guy on the poster. I feel some kind of way about that, J.D. If it walks like a duck and quacks like a duck—"

"Look, Leslie," I said, cutting her off. "I don't need this right now. Of course Howard Harrell and his camp are going to drum up lies and whatever else they can to win this student government election because we are on the verge of beating him. So you can believe all this if you want to, but I'm telling you, none of it's the truth. I've been going through a lot with school, this election, and just life in general. I just really need you to be in my corner right now."

Silence followed. Cemetery-at-night silence. I looked down at my watch. I had approximately thirty-eight minutes to be at the Kappa house.

"Look, I really need a favor," I said. "When you needed me to be there for you, I was."

"That's true," she said, still sounding disappointed. "What's up?"

"Okay, this is gonna sound really weird," I started.

I should have stopped there.

"But I need to borrow one hundred bucks," I continued.

"That's not a problem, J.D.," she said. "I can loan that to you."

"*And*...I need three pair of your panties," I said.

"Three pair of my *what*?" she asked, inflecting her voice in disbelief.

At that point, I knew I'd shot myself in the foot. I couldn't even bring myself to ask her again.

"Did you just ask me if you could have three pair of my *panties?*" she asked. "What the…? Why would you ever in your entire life feel the need to ask me for *one* pair of my panties? Let alone three! I'd *really* like to hear you explain this one."

At that point, I started to just tell her that I was prepledging. But her hatred of frat guys was at an all-time high, plus I didn't want to risk even more backlash with one more person finding out I was prepledging. I figured Lawry was going to rat on me. That was bad enough. But I certainly couldn't risk word of that from a second person.

"You know what," she continued. "Don't bother explaining. This is crazy! I'm so done with this whole situation. 'Bye, J.D."

The dial tone hit me in the chest like an uppercut from Mike Tyson in his prime. It was bone-jarring. It took my breath away. It hurt. Especially after I'd gone to battle with her ex, and jeopardized so much just for her. It was like a slap in the face. I had just under thirty minutes left, when I decided to call the only other girl on campus I was sure would have my back.

"Hey, Kat," I said.

"*J.D?*" she asked, startled.

She had good reason to be. I hadn't called Katrina all semester. She was my last resort.

"Yeah, it's me," I said.

"To what do I owe the pleasure of this phone call?" she asked. "I haven't seen your name pop up on my cell phone all semester. Is it about the campaign? I spoke to your mom earlier today and she was helping me prep for the debate. You know, sometimes I think she's more into this election than I am."

"It's not about the election," I said. "Remember that day

in the library, when you told me if I ever needed *anything,* you'd be there for me?"

"Uh-huh," she acknowledged. "I remember. What about it?"

"There's something I need from you," I said.

"I said anything," she said. "And I'm a woman of my word. What do you need, J.D?"

"I need a hundred bucks and three pair of panties in the next ten minutes," I said. "Can you help me?"

"Oh my God!" Kat said. "I am so stupid. I've been so wrapped up in this campaign, I didn't even notice."

"Notice what?" I asked.

"That you're prepledging!" she said excitedly.

For a second, I wondered how the hell she knew I was prepledging with the little information I'd just shared with her. Then I remembered she was in a sorority. Maybe it was an inside thing or something. I didn't have time to bullshit her.

"Kat, please don't tell anybody," I begged.

"C'mon now," she said. "I pledged! I promise not to tell a soul. I'll meet you out back by the parking lot in ten minutes. Is that cool?"

"That's perfect!" I said. "Thanks, Kat."

FOURTEEN

AGAINST ALL ODDS

MY kneecaps felt like someone was continuously tapping them with the sharp end of an ice pick. The pain was torturous. It was a stinging, unrelenting, throbbing pain that shot from my hamstrings to my knees all the way down to my toenails then back up every few seconds. Both of my elbows felt like they were broken. I didn't even know it was humanly possible to break an elbow until now. But it felt like two grown men were taking turns kicking me in each one with steel toe boots. In reality, I was just on all fours— my elbows and kneecaps—leaning forward, with my ass up, holding my chin in my hand. Fresh was in the same position, just in front of me. My face was directly behind his ass, less than one foot away. We were wearing nothing but our underwear and wifebeaters. Every time I inhaled, I smelled his stankin' drawls. I tried to keep my nose angled to the ground, but Fresh's ass was unfortunately the exact opposite of his name.

"You could've changed your draws, my nig," I mumbled, trying to keep my lips as close to shut as possible.

"I didn't know I was gonna have my ass in your face all night," Fresh said.

The other two guys prepledging with us busted out laughing. I was in so much pain, at that point, I laughed to keep from crying. Fresh laughed so hard, he pooted.

"Damn, blood," I said. "You ain't have to do it like that! Gaaaaatdamn!"

We'd been hovering in the same position, on all fours, for over two hours in a hot-ass, musty basement at the Kappa House. Meanwhile, they were having a party for the graduating seniors upstairs. Every fifteen minutes or so one of the Kappas would come downstairs to make sure we hadn't moved. A few times, they came in through the side door in the basement to surprise us and make sure we weren't cheating. It was our last night prepledging for the semester, so they were trying to make it as hard for us as possible. And they were doing damn good job of that. We'd already been forced to lie on our backs with our hands at our sides while we held our feet up six inches off the ground for thirty minutes at a time. We'd done damn near 500 push-ups and just as many sit-ups. We'd sat in that damn imaginary chair for over an hour. And we'd been stuck in this all-fours position for what seemed like eternity. I was hoping one of the Kappas would come downstairs and ask us to do something different. Anything. But each time one of them came in and saw us agonizing, they all basically said the same thing.

"Oooh!" one Kappa said. "Looks like that's painful. Y'all stay there for a little while longer!"

"Ouch!" another Kappa said. "I remember these days!

Can't feel your arms anymore, can you? Don't trip. You'll be okay in a few days. Just stay there for now."

"Whooooo!" Konceited said. "Man! That's fucked up. Your knees and your elbows feel like shit, huh? They're probably all black and blue by now and all that. You're sweating. One of y'all funky asses farted. That's messed up 'cause I'm about to go outside and get some fresh air, but y'all gon' be down here all night! We're kicking it upstairs, too. The baddest chicks on campus. All the liquor you can drink and wings you can eat, thanks to you guys kicking in so generously. As much as I'd like to stay down here and listen to y'all whine, I got about three chicks upstairs who wanna get freaky with me...at the same time! Ha! I'm out. Dex will be down to deal with y'all in a few minutes."

We hadn't seen Dex since we'd been there. I was actually hoping I wouldn't have to. I wasn't sure if he'd gotten over getting hit by my surprise haymaker. I figured since I'd gotten invited to come back, maybe he'd had time to think things over and realize he was wrong in the first place. But with Dex, you could never really be too sure. And after a few drinks, there was really no tellin'. I hoped for the best, but expected the worst. When Dex came down the stairs, he brought about eight or nine other Kappas with him.

"Damn, you guys stink!" one of them said. "Y'all some ol' funky boys!"

"And pitiful, too," another said. "Look at 'em, shaking and sweating like they've really been doing something. Groaning and wimpering and shit. Y'all ain't even officially on line yet! This is like a three on a scale of ten. Y'all ain't seen nothing yet."

All of the guys were standing behind us talking, so I couldn't see who was saying what. Not until Dex made his way to the front. He was standing right in front of me. He was so close, I could damn near smell his feet through his loafers. For a second, I thought he was gonna do something crazy, like kick me in the face or something. Then it was gonna have to be royal rumble up in that piece. I braced my face for the impact, just in case.

"Y'all can stand up now," Dex said. "You're embarrassing me in front of my bruhs."

It was a struggle just making it to my feet. And standing up straight was even more excruciating. When I finally got my balance, I was looking Dex right in his eye. He stared me down, obviously trying to intimidate me. But it didn't work. I didn't flinch. I did however notice that he was holding what looked like a nightstick in his right hand. Although I couldn't see the Kappas behind me, even with the loud thud of the bass coming from the speakers upstairs, I could hear them murmuring to one another.

"That's the guy who stole on him in Miami," one of them said.

"Yeah, the one he's standing in front of," another confirmed.

"I'd knock him out if I was him," a third said.

That's when Dex started stretching his arms, swinging them side to side as if he was loosening them up to punch me. I held my ground. All of a sudden, a much older, larger Kappa wearing a jacket with a Fall '93 patch on the sleeve came over and stood next to Dex, who was still ice grilling me. The older Kappa had to have been about six-four, at least two hundred and forty pounds. He was twice my size.

"So this is the guy who hit you with the sucker punch out there in Miami, huh?" he asked.

Here we go, I thought.

"Yeah," Dex said, still eyeballing me. "This is him. What you think I should do to him?"

"If I was you, I'd whoop his ass!" he said. "Straight up. But you know you can't do that here, because we don't mix frat business with personal business. Plus, you were wrong in the first damn place. You know better than to put your hands on a lady."

"I know," Dex said. "I could take him outside and wear him out, though."

"You could do that, but there are still people coming and going upstairs," the older Kappa said. "We need to keep our hands clean. You know our chapter stays in enough trouble as it is. Plus, he looks kinda frail. You might break this little dude in half."

"You're right, he does look hella frail," Dex said. "As a matter of fact, all of them do. I hate to see y'all like this. I really do. I remember, back in the day when I was prepledging, I used to be hungry as shit! I was gonna eat this myself, but I guess I will share with y'all. Here you go. Share this with your buddies here."

Dex handed me what I thought was a baton. It turned out to be an eggplant. This time, since it was our last night, I didn't even put up a fight. I just closed my eyes and took a big-ass bite. I tried to chew and swallow before the taste set in, but it was no use. It tasted like spoiled milk. The soft seeds inside it tasted like black licorice. The taste made me heave as if I was going to vomit, but nothing came up. It came back around twice. Each time the taste was just as bitter. It felt like a midget was inside my stomach doing cartwheels. All of a sudden, I felt a strong urge to take a number two. Once I gulped down the last of it, I exhaled a sigh of relief. That's when the older Kappa flinched like he was going to hit me. Instinctively, I threw my guard up in defense. That's when he leaned in and whispered in my ear.

"I ain't gonna hit you," he said. "You are so lucky this ain't ninety-three, though. I woulda been caved your little bird-chest in. Oooooh, you lucky!"

The older Kappa then walked toward the back of the room, leaving Dex in the front by himself again. I just knew Dex was going to come up with something else crazy for us to do. It seemed like he just sat up thinking of ways to torture us in his spare time. To my surprise, I couldn't have been more wrong.

"Well, that does it, fellas," he said. "When you started out, there were eight of you. Now, there are only four. I guess we know who really wants to be here. So far, at least. I know all of you have finals coming up and you need to study for them. And in this frat, education comes first. So we're gonna let y'all study for them, because without at least a 3.0 GPA, you can't even apply to become a member of this organization. That being said, all of you in this room who meet the academic requirement will automatically be on line to become a member of Kappa Beta Psi."

Me and the fellas tried to hold our smiles in, but none of us could. I had mixed emotions. I was elated that this phase of the process was over, but saddened by the fact that we'd done so much, yet we technically weren't even on line yet. And on top of all that, I still had to pull of a 3.0 GPA without the help of Timothy or Leslie. It would take a miracle. More than anything, I was relieved that my fight with Dex in the club in Miami hadn't cost me my opportunity to join the frat. I still had a chance.

"All but one of you, that is," Dex continued. "It has been brought to my attention that we have a snitch among us."

My heart started beating fast. I hoped he wasn't talking about me.

"Unfortunately, I've been informed that J.D. has told others that he is prepledging," Dex said. "And as we all know, the first thing I told y'all is that Kappa Beta Psi is a highly esoteric organization and we have a zero tolerance policy when it comes to loose lips. So, J.D., I'm going to have to ask you not to bother applying for Kappa Beta Psi next semester."

I felt like I'd just been run over by a sixteen-wheeler. I was hurt bad, but I couldn't say I didn't see it coming. I knew Dex had it out for me ever since that fight we had in Miami. Still, the news hit me harder than any punch he could've thrown. More than anything, I was pissed he'd waited until now to tell me he'd heard I'd snitched. If he knew they weren't gonna put me on, they never should have invited me back in the first place. I could have been studying for my finals.

"What you mean, I can't apply next semester?" I asked. "I ain't never been a snitch. You got some bad information, man."

"I can vouch for my guy," Fresh said. "You know we're together all the time. Somebody must have lied on him, 'cause I know he ain't said anything about this prepledging stuff to nobody."

"That ain't what I heard," Konceited said.

"Trust me," Fresh said. "I know for a fact..."

"Look, Fresh," Dex said, cutting him off. "Unless you wanna be in your boy's shoes, you might wanna let this one go. I heard from a very credible source that J.D. was running his mouth, so he can't be down with us. That's all there is to it."

I left the Kappa house alone. I smelled like a mixture of sweat, eggplant and ass. I felt like an idiot. I'd allowed myself to be taken advantage of, so as bad as I wanted to whip Lawry's ass for telling on me, but in the end, I only had myself to blame.

FIFTEEN

THE BIG PAYBACK

Finals were unrelenting. I found it hard to study. I kept having flashbacks of all the things I'd done while I was pre-pledging. The thought of not even being able to apply was sickening. And it really wasn't getting any better with time as I hoped it would. I pressed on anyway. I figured I'd come too far to turn back, so I set my mind to still shoot for a 3.0 GPA. That way, even if I fell short, I'd still make the 2.5 that I needed to be able to return to U of A for my sophomore year. But even that wasn't going to be easy. I needed help, but couldn't find any to save my life. Kat was busy with her sorority business and the election. Timothy still wasn't talking to me, and Leslie wasn't returning my calls. Now that I was sure I didn't have a shot at Kappa Beta Psi anymore, I figured if I could talk to her, I could explain things. But she wouldn't even respond to my text messages. I was distraught. I had nobody to look over my papers and nobody to let me look over their shoulder during the final exams. This time, I was going to have to buckle down and do it on my own.

I had two fifteen-page papers to write—one for English and one for African-American history, and two final exams to take. Somehow, after a couple consecutive all-nighters, and excessive use of Microsoft Word's cut-and-paste tools, I managed to pull both of the papers together on my own. Although they were probably littered with grammatical errors, the fact that I completed both of them on time was enough to put a smile on my face. With Leslie's help, I'd done so well in those classes earlier in the semester that even though my final essays were mediocre at best, I still managed to sneak out with a B in English and an A in African-American history.

Now, algebra was another story. Quite frankly, math bored me. Mostly because I never really understood the point of solving mathematical equations, when I would probably never have to use them again for the rest of my life. I figured, as long as I could count money, I was straight. And for that very reason, no matter how many times I showed up for algebra, I could never stay awake for the entire class. It was by God's grace that I was able to squeeze by with a low C in that class.

When it came to biology, I knew it was a wrap for me. Timothy hadn't shown up to tutor me for biology anymore. In fact, he hadn't said more than two words to me since that night in club. I expected that. But I didn't expect him to sit in the exact same seat he'd sat in all semester when we took our final exam. There were so many seats to choose from, I was almost sure he'd pick one clear on the other side of the classroom. I was fully prepared to eeny-meeny-miny-moe my way through the test and take as many educated guesses as possible. But with Timothy sitting right in front of me filling out his Scantron with his answers in clear sight, I couldn't help but cheat off him. I would have been stupid not to. When I turned in my test, I was certain I'd aced it. I left that class feeling like I was on top of the world. And that feeling stayed with me all day, until I checked my test score on the Internet later that night in our dorm computer lab. Dub-B and his girl were sitting beside me checking theirs.

"*Zero?*" I screamed, slamming my fist down on the desk, viewing my score on his computer. "What the?"

"A *zero,* son?" he asked, looking over at my screen.

"Unless I'm looking at this wrong, it looks like I scored a zero on my biology final," I said.

"That's definitely a zero," he said. "And that C next to it is your final grade in the class. If you would've just got a couple of the answers right on the final, you might've coulda got a B in the class. That's hurts."

"Who you tellin'?" I asked, a lump forming in my throat.

"I know it's not funny," he asked, chuckling, "but how did you manage to get a *zero* on the final? There were *one hundred* questions on the test! That's like humanly impossible, yo. Stevie Wonder could've circled one right answer."

"I know," I said, looking at the screen in disbelief. "This must be some kind of mistake. What did you get?"

"I got a 76," he said. "But you know science isn't really my thing. Did you study?"

"Yeah, I studied," I said. "But when I saw Timothy sit in his usual seat, one row in front of us, you already know I was getting my cheat on! That dude knows biology like the back of his hand. I copied his scantron answer for answer."

"Wait a minute," Jasmine said. "You're talking about your roommate, Timothy, right?"

"Yeah," I said.

"What time did you take your final?" Jasmine asked.

"Eleven this morning," I said. "I'm in the same class as Dub-B."

"That's what I thought," she said. "Hmmm…that's strange. I wonder why Timothy took the final twice."

"What you mean twice?" I asked.

"Well, I took my biology final at nine o'clock this morning and I saw Timothy taking his exam in my class," Jasmine said. "Which was really weird because I'd never seen him in my class before."

"Are you sure it was him?" I asked. "Why would anybody take two final exams for the same class, back-to-back?"

Before I could even finish my sentence, I knew exactly what had happened. I'd been set up. Cold. It seemed too good to be true because it was. And Timothy flew through the test like he'd already taken it because he had. He said he'd get me. And he got me in the worst way. He knew I needed to pass biology in order to keep grades up, so I could get off of academic probation. And he knew I'd copy off of his test if he let me. He threw the bait, and caught me hook, line and sinker. My own roommate stabbed me in the back.

I was staring at my screen, shaking my head in disbelief when I felt my phone vibrate in my pocket. I couldn't believe my eyes when I saw who was calling. It was Dex. He'd never called before. The only time he'd ever contacted me was via text. At this point, I had no idea why he'd be calling me, but I decided to answer anyway.

"J.D.," he said. "I've got Konceited and a couple of my other frat brothers here with me. And we got you on speakerphone."

"Okay…" I said as I walked out of the crowded computer lab to the laundry room, where it was secluded and quiet.

"First of all, I want to let you know that it is highly irregular for me to even be reaching out to you at all," Dex said. "I don't call GDIs. Secondly, let me assure you that my frat does *not* need you in it. However, as a group, my frat brothers and I have come to the conclusion that we didn't give you a fair shake. It has been brought to our attention that the guy who dropped the dime on you is also going against you in the student government election. And after doing our due diligence, we found that he unsuccessfully attempted to pledge Alpha last semester. In other words, we think he may have had multiple motives to hate on you. That being said, we would like to extend the opportunity for you to be on line next semester, under one condition of course."

"What's that?" I asked.

"You still have to meet our academic requirement, which is a 3.0 GPA this semester," Dex said.

"No problem," I said.

"Oh, you're gonna have major problems if you don't address me the way you know I'm supposed to be addressed," Dex said.

"My bad," I said. "No problem, sir."

"That's more like it," Dex said. "Good luck with the election. We're rolling with Kat."

When I hung up the phone, I was overcome with emotions. I fought back tears. I was so excited that all of the hard work I'd put in prepledging wasn't in vain. Even though Leslie was AWOL, Timothy hated on me and Lawry snitched, I still had a chance to make a 3.0 GPA. And if I did, I'd be able to pledge Kappa Beta Psi next semester. But there was only one way for that to happen. Kat had to win the election. That was the only way.

SIXTEEN

THE DEBATE

The final debate was the most pivotal point in the election, especially for our team, since Kat missed the preliminary speeches. Thank God for Dub-B's pops. He really came through for us when it was time to prep for the debate. Without his help, Kat didn't stand a chance. Howard was a seasoned, polished politician. And Dub-B's dad was our secret weapon. Dub-B's pops knew everything there was to know about how to win a debate. After going over the potential debate questions on our conference call with him, I felt confident Kat had what it took to dethrone Howard Harrell.

As we prepared to leave the conference room in Club Woody and head down to the student center auditorium for the debate, I had second thoughts about going. After thinking about the way I'd hammed it up last time I was at the podium delivering the speech in Kat's absence, I questioned whether showing up would actually hurt Kat more than it would help. I was sitting there at the conference table in my suit and tie, mulling over the pros and cons in my head, when Fresh rescued me from my inhibitions. We'd spent so much time together, he knew how I was feeling without me ever even saying it. And he knew just what to say to get me up.

"C'mon, man," he said, tapping me on the leg. "Lets go! Nobody's asking you to speak this time…. Thank God!"

The two of us laughed about my podium meltdown all the way to the student center. I couldn't believe how many students were filing in. The scene outside the student center looked like a clip from a desegregation rally during the civil rights era—except everyone was black, of course. Outside the doors, there was Kat's large group of supporters, comprised mostly of Greeks, faced off with Howard's. The groups stood across from each other holding signs supporting their candidate and trading chants back and forth.

"Don't be a coward, vote for Howard!" one group shouted.

"Be a leader, vote Katrina!" the others responded.

I couldn't help but laugh on the inside as I made my way through their makeshift gauntlet. I had no idea people got so into student government elections in college. The scene literally looked like one you'd see on an old rerun episode of *A Different World*. Inside the auditorium, the ruckus grew to a fevered pitch. You could almost cut the tension in the room with a knife. Our group was ushered into a small, makeshift greenroom backstage. Kat looked nervous as hell. It was the first time I'd seen her look unnerved since that day last semester when she sat in her room with a gun to her head contemplating suicide. Just looking at her, I could tell she was on the verge of a breakdown.

"I'm so nervous, you guys," she admitted.

"It's gonna be okay, girl," Destiny said, patting Kat on the back of her hand for reassurance. "You'll do fine. Didn't you see all of those people outside cheering for you?"

Kat didn't respond. Instead, she checked the time on her watch, then reached in her purse and brought out about four bottles of medicine. I watched as she effortlessly popped two prescription pills about the size of my thumb.

"What if they don't accept me though, y'all?" Kat asked. "I mean with the whole HIV thing and D getting in trouble with the law. I just...I don't know if I should go through with this."

"Now you know we've come too far to turn back now," Timothy said. "Your steps are ordered. Your destiny has been prearranged. It says that right in..."

"Romans eight and twenty-nine," Kat said in unison with Timothy, finishing his sentence. "I know."

"Well, act like it!" Timothy said.

"Yeah," Dub-B said. "We've got a debate to win, ma!"

"Thanks, y'all," Kat said. "I don't know what I was thinking. Just got the jitters, I guess."

Even though Kat was saying she was cool, she still seemed rattled to me. And truthfully, I probably had more riding on her winning the election than she did. I knew I had to do something. In less than two minutes, Kat was going to be standing before the entire student body. And I needed to help her pull herself together before she went out there.

"You guys mind letting me and Kat have a moment to ourselves?" I asked. "Save me a seat. I'll be out there in a sec."

After everyone cleared the room, I cleared my throat. I pulled up a chair and looked Kat straight in the eye. I knew I didn't have long to say what I had to say, so I got straight to the point. Although I already had my academic probation requirement in the bag, I decided to overdramatize the stakes a bit. I knew Kat performed well under pressure.

"Look," I said, "between me and you, the only way my grade point average will be high enough for me to come back to U of A next year is if I get an A in public policy class. So if you don't win this election, I'm out for good. And truthfully, I ain't tryna go back to Oakland on a one-way ticket. The way my homies are getting killed in my hood…"

Just then there was a knock on the door and then it swung open. It was Dr. J.

"Hey, J.D.," he said. "Kat, we're gonna need you on stage in one minute. Good luck."

When the door slammed behind him, Kat whipped her mirror out of her purse, then stood up to check her makeup one more time. I stood up and kept talking.

"The bottom line is I really need you to win," I said. "This school needs you to win."

Kat never responded. But by the look in her eye, I could tell, she was as ready as she'd ever be. On stage, the setup was simple. Two podiums with less than five feet between them. Kat standing firmly behind one in her navy blue, two-piece business suit, Howard cockily behind the other in a chocolate-colored three-piece, a plaid shirt, peach-colored tie and matching pocket square. Dr. J, the mediator for the debate, standing downstage left, cleared his throat before kicking it off.

"I'd like to welcome you all to the highly anticipated final debate between your final two candidates for student body president," he said. "Without any further ado, I would like to introduce your first candidate, to my left. She hails from Athens, Georgia…"

Dr. J's intro was abruptly overwhelmed by thunderous applause. He looked down at his note cards as if he wanted to continue, but paused, smiling for almost a full minute until the cheering died down. Kat remained stoic as long as she could, but couldn't refrain from flashing her pearly whites eventually.

"I'm sure your support for your candidates is flattering, but with respect to our time schedule, let's hold all applause until the end. As I was saying, the candidate to my left is a junior, criminal justice major and member of Alpha Pi Alpha Sorority Incorporated."

"*Skeeeee-weeee!*" Kat's sorority sisters, squealed, totally ignoring Dr. J's plea.

"She has been on the dean's list for the past three years, maintaining a three-point-eight grade point average. Ladies and gentleman, Katrina Turner!"

Again, the crowd erupted with cheers. This time, they didn't stop, more than half of the crowd raising to their feet. Kat blushed, trying to keep her composure. After two failed attempts to get the crowd to simmer down, Dr. J just began talking over them.

"And on my right…"

Before he could eke out another word, Howard's supporters rose to their feet, evoking what sounded like an even louder ovation. I felt like I was at a heavyweight title fight. I was just waiting for Dr. J to scream, "Let's get ready to rumble!" With Howard's lengthy list of accomplishments, I thought Dr. J would be introducing him all night. A few minutes into it, I felt like the touting would never end. Then finally, it did.

"He's served University of Atlanta as class president the past three years in a row. Ladies and gentleman, Howard Harrell!"

Not to be outdone, Howard's supporters—which included the university's entire gay community—stood on their chairs, chanting, "Don't be a coward, vote for Howard!" as loudly as they could. I was still amazed by it all. People were so into the election, it was almost corny.

The actual debate only lasted about thirty minutes, Kat and Howard trading philosophical blows like jabs and uppercuts. For the most part their views were the same. Both of them supported decreasing the price of tuition and student housing. Both promised to squeeze more money out of the administration for homecoming expenses—which ultimately meant better acts to perform at the concert. And after a recent rash of car burglaries, both stood firmly behind an increase on round-the-clock public safety officers around campus. But there were two questions in which Kat and Howard's opinions couldn't have been more opposite. And something told me, their responses could mean the difference between them winning and losing and, ultimately, my making it onto the Kappa line next semester.

"Recently, on campus, a group of gay men inducted themselves into MIAPA—Men Interested in Alpha Pi Alpha, a group imitating the sorority, Alpha Pi Alpha," Dr. J said. "How do you feel this controversy has impacted the University of Atlanta?"

This had to be some kind of trick question, I thought. This was nowhere on the list of potential issues that Dr. J said he may address in the debate. We hadn't gone over this with Dub-B's dad. It was a trap question. A curveball. He had to have known Kat was a member of APA and Howard was gay. I just hoped he wouldn't ask Kat to answer first.

"Katrina," he said. "The floor is yours."

"Damn," I cursed under my breath, taking a deep breath.

Kat didn't answer right away. Instead, she wisely shuffled her papers and gathered her thoughts first. She glanced at her sorority sisters, all of them standing near the front, their arms folded, lips poked out, waiting on her to defend their honor. Then she glanced across the room toward the guys Dr. J was referring to, sitting in the front on Howard's side, clad in their matching pink short-sleeved polos and khakis.

"Katrina, I'm gonna need for you to speak into the microphone," Dr. J said, lightening the mood and evoking a few giggles from the crowd.

"I believe wholeheartedly in freedom of speech and freedom of expression," Kat responded in a very businesslike manner. "But honestly, I think that the recent induction of gay men into this so-called sorority, MIAPA, is disgraceful to Alpha Pi Alpha Sorority, Incorporated, as well as the University of Atlanta as a whole."

As I suspected, Kat's line sisters joined the rest of the Greeks in applause. Meanwhile, Lawry and a crew of gay guys sitting near the front erupted. They booed and shouted obscenities obnoxiously loud. One guy even went as far as standing on his chair, turning around, dropping his pants and mooning Kat on stage.

"Ooooh!" the crowd moaned. *"Aaaah!"*

Dr. J quickly intervened.

"Excuse me!" he said in an authoritative tone. "This is a university, not a middle school. These candidates worked very hard to be up here, and if you can't stand to listen to their opinions respectfully, you are welcome to leave. That goes for all of you!"

Before Dr. J could say anything about the mooning incident, campus security was forcefully ushering the guy out by his collar.

"Howard! Howard! Howard!" the guy shouted, pumping his fist as he left the auditorium against his will.

"As you were saying, Ms. Turner," Dr. J said.

"As a member of Alpha Pi Alpha, I feel that our sorority has dedicated over one hundred years of service to build the upstanding reputation that we have," she said. "And we have worked too hard to have a group of gay guys posing as women, come in and give our sorority and our university a black eye."

After a mixed reaction from the crowd, seemingly split right down the middle, Dr. J intervened.

"And your thoughts on this Mr. Harrell?" he asked.

"Well, it seems *Miss Turner* has just contradicted herself," Howard began. "How can you say you believe in freedom of expression, then in the same breath turn around and say you don't believe in a group of college-educated men expressing themselves?"

Howard paused momentarily, smiling, then continued amid the chatter of the crowd.

"It's just that kind of ignorance that is perpetuating the problem," he said. "If anything, the disgrace to the university was the homophobic backlash from students and faculty around campus. I think the one thing that has become painfully clear is that this controversy is not so much about the sanctity of Alpha Pi Alpha, as Miss Turner would have you to believe, but moreso about homophobia."

Again, a torn crowd responded, some cheering, others booing. I couldn't have disagreed more with Howard's views. But the confidence and intellect with which he spoke made him undeniably cunning and persuasive. I could see why he'd been voted in three consecutive terms. Before things got out of control, Dr. J stepped in one last time.

"All right now, let's pipe down out there," he said. "We are down to our last question. I would like to remind you all that the polls will be open from seven in the morning 'til five tomorrow, so be sure to come to the student center and vote. All you need to bring with you is your student ID."

Dr. J took a sip of his bottled water, before continuing.

"Without any further ado," he said, "I pose the final question of this evening's student body presidential debate. What is your definition of success? Howard, the floor is yours."

In classic conceited form, Howard regurgitated all the

same accomplishments Dr. J had highlighted in his intro. Not that all of the clubs he belonged to and community service awards he'd won were anything to scoff at. But all the same, he was tooting his own horn. And people—at least the ones who thought like me—were sick of it.

"Success is *not* throwing together a free concert at the last second in a last-ditch attempt to win votes," Howard said, taking a not-so-subliminal shot at Kat's Testing For Tickets Day. "Success is definitely *not* making it all the way to college to act like a hoodlum, like members of Katrina's campaign team exhibited today. But I will tell you what success is. Success is an African-American man being able to make people overlook his sexuality and respect him for his character and work ethic. Success is his ability to achieve despite the societal hurdles that have been placed in front of him. So in essence, I would say that *I* am the definition of success."

Howard's supporters gave him a standing ovation, some even blowing party horns in a premature celebration.

"Can you believe this fool?" Fresh asked, nudging my arm with his elbow.

I was so nervous about how Kat would answer, I couldn't respond. My eyes were glued to the stage.

"I've taken fifteen pills today," Kat said. "I took fifteen yesterday. Fifteen the day before that. And tomorrow, I will take fifteen more. For those of you who haven't heard by now, I am HIV positive. Now I could tell you about all of the awards I've won, all the internships I've completed at *Fortune 500* companies or brag about the community service I've done, and you may think I'm successful. But when I got my test results back last semester, I felt like a failure. I felt like I'd let down everyone—my parents, my friends and myself. But the day I decided that I wouldn't let anything—not even HIV—stop me from pursuing my goals, was the day I became successful."

I fought back tears, but couldn't help bringing my hands together to join in the applause with the rest of Kat's supporters. I thought she was finished. But I was wrong.

"You see," she continued, "success isn't what you've become, but rather what you have gone through to get to where you are. So contrary to Mr. Harrell's opinion, success isn't a person. Success is a story. And you can help me make the next chapter of mine a successful one by voting me student body president tomorrow."

This time, nearly every student in the entire auditorium rose to their feet and put their hands together. Everyone except for Howard's most loyal followers, who remained seated, stone-faced and with their arms folded. Even Dr. J had to turn away from the crowd momentarily to conceal his emotion. And the look on Howard's face was one I will never forget. It was one of uncertainty. He'd always looked so confident and sure of himself. But at that very moment, I believe Howard came to grips with the fact that after three years of dominating the student government election, he may have finally met his match. And judging by the look on his face, if he'd had a white towel in his pocket, he may have thrown it in right then and there.

SEVENTEEN

VERDICT

We'd finally reached the point of no return with Kat's bid for student body president. It took endorsements from a rapper to erase the damage I'd single-handedly done to Kat's campaign. And now, she had a legitimate shot to win. But Kat was still stressed out about how the election would turn out. To ease her angst, Destiny thought it would be good to throw a preparty for her in her dorm room a few hours before the results were announced. Nothing too major. Just a little get together for our group and close friends. Everybody showed except for Timothy. Kat said he had some Alpha meeting to attend or something. And to my surprise, neither did Fresh. But Fats came through, probably because he heard there would be food and drinks.

"This is what y'all call food and drinks, cuz?" he asked, standing over the table of party favors.

Highlighted by music, cards, cupcakes, hot dogs, barbeque baked beans, chips and fruit punch, the event turned out to be very PG-13, as I'd expected. I was just waiting for somebody to suggest we play musical chairs. But it was calming, nonetheless. Especially for me. As hard as I tried not to show it, I was at my wit's end. The fate of my future resting in the hands of voters at a damn student government election. As much as I loved Oakland, I didn't want to go back. Not to stay, at least. Over the one year I'd been away in college, I'd changed. The problem is, Oakland was exactly the same. The same guys hanging on the same blocks, trying to holler at the same girls, smoking the same weed, going to the same parties that always get shot up the same way. And I was tired of it. I'd been exposed to more, and I liked it. Of course, I could do without the homework. But even the whole routine of going to class without my mom shaking me out of my sleep in the morning and studying for exams prior to the night before the test had grown on me. Other than my mom and sister, there was nothing for me in Oakland. Nothing but trouble. On the other hand, if I got to come back to U of A and pledge Kappa Beta Psi, I knew that I would be exposed to a group of guys my mom would be proud I called friends. Guys who valued things like high GPAs and community service. Guys who pulled all of the tightest females on campus, not only because of their looks, but also because of their intellect. Waiting on the election results to be announced was nerve racking, to say the least. I had everything riding on the results. My life as I knew it was hanging in the balance.

"Don't worry about it," Destiny said, running her hand along my back as we sat on the couch. "Kat told me about your situation. Trust me. She's gonna win and you will be just fine."

"You can tell I'm stressing?" I asked.

"Yes!" she said. "You dang near haven't said a word to anybody since we've been here. That's not like you."

I would've responded, but something on the bottom of the TV screen caught my eye and diverted my attention. It appeared on the ticker tape seconds before ESPN's anchor Stuart Scott made the announcement. Apparently, I wasn't the only one who'd seen it. I wasn't gonna say anything about it, but Fats apparently couldn't hold it in.

"Hey, y'all turn the music down real quick," he said.

I tried to give him the eye, signaling for him not to mention it, but couldn't get his attention.

"Y'all might wanna see this," Fats said, grabbing the TV remote and turning up the volume.

"Just moments ago, University of Atlanta's Heisman quarterback, Deiondre 'Downtown D' Harris, who in December was notified by NFL commissioner that he would have to withdraw his name from the NFL draft because he was HIV positive, learned more disturbing news today when a federal judge found him guilty of drug trafficking and sentenced him to sixty months in prison," Stuart said. "Sadly, Deiondre was projected as a top five pick in the upcoming NFL draft. More on this later on SportsCenter."

Kat immediately broke down in tears. Her back pressed against the wall, she slid down it slowly with her face in her hands until her butt hit the floor. She sat there with her head buried between her legs boo-hooing like she was at her mother's funeral.

"Thanks a lot, *Fats*," Destiny whispered loud enough for everyone to hear.

"What?" he asked in a mumble, shrugging his shoulders, totally oblivious to his folly. "C'mon, now. It's not like she wasn't going to find out sooner or later. I didn't know she was still feeling him like that."

At first, her reaction struck me as odd, too. Earlier this

semester, Kat had all but sworn to me she was completely over Downtown D. But after I considered the history the two of them shared, not to mention the thirty plus million dollars he was supposedly guaranteed to have in his wallet this time next year, I felt her pain. Her line sisters crouched around her in support. They ushered her into the back room, where they stayed for about fifteen minutes. I don't know what they said to her, but when Kat returned, she looked as good as new money. After Destiny gathered us together for a quick prayer, it was time to report to the student center to hear the results.

While walking there, I don't who was more nervous, me or Kat.

"Hey, why wasn't Fresh at the party?" Destiny asked. "You talk to him today?"

"Nah," I said. "I don't know what's up with him. I don't even know if he knew about the party. I tried to call him earlier, but his phone was cut off. When is the last time you seen him?"

"I haven't seen him since the debate," she said.

"I saw him in the library studying for finals the other day," Fats said. "He was in bad shape."

"What you mean?" I asked.

"I guess from charging ten thousand dollars worth of shit on that credit card and not having the money to pay it back," Fats said. "That's why his phone is cut off now!"

"I can't believe that boy blew ten Gs," I said. "*Ten!* He can't be mad at nobody but himself. I told him. At the end of the day, it's just a credit card though, he can pay it back over time."

"That's the thing," Fats said. "The card he got had a twenty-six percent interest rate on it and that fool didn't read the fine print before he signed up."

"Hell nah!" I said. "Whew! Now, that's ugly!"

"But peep," Fats said. "That ain't the worst part. You know his mom cosigned for it, so he could use the money to pay his tuition next semester, right?"

"Damn!" I said, throwing my hands up. "I had forgot all about that. She sure did. I can't believe that fool just blew his tuition money like that. What was he thinking?"

"Apparently, he wasn't," Destiny said, as we approached the student center entrance.

The hype surrounding the election was unbelievable. Not only were there hundreds of students converging on the student center doors from every angle, but the marching band was outside playing as we walked up. Photographers from the newspaper and yearbook staff were on hand to capture it all. Win, lose or draw, it was a spectacle to behold. A scene I could never forget.

"Can you believe this, cuz?" Fats asked. "I've been here for seven years and I ain't never seen people on the yard get so into a student government election."

"I didn't know you were getting your masters this year," Destiny said.

"I'm not," Fats confirmed. "I'm on the seven-year plan."

"I didn't know there was one," Destiny said, laughing.

"The funny thing is, neither did I," Fats said with a chuckle. "Time flies when you're having fun. I'm graduating next week, though. Believe that!"

"Finally," I said.

"Hey, better late than never, homie," he said.

The moment Kat stepped foot in the student center, the applause kicked up and people cheered. Even though I thought it was kind of lame, especially with us standing right in the front, I joined right in. There was entirely too much at stake for me not to. It wasn't long before Howard made his grand entrance, his cohorts leading the way in their "Vote Howard" T-shirts. I couldn't help but notice that the ovation for Howard was slightly more boisterous and rowdy than Kat's. He stood on the opposite side of the platform near Lawry and the MIAPAs, who held up signs in support. I felt my phone go off in my pocket. Of course, it was my mom sending me a text message. It read *Did we win?*

I was too nervous to even return her text. I decided to wait until the results were in to even hit her back. It was so packed, I hadn't even noticed Timothy had snaked his way through the crowd. He was standing a few feet behind us with the rest of the Alphas. We made eye contact but exchanged no pleasantries. Considering everything, I couldn't even be mad at Timothy for what he'd done. Hell, if it wasn't for him helping me with my homework for biology, my grades would have never been high enough for me to afford to get a zero and still make a passing grade in the first place. And the more I thought about it, the more I came to the conclusion that I didn't have no business relying on his scantron to get me through the biology final, either. As much as I hated to admit it, I was in the wrong. Deep down inside, I knew Timothy was a good guy. I hoped we'd have a chance to talk before he left for the summer.

"Before I announce the winner of this year's student body president election, I would like to say that I have been very impressed by the way in which both the candidates and the voters have taken ownership of this election," Dr. J said. "Judging by today's turnout, this is definitely the most highly anticipated student government election I have ever been involved in."

The chants started low and increased in pitch every go round, drowning Dr. J's intro completely out. The louder it got, the more my stomach churned.

"Howard! Howard! Howard!" folks chanted.

Not to be shown up, Kat's supporters responded.

"Kat! Kat! Kat!" they shouted, fists pumping.

"And now, without any further ado…" Dr. J said as I closed my eyes and clasped my hands.

"Please, God," I pleaded under my breath. "Let her win."

"It is my pleasure to introduce the winner, and new student body president," he said, hoisting the envelope high.

I pooted.

"Katrina Turner!"

I've had my fare share of glorious moments in my life. Winning the little league football championship, hearing my name called at my high school graduation and getting accepted to college among the most memorable. But Dr. J announcing Kat as the new student body president topped them all. Being ridiculed for the entire semester by everyone who assumed I had the package, bombing on the speech in the prelims, being physically degraded and mentally abused during the prepledging process, having my reputation smeared throughout the campaign and being told by nearly everyone that we didn't stand a chance challenging the omnipotent Howard Harrell all made the victory that much sweeter. As Kat stood on stage, tears streaming from her eyes, grinning from ear to ear, Dub-B and Jasmine shared a kiss, Timothy slapped fives with his frat brothers and Destiny jumped up and down clapping with her sorors. I could do nothing more than throw my head back and raise my hands high above my shoulders in jubilee. Then I eased my phone out of my pocket, scrolled to the message my mom had sent me, hit Eeply and typed *Yes!*

EIGHTEEN

EXIT WOUNDS

It was hard to enjoy Kat's victory. I'd waited all semester for this moment to bask in the joy of knowing I'd passed my other classes, I'd been officially absolved from academic probation, my grades were good enough to pledge Kappa Beta Psi and, most importantly, my GPA was high enough for me to return to the University of Atlanta next year. But there would be no celebration for me. For one, my phone call with Leslie really put a damper on things. I'm still not sure what made her finally call me back. I assumed it was because the school year was over and she knew I'd be going back to Cali for the summer. But after spending five minutes on the phone with her, it was clear she didn't want to move forward with our relationship.

"Well, I'm glad to hear you finished with a 3.0," she said.

"That's a tremendous accomplishment. I know your mom is proud of you."

"Yeah," I said, disappointed that the conversation had taken such a generic turn.

"Look, J.D.," she said, "I've heard everything you said about Lawry hating on you and all. And truthfully, I still don't know who to believe. All I know is that you are leaving for Cali in a few minutes, and I'll be out here for the summer. And I'm not too good with long-distance relationships, so I say the two of us just go our separate ways for now. Then when you come back in the fall, if it's meant for us to be together, I'm sure we'll hook up again."

What could I say to that? It seemed she already had her mind made up. And truthfully, as much as I liked Leslie, the fact that she'd left me stranded with no tutor during finals really didn't sit well with me. Plus, I figured if I was going to actually be on line pledging Kappa Beta Psi next semester, seeing her didn't really bode well for my well-being. I was probably better off leaving her alone. At least until after I officially became a Kappa. Then, it'd be free game.

"Yeah," I said, trying my best not to sound disgruntled. "You're probably right. That's probably the best play to run. I guess I'll see you when I make it back."

"Sounds good," she said.

At least Leslie and I didn't end our relationship on bad terms, I thought as I stuffed the last of my clothes into my suitcase. It certainly felt better to have some closure than none at all. I was glad she'd called.

I knew my Uncle Leroy would be pulling up any minute to take me to the airport, so I checked around my room to make sure I wasn't leaving anything behind. That's when I heard my door open. I thought it was Timothy coming in to take his things out, but it was Fresh. I could tell by his facial expression that he was in a rather somber mood. But after the conversation I'd just had, I wasn't really in the spirit to cheer anyone else up. Fresh didn't say a word. He just came in and sat on the edge of my bed with his head down, holding a piece of paper in his hand. At first, I thought he was upset about a girl or something. But by his body language alone, it didn't take long for me to tell he had bigger problems.

"What's wrong, blood?" I asked.

"Man, joe," he said, exhaling deeply as he crashed backward onto my bed. "I really messed up this time, G."

"What you mean?" I asked.

"I don't even wanna go home, folk," Fresh said. "You think your uncle will let me stay at his crib for the summer?"

"I highly doubt that," I said as I pressed my knee down on my suitcase, trying to compress the clothes I'd stuffed inside, so I could zip it up. "Come on, now. Whatever it is, it can't be *that* serious."

"How you figure?" Fresh asked. "How am I s'posed to explain what I did? How am I s'posed to tell my parents I blew ten *thousand* dollars?"

"You're right," I said. "It is that bad."

I wanted to say "I told you so," but I figured now was no time to be condescending. Not with of one my best friends sitting on my bed, breaking down after coming to the realization his college days were over. I could tell by Fresh's voice he was on the verge of crying.

"And just think," he said, "this whole semester we've been worried about whether or not *you* would be coming back. Now I'm the one who's gonna have to sit next year out."

"Can't you return some of the stuff you bought back and get reimbursed?"

"I mean, I could try," he said. "But I doubt I'm gonna

be able to get eighty-six hundred dollars worth of it back. I'll need at least that much to pay tuition."

"Have you thought about hitting up Tiffany or one of your other breezies to see if they'll loan you some dough?" I asked.

"Man, them girls are broke, G," Fresh said. "They're in college like us. Shit, that's probably what was keeping them around. The fact that I was spending my bread. I ain't heard from Tiffany since I went off on her after that incident at Lenox. I heard she's dating some dude at Lighthouse now."

"Damn," I said. "Well, you could get a summer job, apply for some scholarships, ask some family members if they…"

"J.D., I'm not coming back, man," Fresh said, sniffling, his head bowed toward the floor. "What part-time job you know gonna pay me that kinda money, man? I mean, I could apply for some scholarships or whatever, but you know my grades ain't even up to par like that. And my family…they ain't got no bread like that. I'm like you—the first one in my family to go off to college. And I blew it! Bottom line, I doofed myself, G. Straight up. I don't even know what I was thinking. I spent all that money and I ain't got nothin' to show for it. I'm bogus as hell for that. My momma gon' whoop my ass when she finds out."

You had to empathize with the guy. He was pouring his heart out right there in my bedroom and there wasn't much I could say to rectify the situation. Fresh had been my best friend on campus since I arrived at U of A last semester. We studied together, partied together, even prepledged together. The thought of him not coming back had never crossed my mind. No matter how much he loved the Bulls, White Sox and the Bears and bragged about how much fun he had growing up in Chicago, I knew he didn't want to go back home to stay. After going to college in Atlanta for a year, nobody did. I felt his pain. The same thing that awaited me back home awaited him—violence. I knew as well as he did, college was the way out. But Fresh's ticket home was one-way. Even though he'd dug his own ditch, seeing my friend break down like that made me tear up. I searched for the right words to say, but came up with nothing. That's when Timothy came in. More silence followed. It was an awkward moment, seeing him gather his luggage that was already packed up and head toward the door. He was apparently content leaving without saying a thing to me, but I had to say something.

"Look, we need to talk, Timothy," I said just before he got to the door.

"I'm listening," he said.

"First of all, us not talking to each other is really childish," I said. "We've been friends and roommates since we got here."

"We've been roommates," he said. "A friend would tell you if he knows your girl is cheating on you."

"Look, I apologize for not telling you sooner, blood," I said. "That was my bad. You were just so sprung off the girl, I could never find the right time to tell you. Every time I was about to, you'd say something about how much you loved her or how good she looked or how smart she was."

"Well, I accept your apology," he said, extending his hand to shake mine.

"Don't you want to apologize for something too, brotha?" I asked while shaking his hand.

"Apologize for what?" he asked.

"For letting me copy off of your biology final," I said.

Before I could even finish the sentence, I felt funny even saying it. Fresh snickered.

"How do you sound?" Timothy asked. "*I'm* supposed to apologize for *you* copying off of *my* test? I don't think so, J.D. That doesn't even make sense."

"You didn't have to set me up like that, though," I said. "That was hella wrong, blood. You could've told me you were filling in all the wrong answers."

"And you could've told me Amy was creeping behind my back," he said, laughing. "I got played and so did you. So I guess we're even."

I didn't even have a good comeback for that one. I decided to just bury the hatchet on that note.

"I guess so," I said, shaking up with him one more time and giving him a half hug.

"Well, I'm out," Timothy said. "You guys be safe this summer. Keep God first. Stay out of trouble. And I'll see y'all next semester."

When Timothy extended his hand toward Fresh, he bowed his head in shame and broke down crying like a baby.

"Hey, what's wrong with Fresh?" Timothy asked.

"He's just upset about some things," I said, checking under my bed to make sure I wasn't leaving anything behind.

"I'm not coming back next year," Fresh said in between sobs.

"You can't say that for sure, blood," I said, trying to stay positive.

"Yes, I can," Fresh said.

"Why's that?" Timothy asked.

"I don't got the money," Fresh said.

"If you really want to come back, you can get the money," Timothy said.

"How the hell am I supposed to come up with eight thousand dollars over the summer with no job? That's impossible."

"False," Timothy said, sitting down beside Fresh. "All things are possible to those who believe. *All* things. If it's in God's plan for you to be in school here, you'll be back."

"Yeah, but how…"

"How you're going to come up with the cash is irrelevant at this point," Timothy said, cutting him off. "First, you have to *believe* that God can provide it for you. He would never withhold a good thing from you."

"That's real," Fresh said. "I might need you to put in a prayer for your boy."

"I can pray for you," Timothy said. "But I can't believe for you. Do I think you can pull together enough money to pay tuition on your own this summer? Probably not. But as long as you believe God can do it for you, anything is possible. *Any*thing. Just remember that."

I was a firm believer that Timothy was wasting his money in college. With his mastery of the Bible and ability to apply its principles to everyday life, I was certain he was destined to be a great preacher. At times, I was in awe just listening to him. You had to respect it.

"How are your grades anyway?" Timothy asked.

"1 got like a three-point-four," Fresh said.

"Gee whiz!" Timothy said. "With those kind of grades, you'll be eligible for plenty of scholarships. My mom is the director of financial aid for minority students at UGA. That's all she does all day is help students get scholarships. I'll talk to her for you and ask her to e-mail some of them to you. With grades like yours, she can get you ten thousand dollars worth in no time!"

"Really?" Fresh asked, popping up with a smile on his face and hope in his eyes. "Don't bullshit me, G. You serious?"

"If you don't believe me, you can talk to her yourself," Timothy said. "Both of my parents are outside waiting on me right now. I don't think I have your e-mail address anyway. Come on."

"Thank you, Jesus!" Fresh shouted. "Let's go!"

"See you next semester, J.D.," Timothy said. "Be safe out there this summer."

A few minutes later, I grabbed my things and met my uncle outside in the parking lot. Staring at Marshall Hall through the rearview mirror as we pulled off, I got a little emotional as I thought about all of the good times and bad I'd had my freshman year. I couldn't help but shake my head and laugh when I thought about us getting hammered at the foam party and how scared I was walking into the basement at the Kappa house the first night we started pre-pledging. When we passed by the baseball diamond, memories of us running full speed and diving face-first into the bases in the rain flooded my mind. The look on Fresh's face when he turned around to give me that damn garlic was priceless. We were following behind a Neon with a rainbow-colored MIAPA bumper sticker. Instantly, I thought about how Lawry—the last guy on campus I would have ever suspected gay—had done a complete 180 since I'd met him, redefining the term "undercover brotha" right in front of my eyes and sacrificing our friendship in the process. As we drove by the basketball court, I thought about Dub-B. I wondered what would've happened if he wouldn't have ended up in our group, and we wouldn't have had his father's help planning Kat's campaign. Would she have still won or would I be going back to Oakland for good because I didn't make good enough grades to get off of academic probation?

When we pulled up at the light near the student center, I saw two students waiting to use the ATM. I wondered if they were inadvertently plunging themselves into debt, swiping with reckless abandon as Fresh had. Driving by the strip, I noticed all of Howard's posters had been torn down. In fact, only one remained. One that read Vote for Kat. I thought it symbolic. After all of the smoke around her cleared, Downtown D was incarcerated, Howard Harrell was overthrown and Kat was the last one standing. I thought, if Kat—a safe-sex advocate turned HIV patient—could be elected student body president, maybe all that jazz Timothy was talking about anything being possible through God was really true. After all, in a few months I'd be coming back to campus for my sophomore year. And I, of all people, would be pledging a fraternity. This time last year, I didn't even think I'd be getting into college at all. One thing's for sure. Although it still seemed far off, after completing my first year of college, keeping the promise I'd made to my friend T-Spoon before he was murdered now seemed attainable. I was that much closer to finishing what I'd started. One step closer to graduating from college.

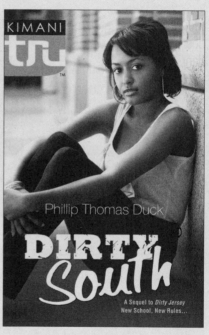

Curveball, coming right up....

Indigo Summer and her best friend Jade are the best dancers on the high-school dance team. Now one of them is going to be team captain—Indigo just never expected it to be Jade. Jealousy suddenly rocks their friendship. And they're not the only ones dealing with major drama. Their friend Tameka is destined for a top college…until one lapse in judgment with her boyfriend changes everything.

Friendships, the team, their futures…this time it's all on the line.

Coming the first week of June 2009 wherever books are sold.

DEAL WITH IT
An INDIGO Novel

ESSENCE BESTSELLING AUTHOR
Monica McKayhan

www.KimaniTRU.com
www.myspace.com/kimani_tru